"First, the 'Saturday People', and then the ..."

by
Bruce Portnoy

Darlene,

It's been great sharing
The MPD Senior Academy sessions with
You. I hope you find my story
As interesting to read As I found it
to write.

Bruce Portnoy

Soft Cover Book* ISBN -13   978-1505990201
Library of Congress Control Number LCCN 2015900306
CreateSpace Independent Publishing Platform,
North Charleston, SC
FIC031060 Fiction/Thrillers/ Political

Dedicated to the following individuals who offered editing suggestions with the intent of making, "First, the 'Saturday People', and then the ..." a meaningful story:

L.R.P., R.J.P., S.L.N., J.J.L., B.I.S., B.Z.L., P.C.B., and W.M.

I am very appreciative for what you did in friendship.*

Chapter 1

Travelling through Halhoula village in the West Bank territory, in route to the "Operation Staging Area," I saw a camouflage painted military Jeep rapidly approaching our limousine. In the rear, were three young Israeli soldiers prominently displaying automatic weapons and flaunting an attitude toward the hostile residents, as if to suggest, "You want a fight? Bring it on!"

Menachim, the Mossad military adjutant, informed me that our armed escort was necessary, as Halhoula was suspected of harboring terrorists.

Once safely past the outskirts of this dusty village, both he and General Charles Orin, Israel's Southern Command senior officer, breathed a sigh of relief. Menachim then returned to reading the "classified" document, he just received on his security rated e-tablet. Finishing, he said, "Jon, I need to clue you and Orin in on the results of some research regarding Jakob Aberdam. Unfortunately, there are no facts as to why this man would use his State Department position to coordinate a terror action targeting Jerusalem's *Temple Mount*."

I interrupted Menachim with a security concern. "Isn't it dangerous to have classified information stored on an e-device that could be easily compromised?"

"Jon, that's a fair question during these insecure times. Keep in mind that this sophisticated tablet operates only when my iris identification is repeatedly confirmed, and my fixation maintained. Should I stop viewing the screen for thirty seconds without incorporating a special code, the document will disappear, without capability of reproduction, and as a last resort, the embedded intelligence drive is programmed to self-destruct. Are you at peace, now? O.K. to go on?"

I nodded my understanding.

Menachim continued, "Let's see what we can learn about the inner man, suspected of planning the accident that took your daughter, Sandra's life, left your wife, Abbie, comatose, and of course, brought you to me."

As I needed to understand the cause of my family's recent tragedy, I asked Menachim to tell me anything learned or even suspected about Aberdam.

"Jon, please keep in mind that I am translating from written Hebrew and my English, may at times appear rough and even grammatically incorrect. Just listen and most importantly, be patient with what I am about to reveal."

"The Aberdam Report--Classified, Level 2":

"Jakob Aberdam is a figure shrouded in mystery. There is no public information on him in any of the traditional record sources. It's as if he never existed. However, some earlier digging by Mossad during their 'Eichmann Extraction Operation' revealed interesting information about his father Klaus Aberdam, which might shed light on the son's attitude toward Jews and Israel and possibly offer some clues as to his next move."

Menachim went on to reveal selected aspects of Aberdam senior's past.

"The father spent his early childhood years, living in pre-World War 1 Munich, within the province of Bavaria. At the age of 18, he enlisted in the Bavarian Army and served on the Western Front as a battalion messenger, rising to the rank of Lance Corporal. What is most interesting is that his tour of duty somewhat paralleled that of Adolph Hitler, having served in the same units in France and Belgium. Klaus was eventually taken prisoner by British forces and because of his English language skills, he was assigned to assist MI-6, British intelligence as an interrogator of captured German officers and German citizens suspected of being spies. The trail then grows cold, until the end of the war when he returned to his hometown in Bavaria. There, it appears Klaus held several part-time jobs, barely making ends meet, until he was offered an opportunity to assist in the establishment of the National Socialist Program. His responsibilities included implementing the means to gradually take away German citizenship from those of Jewish descent. Later, he was promoted to an intelligence unit in Munich, where he was empowered to discover and then eliminate party opposition, by whatever means necessary, including murder.

After Hitler was named Reich Chancellor, Klaus was assigned to the Propaganda Ministry, where in February of 1933; he assisted the elected government to pass laws suspending the civil rights and political freedoms of Jews. By March, Hitler and the Nazi Party effectively ruled Germany. His Ministry of Propaganda position allowed Klaus to travel to the United States where he met with, and strongly influenced powerful, high-ranking State Department officers. Aberdam seized this opportunity to expand the Nazi anti-Jewish policies abroad. He successfully fabricated negative effects of Jewish immigrant issues to receptive government officials in the United States and elsewhere, claiming that Jews were leeches on society and Communists.

He next surfaced in May of 1939, when the German Foreign Office in collusion with the Propaganda Ministry began influencing many nations to decline to admit Jewish refugees from the St. Louis, which sailed on May 13, 1939, bound for Havana, Cuba. On board were 938 souls, most of whom were Jews who had applied for U.S. visas and were planning to stay in Cuba only temporarily, until they could gain the appropriate paperwork to legally enter the United States. It appears that an all too obliging U.S. State Department then assisted Aberdam, as he advocated for the population quotas, formally established within the U.S. Immigration and Nationality Act of 1924, to be enforced and to specifically target Jews.

It was strongly suspected that he, through his high-level government contacts, might have influenced President Roosevelt's advisors against recommending an executive order that would have admitted the St. Louis refugees into the United States, on a humanitarian basis. Reliable evidence also linked him to efforts to block a subsequent congressional bill that would have admitted 20,000 Jewish children above the existing quotas into the United States. Jon, this was nothing short of an eventual death sentence for many European Jews.

Klaus Aberdam's years of fervent anti-Jewish activities caught the attention of former SS officers who served with *ODESSA*, the organization thought to have enabled Adolph Eichmann to flee to Italy and later to enter Argentina. It was suspected, but never proven that *ODESSA* may have worked, in some unclear capacity, with post-World War II American intelligence operatives.

Years after the war ended, the trail picks up with rumors that Klaus was recruited by the early C.I.A., serving in their clandestine services department, while stationed in Jordan and Syria. There he lived with the widow of a murdered former S.S. officer. They had a child out of wedlock, whom we believe to be Jakob. Shortly afterwards, Klaus, his mistress Frieda and Jakob appeared to have vanished."

Trying to digest the ramifications of this information, I offered Menachim an unsolicited thought, "What if Jakob grew up in an environment specifically grooming him to finish what his father was unable to accomplish?"

Menachim interrupted, "We have other pressing matters ahead of us. Don't worry; Israel is not going to let either the father or son go unpunished. Their day of reckoning will soon be upon them. I give you my word."

Somewhat reassured, I looked upwards and saw dark skies looming on the horizon of the mountainous area we were nearing. Within minutes, huge raindrops began pelting our car. Instead of slowing down, our driver actually sped up. A strong sense of danger began to consume me, yet my companions appeared unfazed.

As I looked about, the security vehicle was no longer in sight. A cold sweat overcame me and I began asking myself, "What the hell am I doing here? I'm no hero, I'm just an average man whose wife was deemed a threat to national security, and somebody took steps to silence her."

Suddenly, a powerful jolt altered our limo's direction. The driver lost control and, for the first time, I saw fear in my fellow passengers' eyes. Menachim pulled me down between the rear seats and covered me with his body. At that moment, a second much stronger force flipped our vehicle several times before it came to rest upside down.

The last thing I recall before losing consciousness was being outside the vehicle with rain pouring upon my face and a hazy vision of a decapitated body lying next to me.

Chapter 2

Waking, I found myself groggy and unable to speak. Pain surged through my neck and lower back, accompanied with only brief respites of relief. My eyes were covered with a thick fabric that prevented me from seeing anything, but the faint glow of a light from the sides. A needle poked my right arm and within seconds, the pain miraculously vanished.

Sometime later, I felt someone pinch my shoulder. This roused me. A few moments later I heard commands, in heavily accented English, to move my fingers and to curl my toes. I complied as best I could. Then a different voice told me that a recent surgical opening to my skull probably saved my life. At that point, I began to drift in and out of consciousness.

Awakening from a fright-filled dream, I found my blindfold removed and observed my left hand tightly bound to a bed railing. I felt a catheter within my penis and an I.V. in my free arm.

Two men wearing ski masks entered the dimly lit room where I was being held. One addressed me in Hebrew and I did not respond. He then tried to communicate in French, but without success. Finally, he asked in English if I was an American. I nodded in the affirmative.

"What's your name and what were you doing with those pigs?" he demanded.

Hesitatingly, I replied, "Jon Wolf."

"Mr. Wolf, is it your custom to travel without identity papers in an area where you could easily be arrested for such negligence?" Without waiting for my response, his partner proclaimed in a loud voice that I was circumcised. This prompted a harshly toned follow-up question, "Are you a Jew?"

All too aware of the Daniel Pearl episode, where his last words before being decapitated were a proclamation of his Jewish faith, I thought it best to sidestep this provocative inquiry. Instead, I emphatically blurted out, "I'm with the U.S. State Department!" This was the agency that I held responsible for my daughter's death and wife's incapacitation. Yet, it might now serve to postpone my fate, at least until my fabrication was checked out.

The lead interrogator appeared caught off-guard, and he and his cohort immediately left.

I knew I was in deep shit. However, this diversion might allow me time to get a handle on who held me and more importantly, what they planned to do with me. Meanwhile, I collected my thoughts and surmised my fellow travelers and I had been victims of either an improvised explosive roadside device, or shoulder-fired rockets. In any case, I had been injured and my companions' most likely are dead. My focus now was on survival.

As inconsequential as I had thought my life to be without Abbie and Sandra, I was now more determined than ever to get even with those who had taken so much away from me. Yet, I knew I could not accomplish anything if my true purposes for being in Israel were discovered.

Rather than trying to concoct a complicated bogus story, the details of which I might later get confused, I decided to keep everything simple. With the appropriate inquiry, I would respond that my mission responsibilities were to be revealed to me this coming Monday. That was the day the "Escaping the Abyss" operation was to begin, a fact I hoped was still unknown to my captors.

There was a knock at the open door, and a bearded man dressed in surgical blues entered my room. He introduced himself as Dr. Hassan. Apparently trying to impress me, he loudly boasted that his medical expertise had saved my life. He then went on to discuss the current extent of my injuries, which appeared non-life threatening. Hassan then cautiously looked about and quietly whispered in my ear, "You had best cooperate with your interrogators." He added before leaving my bedside, "I'd hate to see all of my skilled efforts wasted. Do you understand?"

I thought it best not to reveal my medical background. As such, I simply responded, "Thank you for saving my life. I will remember your efforts."

Perhaps it was this calm, respectful attitude that inspired him to converse more gently with me, during subsequent visits. My demeanor actually appeared disconcerting to my captors. "Most prisoners uncontrollably shake and tearfully cry out, while begging for their miserable lives," Hasan would later relate.

I began to suspect my contrived plan might have merit. Nevertheless, it would be hard for me to keep my cool, speak only when asked a specific question, and not look directly into my captors' eyes. Yet, fear of unleashing my anger would remain my biggest concern.

Hassan stepped out of the room only to return a short time later. He informed me that I was to be given 24 hours to regain my strength, before being relocated for further questioning, and that my wrist restraints, penile catheter and I.V. are to be removed within the hour. Finally, I was told that I would be able to get out of my bed, but only in the presence of a guard, who would soon be assigned to my room.

An armed older man quickly appeared, dressed in little more than rags, and speaking only rudimentary English. He passed the time belching a foul smell, while trying to converse with me. His thick accent prevented me from understanding much of what he had said. Purposely, I kept any responses to a minimum, always asking his permission before I sat or stood, all the while never looking him directly in the eye. It was my hope to conserve my physical strength, should an opportunity for escape arise.

Hours passed before the tall, stocky, masked lead interrogator re-entered my room. He ordered the guard to leave, approached, and forcefully took my head in both of his hands. His intense, steel blue eyes then penetrated any defense I could muster. It was clear he wanted it known that my fate hung on his whim. He informed me, "You are lucky to have survived the explosion that killed your companions." He waited for some response, but none was purposely forthcoming.

Then he added, "Until confirmation of your identity, and at least for the time being, I will believe what you say. But, never think me a fool." He then inquired, "Do you know Aberdam?" and followed up emphatically with, "For your sake, he'd better know of you!"

Again, I did not show any emotion.

Turning off the light, he then opened the door and motioned the guard to re-enter before leaving us in a now darkened room. I hoped I could continue to be brave, even though my chain-smoking guard passed the time playing with his automatic weapon, while pointing the barrel towards my head and whispering "dead man," over and over again.

Having been through so much in the past three weeks, I found myself becoming numb to the thought of death. Everything now appeared a grand mind game. Perhaps, with a little luck, I might be able to pull off the ruse and accomplish something worthwhile. As the guard fell asleep, I envisioned taking his weapon and overpowering him. However, where would I go and how far would I get, not speaking or even understanding the Arabic I heard spoken outside of my door?

Chapter 3

A woman completely covered in black garb, which exposed only her dark brown eyes came into my room. She proceeded to take my temperature and blood pressure, while closely observing me. She summoned a tall dark-skinned man, who administered an electrocardiogram and electroencephalograph, the results of which were immediately radioed to Dr. Hassan.

Ironically, the portable heart and brain wave machines were labeled "Property of Hadassah Hospital, Israel." I wondered how these sophisticated pieces of medical equipment fell into the hands of my captors. Never getting the opportunity to guess the answer, Ali the second of the original two masked interrogators barged in. He forced me to a seat in the far corner of the room and took out an inkpad. Rotating my fingers on it, he made crude impressions on a piece of computer paper. Finishing, he informed me that he was sending my fingerprints off to Aberdam.

His eyes narrowed to a squint as he threatened, "Should we find out you misled us in any manner, it will be my obligation, no, my pleasure to slit your throat and watch your life slowly drain away!" He then grabbed a hold of my left hand and said, "I'm told your manner is calm, but, I know you would scream in agony if I cut your finger off and took the wedding band that postponed your fate."

Puzzled by this lunatic's last remark, the only thing I could figure out was that my gold band contained two raised diamond gems interlocked within two carved out diamond shapes. I was impressed that he would know the traditional wedding band amongst Jews is plain, smooth gold. For this infraction, Abbie and I received some heat on our wedding day, yet this lapse may have saved me from immediate execution, or worse, torture.

I began to wonder how long would it take the fingerprints to identify me, not as the State Department representative I'm claiming to be, but as the Jewish operative they suspect? For the meantime, I had a role to convincingly play. A thought of Abbie and my new friend Mehmet came to mind, and I closed my eyes and silently prayed for their safety, as well as my own.

Within minutes, Hassan and the lead interrogator reappeared. This time all were armed. The doctor holstered a small caliber pistol in his waistband, while the others displayed A.K. 47 assault rifles banded about their shoulders. I knew the latter weapon all too well, as I had fired one on multiple occasions at a target range near the Kiryat Arba settlement, during a much earlier visit to Israel.

Initially Hassan started out somewhat pleasant, casually mentioning that I was healing well. Then his demeanor abruptly changed, as the lead interrogator began firing off disturbing questions.

"Think about this Wolf, would you kill, if I ordered you to do so in order to spare your own life? Understand, should we allow you to live, you must prove your allegiance to our cause. There is no middle ground." Hassan and the interrogator then left me, presumably to think about my fate.

I had to reflect on what I was willing to do to stay alive. Yet, there was no way I would kill a fellow Jew to escape my own death. If this scenario should come to be, I would take the weapon presumably loaded with only one cartridge in the chamber and aim it at the most dangerous of my captors before firing. Surely, then I would then be killed, and this ordeal would end.

My reverie was quickly interrupted when my original clothes were delivered, laundered and neatly folded. Presumably, they had been examined for evidence of my identity, with nothing being found.

My guard mumbled something about his shift ending, but he wasn't allowed to return to his home because of me. He became angry and pushed me against the wall. Instinctively, I protected my head. Red-faced, he spat at my feet and left my room. I got myself dressed and lay upon my bed, pondering my precarious circumstances. As my mind darted between unpleasant outcomes, I remembered my earlier decision not to leave this world submissively. At the same time, I wondered if I could hold up under torture.

Starting to perspire, I realized I was sinking into despair. Trying meditation techniques I picked up, while studying Japanese-style karate as a much younger man, I regained my focus and re-established my priorities. With Menachim probably dead, rescue did not seem a realistic option. After all, even if the Israelis were looking for me, how could I be located?

The interrogators came and left my room many more times, each time asking even more provocative questions combined with more serious threats, should they feel deceived by my replies. Without a watch or clock on the wall, I guessed the pattern was repeating itself every 20 minutes or so. They certainly did not want me getting comfortable.

Besides torture, a new fear crept into my mind. Should they use an injection of Pentothal, or some other type of truth serum, I might lose voluntary control over my responses and doom myself. Then I imagined something even more readily available to my captors, which could prove equally damning. Simply "Googling" my name might lead to the immediate end of my charade, resulting in my execution. Suddenly, I realized their intimidation tactics were beginning to wear me down, mentally and physically.

Hassan and the veiled woman reentered my room, closely followed by the original interrogators. They began to converse in Arabic with my guard. I presumed they took turns grilling him about anything I might have said. It was apparent from the look upon his face that at least one of the four was a high-ranking authority figure, if not this cell's leader.

Each then took a chair and sat by the four corners of my bed. Four pillows were placed under my head, raising my position to that of almost sitting upright. Hassan began scanning my charts, while commenting, "You're a lucky man on many levels, Wolf. We thought your head injury far worse than it turned out to be. Apparently, the remnants of a recent head surgery effectively served to relieve brain swelling, and as a result, your vitals are getting stronger. The only thing that's not going well," he hesitated, as his facial gestures hardened, "is your story."

19

"You're most fortunate our brothers in Hamas didn't pick you up. I suspect you know who we are by virtue of our relationship with your employer." Hassan, for a brief moment, cast his eyes downwards, as if submissive. Quickly recovering, he asked me a rather strange question.

"Wolf, do you understand why so few formidable Muslim groups publically acknowledged regret after the September 11 attacks, which clearly demonstrated your country's vulnerability?"

It seemed rhetorical. Yet, this man wanted an answer and an incorrect one might cost me my life. In desperation, I angrily responded, "It's all part of a grand scheme to unite people to oppose what you refer to as 'the great Satan nation,' because of its ongoing friendship with Jews."

With that answer apparently acceptable, he proclaimed, "Israel will be permanently dealt with in short order, and the United States will ultimately succumb to our ways."

A much earlier discussion I had with my friend Mehmet, a retired F.B.I. agent suddenly came to mind. During hostage negotiation training, he was instructed to always encourage the hostage takers to talk on, as they might unintentionally reveal heretofore-unknown intelligence facts. Therefore I responded, "Doctor, you have my interest, please continue."

Hassan did, "With the demise of the former Soviet Union, opportunities came for us to assert ourselves religiously, as well as militarily within the former Soviet states. Finding unexpected success there, we began to formulate sophisticated plans to expand the influence of Islam elsewhere. By initiating gradual Muslim population transfers to other sovereign nations, we found our answer. This increased our influence throughout Europe, particularly in France. Without much effort or sacrifice, we are at long last now converting mixed populations to the righteousness of our ways, and in the process we are gaining strong consensus against the occupier, Israel and its Jews."

Trying to restrain his enthusiasm, Hassan paused before adding, "Even our American foe is slowly recognizing the wisdom of reducing Israel's influence, as well as its Jewish presence in our back yard. However, that task is not easy. For the most part, and even with the assistance of some of their own leaders acting on our behalf, Jews as a group, hold firm to their teachings and resist our ways. That is why severe means are to be employed. Afterwards, other non-Muslim nations will not resist us and soon fall into line. Do you understand where we are ultimately headed?"

Not wishing to reveal my gut level disgust to such ranting, I simply replied, "No."

Gloating, he went on, "America's economic and moral weakness will eventually lead their citizens to internal conflicts. This will provide us the opportunity to secure the ends we seek. Americans, by their nature are spoiled, uninspired, and directionless of higher purposes. Repeatedly, they prove easily led by their politicians, some of whom we have groomed for our own service. They tell their citizens what they want to hear, appealing to their vanity, while proclaiming seemingly righteous utopian goals. It is in this pursuit, we will eventually dismantle the basis of your Constitution, utilizing a carefully manufactured common enemy. Propagandizing will serve to mobilize the escalating rift between the relatively small number of very rich from the growing ranks of the very poor, within your country and elsewhere. Our well-spoken minority figureheads will appeal to the guilt-filled fools and will rise to the top of their leadership, much as a Pied Piper, proclaiming knowledge of a better way, while gradually leading the masses toward the gentle tenets of Islam. Even as we speak, this part of our plan is in motion and winning influential converts. Yes, it may take time, but patience is one of our many virtues. Yet, we shall always hold in reserve our technologically sophisticated paramilitary cells, which are strategically placed throughout all of the western nations, many within the framework of liberal university systems. Wolf, our vision for the future will prove inevitable. Surely, by virtue of your association with our mutual benefactor, you must see this for yourself."

He re-emphasized, "Over the years, we encouraged migrations of our dedicated populations away from their homelands, as a calculated measure to foster conversion. And their numbers will soon be heavily supplemented, once Israel is relegated an uncomfortable memory."

He ended with, "Islam will flourish in the West with much credit due to your country's views on political correctness and to the legal rulings stemming from multi-culturists. Without knowing it, you have handed us the opportunities we never dreamt possible, but for which we will certainly take the advantage."

Hassan hesitated for a moment as if to accentuate the following point, "Wolf, none of the powerful nations that once exploited us recognize that they, much like Israel, are in a struggle for their very existence. This flaw will prove to be their ultimate downfall. In the meantime, the United States will soon turn a blind eye toward Israel and Jews."

I was in shock after hearing these cold, calculating words, fearing the depth of the influence these diabolical forces might gain worldwide, should Israel succumb.

There was an extended silence in the room before someone unfamiliar to me entered and briefly spoke to the others in Arabic. Hassan then stared at me in anger, "Wolf, our contact within your State Department does not acknowledge you. Are you C.I.A. or an American working with Mossad? Actually, it doesn't matter. Your death will be soon and very slow, and incredibly painful!"

I began shaking, thinking my throat would be slit. Summoning up some courage and hoping to stall, I told them I didn't know what they were talking about. I then asked for time to make my peace with the prospect of my upcoming death. Hassan translated my request to the others. The mood turned ugly, as they demanded immediate vengeance. One man pulled a knife from his belt and held it to my throat. The veiled woman at the head of the bed then spoke in a firm tone, the man reluctantly backed off and they unexpectedly left.

If their aim was to scare the shit out of me, it was working. I had nothing left in reserve. Yet, I hoped I would not meet this last great adventure a compliant victim. Only in the last minutes of my life would I come to know the true me.

Thoughts came to mind of Abbie, Sandra, Menachim, and other Jews throughout history, who were forced to make the ultimate sacrifice of their lives, at the hands of cold-blooded murderers, just for being Jews, and I certainly would not be the last to fall. The Good Lord had saved my life on too many occasions, perhaps so I could face this moment with courage and faith.

In what seemed only minutes, the four burst through the door and two men held me flat on the bed. The one who, just moments earlier had placed a knife to my throat said, "We don't care if you made your peace. In only a short time, Aberdam arrives. We want to hear you beg for your worthless life! Then we may just dispatch you in a less painful manner," he said, while flashing a smirk to his cohorts.

The interrogator who had been quietly listening then piped up, "Tell us why you were with the Israelis in the car we attacked." Suddenly, it became clear to me that if they knew more than they let on, the questions would have been more direct and in all probability, I would have been executed by now. A strange calm came over me, even as my shirt was ripped open, and a sharp knife-edge placed upon my bare chest. The blade began to make deep cuts, drawing beads of blood, as it traced out a Magen David, Jewish star.

"Well, do you still love your Israel? Now you will share its symbol, until your body rots. Tell us who you are, who you are working for, and what you are doing here!" he demanded.

While I felt pain, I sensed, at least for the present, they were done torturing me, and that I had stood up to these bastards. Responding in a very low tone, I replied, "What I told you earlier, still applies. I work as an observer for the U.S. State Department and will be told my final objectives on Monday. I don't know the day of the week or for that matter if it is night or day. However, what I do know is that if I am not available, an inquiry is sure to begin and you will have hell to pay!"

The veiled woman spoke and all I could understand was the name Aberdam. She and the interrogators left, leaving Hassan to dress my wounds. "Look Wolf, I had no choice but to follow orders. Are you sure there is nothing else you want to tell me?"

The pain of the antiseptic tracing my wound caused me to cringe. As tears filled my eyes, I gritted my teeth, while saying, "Tell your friends, I will see all of you in Hell!"

Hassan took on a scared appearance at the sound of these words. "Wolf, before converting to Islam, I was a Christian. Is my soul truly damned?"

"God knows what you have done. What do you think?" I answered.

"If I tell you something important," Hassan hesitated, as he continued to attend to my cuts, "do you think I might receive some compensation from Heaven?"

To this, I just shrugged my shoulders as if to say I didn't care.

"This was just a tactic, a reminder of the seriousness of what we have to accomplish. We don't intend to kill you, at least not yet. In fact, we don't know exactly who you are. However, we can't jeopardize our relationship with your employer. That is why we summoned Mr. Aberdam." Hassan appeared relieved to have conveyed these thoughts. He added, "I am arranging food to be sent to you. Let's hope you will be let go and brought to an Israeli checkpoint, alive."

Shortly after Hassan left, the original guard with the bad breath returned with food. It appeared untouched by him. At this point, I didn't care. I required sustenance and savored the hummus, Jerusalem salad, and brown rice placed upon the table next to my bed.

Even if all of this was just an act, I understood my fate could change on a dime. I reasoned my only choice now was to escape. I asked the guard for permission to go to the bathroom and then to get some exercise, walking the hallways. Understanding my request, he excused himself to seek permission for me to do so. He came back and with a smile, saying it was okay, so long as he accompanied me.

It felt good to be able to leave the tight confines of my tiny room. Except for the one I occupied, this was indeed a medical care facility without private rooms. The hallway was narrow and dimly lit by low wattage bulbs, dangling every 20 feet or so from a tall ceiling. The windows had thick curtains covering them. There was no visible sunlight showing through the edges of the material. I walked slowly, feeling my strength starting to decline. As I made my way, I observed hospital beds lined the corridors, and orderlies were attending to patients of all ages. Then I caught a glimpse of Hassan, he was treating an elderly man. He turned and waved his hand, as if to greet an old friend. Getting very tired, I made my way back to my room. That was enough reconnaissance for today.

Chapter 4

As I was lying down, I heard a series of loud explosions that seemed to be getting progressively closer. At the same time, I heard what sounded like helicopter propellers hovering above. Through the open door, the patients and staff in the hallway appeared frightened. My guard told me to get off the bed and lie on the floor, with him on top of me. "See, I protect you," he said, while shivering.

This whole experience was schizophrenic. One minute they're cutting me up and threatening me with immediate execution, and now I am invaluable, and in need of protection. No matter, I had no idea of what was actually occurring.

Just as quickly as it began, the explosions stopped and my guard got off me. Then I heard sirens approaching, presumably from ambulances. My best guess was that injured people were being brought in for assessment and treatment.

Hassan opened the door and screamed, "You see, those damned Israelis' must have targeted one of our leaders with their helicopter gunships. They rocket the area and, no doubt, innocent civilians are hurt. You see why we hate those sons of bitches. Stay inside your room," he cautioned, as he closed the door and abruptly left. I got up and reopened the door just a crack to observe white-coated ambulance drivers shouting in Arabic while hurriedly carrying stretchers holding wounded individuals covered in blood.

Then an unbelievable scene unfolded. Four men on the stretchers threw off their blankets, jumped off the carts and brandished Uzi submachine guns. An exchange of gunfire with building guards immediately began. One of my masked interrogators then pointed his weapon directly at me and I froze. Almost immediately, one of the intruders shot him in the head. The shooter then approached me and demanded that I seek cover, while the building was being secured. The whole confrontation was over almost as quickly as it began.

Early on, the guard in my room had thrown down his weapon and lay face down upon the cold floor, placing his hands, fingers clenched behind his neck. I was asked who was in charge, and replied that I wasn't certain, but did say I had dealt primarily with Dr. Hassan, who at this point, was quietly kneeling with a group of Arab patients in a nearby corner. The intruders began to cover the heads of the patients and staff with loose fitting white cotton hoods.

During the commotion, several-armed Arab guards had been killed, and one of the attack force members seriously wounded. His condition appeared grave with a gaping wound to his head. He was intubated and given an IV, while I was instructed to put on a blood soaked lab coat. Both of us were then strapped to stretchers and quickly carried out.

Hassan was instructed in Arabic to accompany us, but he refused. He stated that his patients required his care, and that he would not leave them unattended, as he was the only doctor assigned to the building. I interceded on his behalf, indicating that he would probably be too busy taking care of his own hurt people to interfere with us. His hood was then removed and we began to leave. To my dismay, as we started down the stairs, Hassan picked up a discarded assault rifle and before anyone could determine the reason for such action, he was shot dead. "What a waste!" I shouted, as we filed out.

The rest of the building staff were bound, gagged, and told not to move for 15 minutes, or they would risk being shot. In passing, I caught a glimpse of one member of the attack force placing what appeared to be timed charges against the stairwell. It all was proceeding too rapidly; I never had a chance to question anything.

We made our way down poorly lit corridors to the street level where I saw "Crescent" marked ambulances waiting. The area was filled with people. The crowds began to part for our ambulances, as directed by our Arabic speaking drivers. Suddenly, several armed militiamen approached and demanded to know why we were leaving with men on stretchers. They were told that the doctor inside the building was killed and these gravely wounded patients required transport to another medical facility, less than a mile away. Fortunately, we were allowed to pass. Afterwards, these same militiamen entered the building from which we had just come.

I heard an explosion and the entrance to the building fell to rubble. As our ambulances raced away, shock began to set in. I began shaking and couldn't stop. I vomited into a paper bag. When that stopped, tears started flowing uncontrollably. Within minutes after arriving at a tree-lined gully, two helicopters landed. The seriously wounded attack force member and I were secured in one craft, while the remaining rescue force boarded the other. At that point, I passed out.

Regaining consciousness, I awoke in a hospital room. Someone in street clothes was checking my vitals and conversing with a nurse. I overheard them say I was fortunate, but dehydration had worsened my infection.

I was about to drift off when I was abruptly jostled. "Hey Wolf, you don't get the luxury of resting, while others have to shoulder your responsibilities. Say *Shalom*, to your concerned friend."

Opening my eyes, to my amazement, there stood Menachim, apparently physically well. I told him my Arab captors informed me that he had been killed, along with General Orin and our driver.

"Fortunately, they were only partially correct; the driver and I were not seriously injured," Menachim responded.

I was glad to see him.

Anticipating my next question, he told me he was able to track my whereabouts with a homing device he had previously glued within the sole of one of the shoes I had been given by his neighbor.

"Standard practice, when the Mossad is entertaining such a valuable person as you," Menachim joked. "The signal was GPS traced to your location. Luckily, your other hosts didn't do a sweep for these devices, and you didn't set off any car alarms, as can sometimes happen. It was then necessary to figure out the best tactical diversionary action to rescue you, before you were disposed of or shipped off to Iran. That was very possible, as they were bringing in Aberdam, a chief U.S. State Department operative with known ties to Middle East terrorist organizations.

Wolf, you missed all the fun here in Israel. While you were getting pampered, the rest of us had work to do." It was at that moment Menachim saw the handiwork imprinted upon my chest.

"That explains your infection. Do you think that scar is something? I should take you down to the civilian amputee and burn ward. Those poor souls carry a reminder of terrorism that can't so easily be concealed."

I quickly interjected, "I'm not complaining, I'm just happy to be alive and to see you alive. Are Abbie and Mehmet all right?"

He hugged me and kissed my cheek. "Typical nice Jewish boy always concerned about family and friends first and foremost. Your dear Abbie appears to be stable." Intentionally avoiding answering about Mehmet, he diverted, "I think that you will find my other news of great significance."

A military attaché then interrupted and Menachim translated for my benefit.

"Jon, Aberdam discovered your identity. However, he didn't know if you were killed in the building entrance collapse. A reward equivalent to ten million dollars in United States currency is currently payable upon physical proof of your death."

"Ten million dollars, is that all I'm worth? What happens next?" I quickly rattled off.

Menachim disregarded my weak attempt at humor. "First, we'll arrange to get your fingerprints altered and give you a new identity. How does the name Roberto Simon sound to you? For a career choice let's consider a research biologist's assistant, or something on that order."

I chuckled, "You would pick something boring."

"My friend, that's exactly the type of work witness protection programs seek out. You might be surprised about your opportunities. Now, I have other matters to go over with you."

Assured we were alone, Menachim then told me details of the "Escaping the Abyss" operation.

"We were able to gain access to the suspect areas beneath the *Temple Mount* without being compromised. Utilizing the flexible tubing we had discussed, heavily salinated water transported from the Dead Sea was injected into the caverns, successfully flooding a large number of them. Simultaneously, a mixture of an inert gas combined with a short-acting nerve agent was pumped into the rest, diluting breathable oxygen. All appeared to be going well, until an alarm sounded and armed Arab guards entered the higher levels and began firing their weapons wildly. Within moments the shooting ceased as the gunmen lost consciousness."

"In several remote areas within the tunnel complex inaccessible to the gas or flooding, we detected explosive triggers. Fortunately, they were situated amongst smaller numbers of the graphite encased enriched Plutonium balls. Units of our Special Forces wearing gas masks broke through to these sections. They radioed back that fierce hand-to-hand fighting cost many lives on both sides. That said, there was one narrow tunnel that could not be secured and its contents were remotely detonated. Thank God, there wasn't a nuclear reaction."

Hesitating, Menachim took a drink from my water glass before continuing, "However, the explosion was sufficient enough to weaken the support structure of the *Temple Mount* and irradiated dust clouds began leaking from the resultant surface openings.

We had no choice but to clear the surrounding mixed population of Arabs, Christians, and Jews. Arab leaders immediately began spinning a fabricated story that the whole nuclear mess was planned by the Israelis."

Menachim then looked directly into my eyes, "Jon, we had to release all the information that you and Agent Mehmet found on Abbie's laptop to a United Nations commission, charged with investigating the incident. Unfortunately, Israel is expected to go on trial for planning an attempted destruction of Islam's Holy sites."

Exasperated, he continued, "We are impotent in participating in the actual fact-finding investigation, other than by supplying what we knew and how we knew it, through our Foreign Affairs representatives. Formal proceedings against us are expected to convene within a month. However, we did learn through one loyal source that several prominent U.S. State Department officers were taken into custody for questioning regarding their involvement with known terrorists who possessed expertise in nuclear detonation.

Currently there are also uncorroborated allegations of involvement by Israel's President with various Arab and Muslim nationals, including Iranian and Palestinian agents. Wire taps revealed that the latter plotted to bring down Israel and to establish a subsequent larger, one-state entity, overseen by a joint Muslim and Arab Authority.

Lastly, the Arab engineer who you spoke with at the planning site appears correct in his allegation that a small number of Israeli officers' were also complicit in the planned nuclear destruction of Jerusalem's *Temple Mount*. That brings shame upon our nation. How could Jews born and raised in Israel sell out their heritage and put in jeopardy so many innocent lives? Apparently Arab terrorists don't have a monopoly on evil."

"Jon, you must understand that your rescue was unauthorized and unrecorded. In fact, your identity and whereabouts are unknown except to a few trusted souls. I must also inform you that the press found out that you had full knowledge of the contents of your wife's correspondences with Jabr Mahjub, son of a terrorist-linked Lebanese Foreign Service officer.

Regrettably, his entire family went missing and, we suspect, were eliminated, as they could have provided independent verification of our side of the story. They were our best hope, as Abbie remains non-communicative. Incidentally, her hospital room is under 24-hour guard. No one gets in or out without verifiable credentials. Soon she will be moved to a more security favorable location.

There is one other potentially supportive speaker on our behalf that we can't seem to locate. Your friend, Agent Mehmet has effectively disappeared. He was in our protective custody, in what we thought to be a 'safe house' in the Chicago area. However, the apartment was raided and two of our best agents were killed. Yet, there was no trace of Mehmet. Even his D.N.A. was wiped clean from the apartment. The F.B.I. and we are at a loss as to who was responsible.

One possible suspect is the branch chief of a small State Department sub-agency, whose background check intimates suspicious political leanings and long-term hostility to Jews. Therefore, our Intelligence agents are actively seeking a Mr. Aberdam. Interesting, he too is nowhere to be found."

I then asked about Mehmet's daughter Malak Abbas, and his granddaughter Eryn.

"Jon, they're okay, but sorely missing Mehmet."

"They are not alone," I added.

"We know for a fact that you are being actively sought out. With you dead, the international case against Israel could proceed without much obstacle. You pose a threat to all of the conspirators. It will be hard to protect you here, so we have decided to move you, as inconspicuously as possible, and keep you safely concealed, until your information can be independently verified.

You should also know that the U.S. State Department, through the offices of the F.B.I. and Interpol, has issued a warrant for your detention and questioning, labeling you a suspected national security risk. As you can see, it may be some time before this mess is straightened out. In the meantime, you have to vanish. We are taking you to a small airbase tonight and will relocate you to a European safe house, where you will remain hidden, until the world proves more receptive to hearing the facts. Exactly when that will be is anyone's guess. Naturally, you won't do yourself or us any good if you turn up dead."

With an intentional pause followed by a muted laugh Menachim added, "And now for the bad news."

He continued on, in a more somber tone, "Jerusalem is in a state of near panic. There are international groups capitalizing on the chaos. It reminds me of your 1968 inner city riots, after the Martin Luther King assassination. Crowd control is not going well. Our people are turning on the government and out of frustration are placing unjustified blame upon our side. With only one-sided hostile information on the table, previously neutral nations are beginning to line up against us. There is a call for Jerusalem to be internationalized. If allowed, this could be the beginning of the elimination of our biblical heritage. We may be in a struggle for our very existence. Rumors are circulating that Jews may have to be rounded up, allegedly for our own protection. A witch hunt has begun for a scapegoat and once again it is us."

I inquired about Menachim's wife and daughters.

He responded, "For their safety, my family is staying in Netanya with distant cousins."

Changing the subject, Menachim pointed out, "Jon, once you are abroad you will have the option to undergo facial reconstruction to further facilitate your safety." He then added, "If I were offered the same opportunity to leave, even for a short while, I might take it, especially with the prospect of facing months, if not years, of the insecurity and confusion that lies ahead of us."

I replied, "Like hell you would leave. Look, I didn't ask for any of this either. Menachim, I will return and help you straighten out this mess whenever you call upon me. Nevertheless, promise me that you will not stop searching for Mehmet. Israel owes this man and Arabs like him, great respect. Most importantly, watch over my dear wife, Abbie. Do not let any harm come to her."

As I was being led away, Menachim said, "Don't do anything stupid, Jon. Don't be a hero! Remember our national future may well depend upon you."

That being said and heard, I cannot so easily forget who I am and what was done to my wife and daughter. I will play by Menachim's rules, until I complete my part. Then I'm heading back to be with Abbie and if at all possible, to search for Mehmet, no matter the risks to my well-being. When it comes down to it, without the people I love, and who once loved me, I might as well have been killed in the accident that brought all this about, not that long ago.

Chapter 5
(Three Weeks Earlier)

Dr. Miller entered the emergency room where, only minutes earlier, Wolf was brought in unconscious. After assessing the strength of his pulse, respiration, and pupillary reflexes, Miller repeatedly tapped Wolf's shoulder while asking, "Can you hear me?" Not getting a reaction, he looked at the overhead monitors and observed Wolf's blood pressure rising, while at the same time his heart rate began to slow significantly. Miller ordered Megan, his assistant to schedule a cranial scan. She immediately alerted the on-call radiology tech, who quickly put everything necessary into motion.

Picking up the chart, Miller read that Wolf's car hit a concrete barrier, while travelling an estimated 55 miles per hour. The nearest fire department dispatched E.M.T.s who found him unresponsive but stable. During transport, they drew a sample of his blood to facilitate a transfusion match and for logging the blood alcohol level. The report indicated there had been two other passengers, but was unclear as to their status.

Miller then looked up and saw what he presumed to be the accompanying police officer waiting outside the E.R. He motioned her in.

A petite, dark haired woman in her late 30's entered. She identified herself as Malak Abbas, a police criminal investigator who happened upon the accident scene, just as the ambulance was arriving. She immediately inquired if Wolf's blood alcohol level had been determined.

"Not to my knowledge," Miller replied. "What can you tell me about the other passengers?"

Abbas indicated that one was Abbie Wolf, the driver's wife, who had suffered a serious head trauma and was airlifted to the Level One University Hospital facility. A young unidentified female, presumably their daughter, appeared to have been thrown from the crushed vehicle. Unfortunately, she was pronounced dead at the scene, and subsequently transported to the county coroner's office, also located in the same facility.

Although a veteran of this type of situation, Abbas appeared unexpectedly distraught. She took in a deep breath and slowly let it out, while trying to regain her composure before going on to describe the extent of the child's injuries. In passing, she mentioned having a daughter about the same age as the victim. Then her features hardened as she stated, "If alcohol were involved in this accident, I'll make sure someone pays for this waste of precious young life."

Wolf was returned to the E.R. with his imaging scans lying upon his chest. Miller grimaced as he read them. "Damn, an occipital subdural hematoma with brain swelling," he mumbled.

Only one other time, many years earlier during neurology rotations, had he observed the treatment necessary to resolve the problem. Unsure of his current skills, he immediately requested a telephone consult with Dr. Brownstein the head of emergency services, who because of the late hour was thought to be home and most likely asleep.

Taking another glance at Wolf's vitals, Miller knew a trip by ambulance to a skilled trauma center with an experienced neurologic attending could prove too risky, at this stage. He politely asked Abbas to leave. The E.R. suite phone began to ring.

"Bob Miller," he answered.

"This is Brownstein, what do you have?"

Miller went on to describe the situation and his treatment plan. Brownstein asked if Miller wanted him to return to the hospital to assess the situation.

Understanding the urgency, Miller simply sighed. He knew he had to quickly relieve the intracranial pressure. His plan involved first accessing and then expressing any suspected clot or clots. Then he would seal any leaking blood vessels.

"That's why we got into medicine." Brownstein commented before adding, "Go ahead, do your best, and call after you have finished. Miller hung up and immediately ordered a Cranial Drill Kit. The only piece of luck was that the E.R. was atypically slow and therefore a surgical suite was sure to be available.

Wolf's condition quickly worsened, his mobility to a surgical suite at this stage was too risky. Time was of the essence. Everything would have to be accomplished now, and within the Emergency Room.

Megan, standing alongside Miller, had served as a combat surgical nurse and understood what had to be done. She knew that there would be little hope, if they delayed their surgical intervention. Wolf's occipital pictures were quickly slipped into the light boxes, in the hope that they might serve as a roadmap to the suspected clot.

Meanwhile, Wolf was firmly secured to the sterile transport table with only a thin cotton sheet separating him from its cold metal base. An operating lamp was brought in and set up, as a surgical diamond drill bit was secured. Not knowing if the procedure would ultimately be successful, Miller decided to request that a "Medivac" helicopter be made available.

Miller's face began to flush. Megan grabbed his gloved hand into hers and calmly said, "Let's start."

Across town, Abbie's parents, Jim and Marney Silver, arrived at the University Hospital and Teaching Center. At the front desk, a security guard directed them to a waiting area where they would meet with the Chief of Neurology when he became available. The room was warm, yet both began to shiver.

They had only been in an emergency situation one other time. Abbie was 15 years old and hit in the leg with a fast pitch league ball. She was in excruciating pain, but conscious. This time it was frighteningly different.

Marney suggested that Jim telephone their rabbi and ask him to join them at the hospital, while they awaited news on their daughter's condition.

"Are we to lose Abbie, as we did our only grandchild Sandra?" Marney questioned under her breath.

Unaware of their son-in-law's circumstances, Jim commented, "Jon's loss must be unbearable, especially with no family by his side. But Abbie is our immediate concern." They sat down on a large couch in the empty room and passed the time praying silently for their daughter's recovery.

Moments later a uniformed police officer knocked at the entrance before entering. "My name is Officer Malak Abbas. I was first at the scene of the accident. Please call me Malak."

Marney quickly asked, "Did our granddaughter suffer?"

"No," Abbas replied, believing that under these tragic circumstances, these people needed to hear some reassuring words. She knew that would be what she would wish to hear and she didn't hesitate to ease their pain, even if for only a brief moment.

Noticing her dark complexion and detecting what she thought to be a possible Middle Eastern accent, Marney casually asked Malak if by chance she were Israeli.

Abbas flashed a smile and informed the Silvers that she was a second generation Arab-American, adding that her family roots stemmed from Jerusalem and the Gaza strip. To lighten the mood, she told them her name in Arabic meant Angel.

Sensing embarrassment from Marney's reaction, Jim quickly stepped in and expressed appreciation for what Abbas had done. "Thank you," he said as tears began welling up in his eyes. Silver had been through World War II as a bomb disposal specialist and was familiar with death. Nevertheless, Sandra was their first and only grandchild. It was a particularly hard time, as it wasn't that long ago that they lost their son to complications from kidney disease.

Jim and Marney had been high school sweethearts, who were parted by war and married in the peace that followed. He returned to his sales job and quickly rose through the company ranks. Ever ambitious, he went on to further his education at night, eventually earning a B.S. in political science. That served as his stepping-stone into law school where he graduated in the top ten percent of his class. He subsequently secured a position working for the State's Attorney, in the criminal prosecution division, where he practiced for 30 years, until recently choosing retirement.

Marney, on the other hand, never did fulfill her childhood dream of attending college. After her marriage, she did what was the tradition of the time. She raised a son and a daughter, giving each the encouragement and financial support to accomplish whatever they wished.

Both Jim and Marney Silver knew how important family was in the scheme of things. Now their family was in crisis. They had been unprepared for the telephone call that came in the middle of the night. An Illinois state trooper informed them of the seriousness of the crash. Yet, he didn't reveal the extent of the injuries suffered.

With one subsequent telephone call to an influential colleague, Jim was soon able to get the details of Sandra's passing and Abbie's incapacitation.

"Officer Abbas," Marney went on, trying to control her emotions.

"No, it's Malak, please, call me Malak," she insisted.

"What can you tell us regarding our Abbie? Was she lucid when you arrived on the scene? Did she call out for either Jim or me?" Marney rapidly questioned.

"No ma'am. Your daughter was in an unresponsive condition. Luckily, the E.M.T.s arrived quickly. We were also fortunate that a passerby called in the accident moments after it occurred."

Now, it was officer Abbas who asked the questions, the first of which was to inquire if their son-in-law ever drank to excess.

Abbie's parents were at first flustered by the question. They had never been overly fond of Jon, as he had not come from a base of wealth or social standing. Yet, he loved their daughter, shared their work ethic and appeared to be a responsible husband and caring father.

The question continued to filter through Marney's anxious thoughts. "Do you think he was responsible for this tragedy?" she asked. "He always had a temper," she exaggerated, as she focused her eyes away from Abbas and toward her husband, who sat quietly by.

Jim understood that he would be called upon to be the strong, sensible one. It was expected of men of that generation. "Honey, let's concern ourselves with Abbie's welfare and what we are going to have to face with Sandra's funeral. Let's give Jon the benefit of the doubt, until evidence proves otherwise." Still, from his long career with the State's Attorney, he had prosecuted good individuals, even highly connected and powerful people, who had D.U.I.'s that resulted in serious injury and even loss of life. Jim knew that this question would have to be addressed, eventually. However, later was preferable.

Seeing an approaching doctor, Abbas went into the hallway, introduced herself, and asked for an update on Abbie's condition. The physician requested she accompany him back into the room with the Silvers present. There, he would only have to answer the obvious questions once.

Chapter 6

With the prepping completed, it was time to start the surgery. Dr. Miller steadied the drill, took a quick reference look at Wolf's brain scans, and began to rotate the hand crank. "Slowly," he muttered to himself, almost imperceptibly. "Steady," he spoke louder. The only thing not audible was his silent prayer that he saves this man's life.

He knew by feel that he had just passed through the rigid skull. Now his major concern was rupturing soft brain tissue, which might result in permanent damage. With each turn of the drill crank, fragments of skull were starting to fall onto the white receiving cloth placed beneath Wolf's head.

Aware that sweat dripping into his eyes would cause a loss of focus, Megan dutifully swabbed Miller's forehead. He was at a particularly difficult stage in the operation; yet knowing Megan was there bolstered his confidence.

Believing he was at the probable location, he put down the drill and began to probe for the clot suspected of contributing to Wolf's life-threatening problem.

"Megan, we should have hit the 'hot area!' Where in hell is the clot?" The increasing pool of blood, within the sub-Dural sheathing, was continuing to threaten Wolf's vitals and Miller wondered how much longer his patient could withstand the pressure upon his brain.

He turned the probe slight lateral from its current position. Nothing happened, so he went back to the original position and this time turned it slight nasal and suddenly a gush of blood burst forth, splattering his face shield. "Thank God!" he yelled and repeated these words two more times. His eyes sparkled, Megan would later relate to the Chief of staff when they reviewed the case. Even through his surgical mask, she recognized his happiness. "Megan, this is why I went to medical school, not to make money, but to make a difference."

Wolf's heart rate and blood pressure began to stabilize. Yet, he was not out of danger.

Chapter 7

Dr. Shah asked Jim, Marney, and Officer Abbas to follow him to a more remote area of the urban high-rise hospital, as he was unsure of their individual reactions to what he was about to reveal. "Let's go to the chapel," he suggested; which he thought most appropriate for his purpose.

He motioned for them to sit together. In a concerned, yet professional demeanor, he went on to explain, "Your daughter was very seriously injured in the auto accident. Her tests indicate her brain may have been deprived of oxygen for several minutes subsequent to the crash." He paused and waited for the response he expected.

"Will she recover?" Marney asked.

"It's too early to say with certainty, but she appears stable at this point in time." He continued with a more cautious tone, "She's in a trauma induced coma and her brain wave pattern is erratic." He put a hand on each of the parent's hands and said, "I am afraid we will have to wait this one out."

Of course, she will not be able to attend Sandra's funeral, Marney thought to herself.

The impact of what Shah had said to these already grieving grandparents had yet to settle in. He proceeded. "I expect that the patient…"

Marney then cut him off, "Abbie, doctor, her name is Abbie. We would appreciate it, if that is how you would refer to our child."

"Very well," Shah continued, "I suspect Abbie will be with us for some time. However, I can't say with certainty when she will be off feeding tubes, monitors, or assisted breathing. As I said, her brain wave pattern is questionable and neurologically her reflexes are not normal. Does she have a designee to address her health care wishes?"

Shah's words were traumatizing. A look of total dismay came upon Marney as she said, "Abbie is in the prime of her life and now appears to be cut off from what was expected to be a promising future."

"I think it best that I leave you to gather your thoughts and perhaps to pray for your child." Shah said as he left the room, followed by Abbas.

Praying was exactly what Jim and Marney continued to do, as they held each other and sought heavenly intervention. They understood that the fate of their daughter rested with a higher power.

Leaving the chapel, a floor nurse approached and informed them, "Excuse me folks, your daughter Abbie is being transferred to the intensive care unit."

As they neared the elevator, Marney's knees began to buckle. Jim braced her up, until she regained her footing and then both went to see their child.

Chapter 8

Serena, the critical care unit nurse shouted, as she tried to get a response from Jon Wolf.

She firmly pinched his shoulder and he tensed. "Good job, Wolf," she said in a West Indian accent.

My eyes opened and I began to make inaudible sounds.

"Mr. Wolf, my name is Serena and together we are going to get you well. Can you see the T.V. camera by the corner ceiling? From there we can observe your progress, check your vitals and administer medication remotely without personally having to come into the room all the time. Isn't technology marvelous? Now, don't attempt to get out of bed or you will trigger an alarm, which will upset us, as we have many patients in far worse condition than you to deal with today."

She left as Dr. Brownstein entered my room, accompanied by three interns; I asked him where I was and what had happened to me.

He replied with emphasis, "You are a very lucky man who had an emergency room doctor named Miller save your life! I suggest you remember that."

"It says on the arrival slip you are a doctor. What's your specialty?"

I replied, "Optometrist."

"Oh," Brownstein responded.

I had seen that look before and even in my weakened condition, it irritated me. It appeared as a look of diminished respect for a medical profession this physician most likely didn't fully understand.

Suddenly my thoughts shifted to my wife and daughter. "Where are Abbie and Sandra? Are they all right?" I asked.

"All in good time," Brownstein replied, while passing my post-surgical reports on to the interns.

All the while, I was thinking, "What a lame response. What's with this guy? Is he trying to push my buttons?" Then I heard one of the young interns instruct me to stay awake for what was hopefully to be my last visit to nuclear medicine, at least in this facility.

Having completed the tedious imaging procedure, I was escorted along the hospital corridor that was beginning to fill with people, I wondered about my family. I looked at everyone who came my way, but didn't recognize any familiar faces. At the same time, I tried to recall what had happened the evening before, but without success. It was as if a closed gate separated me from my immediate past.

I returned to my C.C.U. bed and re-hooked to those annoying monitors. Although my actual physical discomfort was minimal, I was growing increasingly anxious about the uncertainty of my family's status. This time and with more vigor, I bellowed out, "Nurse, Doctor whoever the hell is out there, get in here!" I was ready for confrontation.

The station nurse was the first to arrive and inquired as to my problem.

"Where are my wife and daughter?"

The nurse firmly replied, "Be calm Mr. Wolf."

"That's Dr. Wolf, Nurse!" I angrily stated.

"All Right!" she forcefully responded. "Your physician will be on his way back to speak with you after he reviews the results of your imaging tests. You're not the only patient he has to see," she added with attitude.

"Bitch," I said under my breath. She turned towards me and gave me a menacing look. That apparently was not the first time she heard the word in reference to herself.

Through the glass partition, I could see Brownstein approaching, but this time accompanied by and conferring with a uniformed police officer. Walking together, they stopped just outside of my door. I could not hear anything, yet a sudden chill came upon me.

Dr. Brownstein entered alone and inquired in a kind tone if he could call me Jon.

This time I calmly replied, "Please tell me about my family."

Almost apologetically, he informed me, "I am sorry to tell you this, but you and your family were involved in a very serious auto accident. Your wife and daughter were taken to a level-1 trauma center, and you were brought here. I don't know their status. However, I can tell you that they are in a respected medical center and are receiving the best of care and you will soon be joining them. I signed your transfer orders and a helicopter is on the roof ready to transport you. Please remain calm. I'm sure everything will work out. We have done all we can for you here and that's it." He turned to walk away as I called out for him to answer more questions. Ignoring me, he closed the door behind him.

Again, I saw him speak with the same police officer. However, fatigue was setting in and I soon fell asleep.

Meanwhile, Brownstein shared with Officer Abbas the report on Wolf's blood alcohol level. It was just above the legal limit at .082, enough in the State of Illinois to consider him functionally impaired at the time of the accident.

"Did you tell him anything regarding the specifics of the accident?" Abbas questioned Brownstein.

"Look," the doctor replied, "he has a full plate and he'll find out soon enough about the situation he may or may not have caused."

"May I quote you on what you just said?" she questioned.

"Cut the crap, Officer! I have another patient waiting and I have to leave."

"May I have a brief word with your patient, the good doctor Wolf?" she sarcastically inquired. Eager to put the pieces of her case together, she was getting frustrated with the delays traditional medical routine dictated.

Brownstein asked, "Are you going to charge him, right now?"

Abbas shook her head no.

"Then wait until he is transported to and evaluated by the University Hospital Neurology Department. Post-surgical complications are not that easily foreseen. A comatose or dead patient is not going to be of much use to you. Correct, Officer Abbas?"

Knowing very well that his blood alcohol level was enough to charge him, Abbas thought it best to allow events to unfold as Brownstein dictated.

"Wolf will keep," she said to herself as she entered the elevator and contemplated the strength of her case against him.

Chapter 9

Approaching the helicopter, hospital staffers helped me from my gurney and onto a stretcher mechanism before covering me with several layers of blankets. Once on board, I was secured with belts and hooks, to minimize jostling during the estimated 15-minute flight time.

"Enjoy the ride," one orderly said.

With noise-muting headphones placed upon my ears, I heard the pilot say, "It's not too often I get a conscious patient for company. I'll try to keep the aircraft from shaking too much, and you must try not to get airsick. However, if worse comes to worst, there's a small paper bag next to you. Use it, if you feel the need."

"Shit," I said. "All I need now is to puke my guts out on myself."

The helicopter took off and hovered above the roof before getting final instructions from the regional flight tower to proceed.

During the trip, I repeatedly tried to recall the events leading to the accident. I began talking to myself to jumpstart my cloudy memory. "I was getting ready for the party. Every year the boss throws a great affair and Abbie and I always looked forward to it."

Suddenly, I had a recollection of my wife in her black cocktail dress, the one that accentuated her cute figure. It's amazing, that after thirteen years of marriage, she still excited me. Moreover, our daughter Sandra was her spitting image, and I loved both my girls even more because of that.

Bits and pieces of the past were slowly returning. Sandra was not supposed to accompany us to the party, but her sitter Maxine came down with the flu. When she called to cancel, Maxi also informed us that none of her friends could fill in as a flu epidemic was working its way through the neighborhood junior college that she attended.

When our daughter found out she would have to join us, she was excited and fantasized a great adventure especially since my boss Andy's daughter Angie would be there. An only child as well, and only a year older than Sandra, Angie had a lot in common with our daughter. However, Angie is too much into boys for her own good, a trait I hoped wouldn't rub off on Sandra.

Then I recalled that at the last minute we were forced to drive Abbie's Honda, a recent present from her parents. Unexpectedly, my car required some repair work that day.

"Five minutes before we land," the pilot spoke into my headset.

That brought to mind we had arrived five minutes late for the party. Andy's wife Julie welcomed us, as Angie ran to Sandra. The two girls went up to her room to no doubt discuss the critical teenage issues of the day.

I remembered Julie saying, "Abbie, join me in the parlor where the women have gathered and Jon, you go into the den with Andy and the other docs. I am sure you will find shoptalk much more interesting."

The house was huge. Andy was a very successful eye surgeon who at the same time was not full of himself, like so many of the other M.D.s I had the displeasure to encounter in my daily work. He lived well, but not ostentatiously and, more importantly, always treated me with respect.

I don't remember having too many drinks that evening. In fact, compared to the others at the party, I recall being one of the more temperate abusers. The food issue was another story. I always had an overeating problem. Abbie was my polar opposite. Ever conscious of her brother's premature passing from kidney disease, she was sticking to a strict diet and it showed.

My reverie was interrupted, when I heard through the headset, "Dr. Wolf. Are you all right?"

"Yes," I replied.

"We'll soon begin our descent to the University Hospital's landing port. I suggest you remain as still as possible."

That was too much to ask of an anxious husband and father.

Chapter 10

The Silvers were approaching the hospital floor elevator when a nurse suddenly called out to them. "I am sorry folks, but I need one of you to go down to the morgue to identify your daughter's body."

Beginning to lose her color and feeling faint, Jim promptly settled his wife into the nearest chair. He then pulled the nurse aside and asked, "What the hell are you talking about? The Chief of Neurology just told us our child was holding her own. Now you tell us our daughter is dead. Where did you get your authority to say that?"

Frightened by Silver's heated response, she excused herself to find out whether or not her instructions were accurate. Within minutes, the I.C.U. medical director approached and apologized for the error. He clarified it was their granddaughter's body that required legal identification.

Jim demanded that the director provide a medically trained companion for Marney, while he attended to what had to be done. Attempting to remain composed under these trying circumstances, he still chastised any hospital system that would permit such an unverified statement, especially at this most stressful time. The Medical director agreed and pressed the elevator's basement button.

It sped both men to the lowest floor where the bodies were held. As the doors opened, Silver couldn't help but notice the obvious differences between this area of the hospital and the other floors. The walls were not painted; the plumbing pipes were exposed on the ceiling and the room temperature was at least 20 degrees colder. He had not brought his coat and began to shake, mostly due to the task he was about to perform. Proceeding through two wide automatic doors, he saw five tables with sheeted bodies.

The Medical director paged the morgue attendant and excused himself, telling Jim he had to get back to his regular duties. However, he agreed to personally check on Marney, adding; "Again, I am truly sorry for what was said. Call me if I can be of any further service."

As he began to walk away, Jim muttered in a low, but still audible voice, "Have you ever had to identify the body of someone you once loved?"

The Medical Director hesitated for a moment and then resumed moving toward the employee's elevator. He didn't want to engage this stressed man any further.

Chapter 11

The helicopter landed without incident and the pilot wished me luck.

Having heard the word "luck" used so often, its use now was starting to concern me. Maybe mine was about to run out.

The receiving staff immediately transferred me to a gurney and quickly brought me the short distance to, and then through, the hospital rooftops sliding doors. Even with a thick blanket, it was freezing outside and I was glad to get into a warm area.

Finally, I'd be reunited with my wife and daughter. It was a wonderful thought even though a strange foreboding came upon me. Nevertheless, I looked forward to getting resolution as to what actually happened at the time of the accident.

Before being assigned a room, once again I was taken for what I hoped to be my final brain imaging series. Although I understood their necessity, this additional delay was frustrating.

Secured on the M.R.I table, the tech read the medical history that accompanied me on the flight and said, "I guess you doctors really have nine lives, unlike the rest of us."

I heard the machine start to hum and pound and was reminded to remain as still as possible.

For no obvious reason, details of an accident that occurred much earlier, when I was just 15 years old, suddenly came to mind.

Shortly after my August birthday and just before school began, I crept into my parent's bedroom and took the car keys my Uncle Mort had left with us the evening before. He and my Aunt Charlotte were to be vacationing in Florida for two weeks. Without a garage, Mort thought it best to leave his prized, "1955 Cadillac" car with my father.

I remember opening the car door and starting the ignition. This shiny vehicle was just begging to be driven by a 15-year-old without a license.

With no thought of consequences and relying only on luck, I picked up my best friend Kenny who brought along his father's bottle of Seagram's whiskey. We saw ourselves as real men. "We have a 'cool' car, an open bottle of liquor and only need at least one cooperative lady to fulfill our fantasies." I boldly suggested.

Arriving at our last accomplice's home, we didn't see Howard outside waiting, as planned. To pass the time, we opened the bottle and shared in the prize. Finally, he stumbled from his apartment building stairwell, while walking towards our car. "You guys are really doing this. I can't believe it. This time you fuckers really came through," he laughed as he crawled into the back seat.

"Let me drive," Kenny demanded. "After all I am three months older than you assholes. That means I'm also smarter, as well as better looking!"

At this point Howard glanced up and saw the light in his bedroom window go on. "Shit," he said, "I bet that's my father. He must have heard me shut the front door. He has hit me with his belt for less. I'm going back upstairs, before I catch worse."

As he opened the car door and ran back into his building, we heard him loudly utter that oft-used, yet nevertheless stupid saying, "Don't do anything I wouldn't do!"

Howard's father opened the window and shrieked, "Get out of my neighborhood, or I'll call the cops on you sons of bitches!"

Kenny shot him "the bird" as our car slowly moved forward. "After all, we were not going be intimidated that easily, especially by a jerk."

I looked at my best friend and asked, "What happens if he does call the police?" Kenny replied with a smile, "Then I guess our ass is grass."

He and Howard were always bolder than I was. While, I would be the "idea man," almost as quickly, my conscience would temper my actions, and Kenny would joyfully egg me on. We had been friends for many years, having gone through elementary school together, before his family moved to the Roosevelt High School district. His father and mine had been fishing friends forever. That tight bond was rarely challenged, except when our moms got into a loud argument. Even then, the men wisely chose never to take a side that could have put a wedge between them. Nevertheless, what was important to us kids was the example of the male bonding they set for us.

Now, here we were in a mint condition "1955 Caddy." Poor kids like us rarely got such an opportunity and we were determined to take full advantage of it, common sense aside. Easing the car from 1st into 2nd gear, we were on our way. Where to, it really didn't really matter, as we were certain this would be the adventure of our lives.

However, we didn't get very far when we began to feel the effects of the hard liquor we had sipped earlier. Kenny suggested we pull into the neighborhood park to plan our next move. Howard had let us down and the odds of finding willing women to accompany us were zero. With no other options, we decided to take another drink before heading home.

At the far end of the park, a car slowly made its way toward us with its headlights off. Could this be the police, we wondered? After all, it was well beyond curfew. Agitated, Kenny shouted, "Jon, start the fucking car, let's get out of here! Maybe we can beat this."

Somewhat relieved at the thought of having this misadventure end, I slid into the driver's seat, started the engine, and said, "I guess no hot sex tonight." We both giggled, as I proceeded out.

Unknown to us, two unmarked police vehicles with their lights off were dispatched to block our exit from the park. Suddenly my left front bumper hit one of these cars. I heard the crunch and felt a sick feeling enter the pit of my stomach, especially when I saw the man inside pull out a gun and point it towards me. Reason did not enter my mind, only adolescent intuition, and in a moment I would later regret, I began to bear down on the gas. Looking in the rear view mirror, I saw the car we just struck attempt to follow, but its engine died. "Great luck," I thought. At the most, some excuse could always be made for the damage to my uncle's vehicle. That relief was short lived, as the other car in the park turned on its flashing lights and began to chase us.

In the turmoil that followed, I chose to stop and face the consequences. Suddenly and unexpectedly, Kenny put his left foot on the gas and the car lurched forward. That moment would serve to change my life and all whom I had ever cared about, forever.

Chapter 12

The morgue tech approached Jim and offered him a lab coat that he gratefully accepted. The tech, Ronnie, read the medical report and asked Jim if he was prepared to view the aftermath of the accident.

Silver responded, "I have no other choice. Her father's not available."

Ronnie cautioned the man that he mustn't try to be too brave and tears can be a wonderful stress relief mechanism. He then slowly began to pull away the white linen sheet and expose Sandra's face. Jim gasped, as he looked into the lifeless eyes that days earlier were filled with limitless wonder. It was hard for him to imagine this to be his once lovely little grandchild. Yet, her curly hair and general contour gave him the inner assurance it was indeed her.

"Enough!" he shouted with tears streaming from his eyes. "That's my Sandra."

Ronnie re-covered her and gently took hold of Silver's arm after noticing his color pale.

"I'm alright. What's next?" Silver asked.

The tech replied, "It's typical that in these cases an autopsy is performed. It's a requirement from the medical examiner's office to prove that the victim was not dead before the accident."

Jim nodded his understanding, as the legal requirements had not changed since he was with the prosecutor's office. The only thing different was his granddaughter would have to be the one cut up and each of her organs assessed.

"Is there any way we can avoid this?" he questioned.

Ronnie suggested calling a connected official who might be in a position to intervene. Then he asked Silver's religious affiliation.

Jim responded, "I'm Jewish."

The tech then pointed out that an influential rabbi might also be of assistance.

Silver was then escorted outside of the double doors and to the elevator. Putting his hand on Jim's shoulder, Ronnie asked if he needed any water or anything else before leaving.

Jim returned the lab coat and sat down for a moment to collect his thoughts. He pulled out his cell phone and while dialing, uttered a quick prayer that his rabbi of 30 years would be home to answer the questions he and Marney desperately needed addressed.

Although typically the call would have gone to his answering machine, Rabbi Ford picked up. After exchanging formalities, Jim broke down and began to sob. Neither his history in war, nor his prior job viewing murder scenes, adequately prepared him for what he had just seen.

Regarding the autopsy question, Ford reinforced what his congregant already understood. "The law of the land is the law to be followed."

Silver explained the circumstances of Sandra's death and Abbie's current coma as well as Jon's indeterminate status.

Rabbi Ford thought all of this appeared too much for any one individual to bear. Trying to spare his congregant further hardship, Ford intervened, "Jim, let me help you and Marney. I have a contact in the Medical Examiner's office that might be able to stay an autopsy. I cannot promise anything, but I think the auto accident by itself should be clear evidence of death upon impact. In all probability, the coroner would not find a secondary cause. Let's see if this can be resolved with the authorities."

Rabbi continued, "Although Jewish custom requires a prompt burial, this may not be the case now. I will also contact the Bet Din, the Jewish Court, as well as get in touch with a Jewish mortician." He reminded Jim not to say Kaddish, until the formal burial. "I will call you later and, hopefully, we will be able to arrange Sandra's funeral soon. I am truly sorry I can't be with both of you now."

Rabbi and Mrs. Ford were long time friends of the Silvers, as well as Marney's parents. He officiated at Abbie and Jon's wedding and named Sandra shortly after she was born. However, for all of this, his final act of loyalty would soon follow.

Not leaving anything to chance, Jim telephoned his old boss, Bob McNamara, a former State's Attorney. Although recently retired, Bob was still very influential. Unfortunately, he didn't answer the call, but Silver left a detailed explanation as to what he needed, and within what time period it had to be done.

Chapter 13

The radiologist informed me the scan did not show any new blood pooling in the labeled "hot area" of my brain. The only thing he mentioned in passing was an observation of a tiny frontal lobe lesion that appeared decades old. He asked if I ever experienced unreasonable behavior outbursts, or delusions of invulnerability. Not being devoid of common sense, I responded, "No."

Changing the subject and hoping this doctor might be able to assist me, I asked if he were able to check on the status of my wife and daughter. He said the best he could do was to leave an e-mail for the hospital ombudsman.

I understood he meant well, but at the same time, I was tired of excuse after excuse. I needed to know about my family and no one appeared to have the information or was willing to get it for me.

Later that day, I was transferred to the fifth floor general patient ward. The orderly commented as he angled me onto the elevator, "You must be a popular man."

I asked him why he thought that. He replied, "There are a number of people asking about you."

Perhaps it might be my in-laws and that would be just great, I thought. As the elevator doors were shutting, I thought I saw Abbie's father in the hallway, but I was too weak to call out.

As I was wheeled into my new room, I saw three nearby uniformed police officers look at me in a strange, somewhat menacing manner. At the same time, a very well dressed man approached me. His tag indicated that he was from the hospital ombudsman's office. Before he could speak, the officers rushed up and asked him if there might be a private area available. He pointed to a corner lounge and they began to take me there without saying a word.

The female officer flashed a badge and asked an older couple who were in the area to leave. I found myself surrounded by a male officer on either side of me and the female officer standing so close to me I could feel her warm breath. Speaking in a harsh tone, she identified herself as Malak Abbas, the police investigator in charge. The other officers were assigned by the State's Attorney to assist her.

Before I could say anything, she informed me I was under arrest and began to read me my rights. I attempted to interrupt her to find out what this was all about when one of the male officers firmly grabbed my right arm. He turned to Abbas and inquired if she wished me cuffed to the gurney. She looked me in the eye and asked if this would be necessary. Nervously I responded, "No." The officer then let go of my arm. She finished reading me my rights and asked if I understood them. She then asked if I wished a lawyer present, while she questioned me further. Although in shock, I stated I understood my rights. Knowing I needed my own questions answered immediately, I replied. "At this point, I don't want a lawyer, but I do want to know about my wife and daughter."

The officer who previously grabbed my arm said in a guttural tone, "Shut up! We do the talking. You listen and you answer!"

A staff doctor, apparently sent by the ombudsman rushed to intervene. He asked, "What do you think you're doing?"

Abbas handed him the arrest warrant. The doctor informed her and the other officers, "This man has just been through a great deal of physical stress, including brain surgery. If you push him too hard, he could have a stroke. Do you three understand me?" He focused on the officer who by now was painfully squeezing my arm. To my relief his grip relaxed. Both male officers took a step back.

Sizing up the situation, Abbas decided upon a different approach. She asked the physician if he wished to be present, while they questioned me. Anticipating his next question, she stated, "Dr. Wolf has formally declined a lawyer."

The doctor interjected, "I am not so sure he is in any condition to understand enough to legally waive his rights."

She commented, "If he is well enough to be discharged from the I.C.U. and to be placed in the general patient ward, I assume he is not at acute risk and can answer some simple questions."

The doctor nodded and asked if I felt up to this. Abbas told the two male officers to have a seat, while she spoke with me. I wanted to proceed and nodded back to the doctor indicating I was okay talking with Abbas and that it was okay for him to leave as well.

"Is this about my wife and daughter? Are they all right?" I asked.

"Your wife is being treated here, but I am not sure of her present condition. However, her parents are with her," Abbas replied.

"What about my daughter? Is she all right?"

"There is no easy way of telling you this. So I am just going to say it."

Without her uttering another word, I knew. Tears began to flow down my cheeks. She gently took my hand into hers and mumbled something about being brave.

"Your daughter Sandra died instantly, when your car hit a concrete barrier and she was thrown from the vehicle."

One of the seated officers shouted out, "Don't forget to tell the asshole, he was responsible for what happened!"

Abbas flashed a stern look of disapproval, "It's time for you to shut up, Bill. I am in charge here. Keep your comments to yourself."

Under his breath, but still audible to me, Bill said to the other male officer, "It's always because we go too easy on these bastards they think they can drink and drive drunk, ignoring any consequences."

When I heard this, I raised myself up in the gurney. I saw the two male officers tense. Abbas said quietly to me, "Where do you think you are going?"

I replied, "I have to find Abbie. She must be sick with grief. Sandra was our only child. My wife needs me. Can't you understand that?"

Abbas could understand, but knew better than to appear vulnerable to someone she had just arrested.

Her facial features hardened as she stated that my blood alcohol level was above the legal limit of .08. Until proven differently, my culpability was presumed.

I cried out, "Not again. Please Lord not again!"

Abbas responded, "What the Hell are you talking about?"

Chapter 14

When Marney and Jim entered her room, Abbie appeared to be peacefully sleeping. There were no obvious marks on her face or head, yet she was unresponsive to their hugs and kisses. Her parents decided to sit and just gaze upon their only surviving child. All of their dreams for her took a back seat to the fear her very survival was in jeopardy.

The blame game was about to begin. It was to be directed at their son-in-law. Marney had long hoped to quell the relationship between Abbie and Jon. She decided during her daughter's junior year at college to send her to study in Israel. This "nonsense," as she referred to their relationship, would then end and Abbie could find a more suitable man in due time. However, within a year of her return, she and Jon married. Now Marney thought Jon likely responsible for this terrible tragedy.

Jim's cell phone rang. As soon as he saw it was his former boss, he knew he could not take the call in Abbie's room. He asked his wife's permission to leave. Marney responded, "Go ahead; I need to speak to our little girl, alone."

Stepping into the hallway, Silver pressed the answer button and heard, "McNamara returning your call. Jim, how is it going?"

He replied, "Not well Bob, Abbie appears to be in a deep coma. Can you tell me something good?"

Bob replied, "Your son-in-law is being arrested as we speak. He is charged with impaired driving under the influence of alcohol and vehicular manslaughter. Have you spoken with him?"

Jim replied, "Not yet."

Bob added, "Although the blood alcohol level was higher than the state limit, unfortunately, there's little other supportive evidence of impairment. Meanwhile, the involved vehicle is being inspected at the auto pound."

Silver's cell phone again beeped its call waiting tone. When he saw it was Rabbi Ford, he asked if he could call McNamara back.

The former State's Attorney said he would hold for as long as necessary.

"Rabbi, what can we do about poor Sandra?" Jim questioned, as he held his breath awaiting a response.

"Good news, if one can say there is any good news under these circumstances. My friend in the Medical Examiner's office has spoken with the responding police officer, who indicated the potential for suspicious circumstances appeared remote. This, combined with the E.M.T. and hospital reports, as well as a telephone call from a Mr. McNamara all served to eliminate the need for an autopsy. Sandra's body will be released, and she can be buried as soon as tomorrow. I took the liberty to contact a local Jewish burial society and they will prepare Sandra's body. My schedule is at your disposal. Do you think all of this will be okay with her father?"

"Frankly, Rabbi, I don't care whether it is or not. Abbie is still comatose and Jon has been arrested for being the suspected cause of the accident. Thanks for your efforts. Go ahead and do what you have to do. I

75

will take the responsibility for dealing with my son-in-law. I will call you later to firm up the burial details. Is that all right? I have Bob McNamara from the office of the State's Attorney on the other line."

Silver switched back to the holding telephone call. "Bob, I am sorry. The other call was from the rabbi and, before I forget, thank you for helping to stay the autopsy on Sandra. Quite frankly, I am not so sure my sanity would have held up." Silver went on to relay the rabbi's question regarding Jon's approval.

"Jim, this is a legitimate concern. It's possible, the father, Jon, could demand an autopsy should he be charged with manslaughter. In order to proceed as safely as possible, it's my recommendation that you get a power of attorney authority in regards to both Sandra and Abbie's affairs. I will fax a copy of these forms to the hospital. Go visit with Jon, but put your emotions on hold, until this matter is taken care of. Say what you have to say and get him to sign the paperwork. Lastly, from my discussion with the current S.A., he wants to personally go after Jon and make an example of him. Something else may also help you to get a leg up, should your son-in-law buck your requests. When he was a minor, there was a sealed criminal action against him, involving another alcohol related fatality. I don't have to tell you that it's election season and the S.A.'s record is up for scrutiny. He is not exemplary and has a strong challenger. This could be a great case for him. How do you feel about what I am trying to tell you?"

"If you are asking me to care about Jon going to prison, let me put it this way, I put away bastards for lesser crimes. He took away our precious Sandra and possibly Abbie as well. He's lucky I don't take him out myself." Silver's demeanor hardened, especially as he and Marney had been unaware of Jon's prior history. He meant what he had said and he knew his friend would not repeat it.

Jim assured his old friend. "With just a little luck, the justice system should give Wolf exactly what he deserves and maybe more."

Bob made the following suggestion. "Volunteer your legal services to Jon. In that way, you can ensure the odds of success. Get him to tell you about his earlier court case. In the meantime, I'll call the S.A. and request a hold on the actual incarceration, until you gain total control of the situation."

Chapter 15

Abbas reminded me that even though I had declined a lawyer, I still had a right to reconsider before her interrogation proceeded. At that moment, Silver knocked on the door, entered and introduced himself as my legal representative. He turned to me and told me to shut my mouth.

She showed my father-in-law the arrest warrant.

He told Abbas to call the State's Attorney, as her boss had new directives. She looked him in the eye, but thought better than engage in a power struggle. As she stood up to leave, she instructed one of the accompanying male officers to cuff me to the bed frame. That done, Silver asked the other officers to wait outside during his conversation with me, his client.

Trying to control his inner rage, he quietly asked me for my understanding of the events surrounding the party and the accident. I told him I had no memory of the accident or what led up to it. The best I could do was to relate some sketchy details that had come to mind earlier that day.

Jim looked around to assure we were alone and the door closed, before saying. "Let me tell you what I found out. First, you were witnessed to have consumed four glasses of wine without eating much food. Your attitude was generally hostile to your hosts and your locomotion appeared impaired, having bumped into several other guests, while knocking down a serving platter. In fact, you were openly hostile to Abbie when she asked for the car keys. You shouted down her request to drive. You became obnoxious when your host suggested Abbie or one of the other guests drive your family home. Furthermore, you were observed to have forcibly grabbed both Sandra and Abbie's hands, while dragging them towards the front door, before they had time to say a proper goodbye to the hosts and other guests. Does any of this ring a bell?"

It didn't sound familiar or even like me, at all. Therefore, I shook my head no. At first, I thought Silver was joking, but his demeanor hardened as he was speaking. He told me I had to sign a temporary power of attorney so he could act in Abbie's stead, while arranging for Sandra's burial in the family plot.

He convinced me that I and I alone was solely responsible for the death of my daughter. Silver asked if I could live with that fact for the rest of my life. He then asked if I felt any guilt for the other death I caused as a youngster, again under the influence of alcohol.

This proved overwhelming. I began to experience difficulty breathing.

He saw the helpless expression upon my face and took advantage of it. He went on to state that he was going to seek out the previously sealed records to help defend me from the current D.U.I., as well as the vehicular manslaughter charge he expected to be filed.

At some level, he must have understood this may not have been proper, yet requested that I also sign a release on this issue as well. Nothing made sense. If anything, my prior history might raise the probability of my guilt and result in a stiffer sentence. However, he was my lawyer and knew best, so I thought.

I asked for a doctor, as I was feeling ill. However, Silver ignored this request and instead began to pump me for additional information. With the little energy I could muster, I relayed the details of the events that culminated in the death of my best friend Kenny, as the car we had taken hit a tree, while trying to evade the police.

I must have accidentally hit the medical alert button, as the floor nurse came rushing into my room, closely followed by the two police officers stationed outside my door.

"Are you alright?" she inquired, noting my elevated blood pressure, rapid pulse rate, and labored breathing. Emphatically she stated, "I think that's enough questioning for now!"

Although the two officers returned to their prior duty, Jim obnoxiously replied, "I am his lawyer and we need to prepare his defense case, as he is going to stand trial soon."

"I'm his nurse and I said wrap it up. You have five minutes more. I mean it!"

Silver began to belittle me. "Jon, be a man and get your act together! We have a lot to accomplish in a relatively short amount of time and you're not helping yourself with these bullshit antics."

I felt I had no choice but to do whatever he requested. He was Abbie's father and I could not imagine he might act in any other manner than to do his best to help his daughter's husband.

"Let's get these forms in order for the funeral and Abbie's care. Don't even bother to read them. They are just routine paperwork."

The nurse returned and was asked to witness my signature on the various Powers of Attorney papers and documents I was signing. She complied, but inquired if I knew what I was signing. I nodded and that was that.

Jim told me Sandra's funeral was to be held tomorrow and under the circumstances, it's best if I don't attend. After all, I was under arrest as the cause of her death. It would bring up too much pain for the others in attendance. I again nodded my understanding and thought to myself what other choice do I have?

Shortly after he left, the same nurse returned. "You've been through a lot. I think it best you eat something, to regain your strength. Also, I am going to speak with the officers outside, to see if you still require restraint to the bed railing."

With one hand cuffed, it was a constant struggle to drink water, even with a straw. I had to change my position frequently to avoid choking.

Finally, I reviewed everything I had been told and decided it was for the best that Jim and Marney take care of Sandra's funeral and look after Abbie. Clumsily, I knocked my food tray onto the floor. One of the outside officers heard the commotion and peeked inside. Seeing my predicament, he laughed and loudly asked, "What's the matter, loser? Having problems?" His partner smirked and added, "I think this one will get what's coming to him. I'll get Abbas. Maybe he has something to say."

As the taller officer left, he asked his partner if he wanted a cup of coffee.

Abbas literally bumped into Bill. "Perfect timing, boss, I think your boy might be in the mood to talk facts."

"What a pig," she thought, resenting the need for such goons to help control prisoners. Abbas was proud of her hard-earned reputation as a respected criminal investigator. She understood the job stresses including turning a blind eye to the pranks of a number of her male colleagues who resented her promotions and citations. However, one thing she was determined never to overlook was the crude sexual comments intended to knock her down to size. In the early days, she had to put up with a lot of shit, as women held minority representation within the department. Recently, that appeared to ease off a bit, but some hostility always seems to linger under the surface.

She opened the door and saw me wet and distraught. Immediately, she grabbed the key for the handcuffs and released me to go to the bathroom and put on a dry gown.

Through the closed door, I heard her ask, "Is everything okay?"

I responded, "Yes." When she asked if I wanted to talk, I ignored my father-in-law's advice and told her that the accident and its consequences were my fault. Perhaps this admission might also serve to be an opportunity to unburden my conscience from the other deadly auto accident that I was involved in as a teen, for which I was never, in my opinion, adequately punished.

The earlier incident was never spoken of, since my parents' demise. The scar was so deep and its consequences so severe I chose to file it away, fearing if I revealed it to Abbie, she could never love me and her parents would most definitely reject me.

I stared into the eyes of this kind police officer and whispered, "I destroyed my family, didn't I? I want to dispense with a formal jury trial, and to schedule a hearing with a judge, as soon as possible."

"Are you sure you want to proceed in that direction?" she questioned. From her body language, I surmised a warning light appeared to have gone off in her mind, suggesting I might try to take my life.

For the first time since this ordeal began, I smiled.

"What is so funny?" she inquired.

"Don't worry," I replied. "I'm not going to kill myself. Not that the thought hadn't crossed my mind, but I needed to face the system to finish this."

Abbas then followed up with a strange question, "Did you or Abbie have any enemies that might wish either of you harm?"

"What a silly thought, everyone loved Abbie. Although, I must admit few felt the same about me. Yet, no one ever expressed a desire for my death, at least not to my face. What makes you ask that?"

"Routine," she replied, knowing earlier in the evening she received a call from the police auto pound where a comprehensive check of Abbie's car revealed a small puncture hole in the brake fluid hose. It was not frayed, as one might expect from such an accident, but rather appeared deliberately cut. Yet, this might be difficult to prove without a motive. "Well, answer my question," she persisted.

"Not that I am aware of," I finally replied.

"Look Wolf, I think it's in your best interest to have your lawyer present when discussing this further."

"My lawyer, my father-in-law is probably attending to Abbie and Sandra now. Did you know he advised that I not attend my daughter's funeral?

Somewhat surprised at hearing this, she answered, "I am sure that must be very troubling; however, your lawyer also advised you to shut up. Do you remember that?"

Because of his obvious vulnerability, and to offset any potential claim in the future that he was coerced into a false confession, Abbas decided to reinforce upon Wolf the need to think before speaking.

Before leaving, she apologized as she cuffed me to my bed railing. "Rules are rules," she mumbled.

Chapter 16

Marney and Jim were sitting at their daughter's bedside when a man wearing a white lab jacket entered the room. Without introducing himself, he approached Abbie, took out his stethoscope, listened to her heart and checked her pupillary reflexes. He then assessed her knee and ankle reflexes with a rubber tipped mallet. Lastly, he pinched her arm to see if he could elicit a response. When none was forthcoming, he turned his attention to the E.E.G. brainwave monitor and its printout, all the while not making any notes on her chart.

Marney was becoming disturbed with this man's behavior. Finally, she asked, "Has there been any change from what the other doctor saw just moments ago." Without looking at either parent, he simply replied, "No" and left the room as quickly as he had entered.

"They certainly didn't teach that guy bedside manner at medical school," Jim said, trying to lessen the tension that was beginning to build. "Marney, did you catch his name?" he added.

She was brushing her daughter's hair, stopped for a brief moment and mumbled, "Abermen… or something like that," and then whispered in her child's ear, "Please wake up honey. I am so sorry."

Abbas was making her way to Abbie's room when she noticed a male figure wearing a lab-coat with his back to her, texting on a cell phone in a clearly posted area forbidding such activity. Her investigative instincts were alerted, yet she let it go. When she had second thoughts and turned back to speak with this man; he stood up, sped away and blended into the crowd entering the elevator.

She knocked and went into Abbie's room, asking how everyone was doing. The mom and dad's sad faces were answer enough.

"Are there any signs of improvement at all?" Abbas inquired in a hopeful tone.

Marney simply shook her head. Meanwhile, Abbas thought she heard Jim say under his breath, "The bastard will pay," and wondered to whom he was referring. She then asked what the plans were for Sandra's funeral. Jim Silver indicated it was to be a small gravesite service with only immediate family present.

"Mr. Silver, I know you are representing your son-in-law, but are you aware he plans to sidestep the customary process with a pre-trial admission of guilt? I warned him not to say anything else without you present. He seemed genuinely remorseful, willing to shoulder the total responsibility for the accident, and wants resolution."

At first, Jim cast an icy glare at Abbas, but then masked his feelings, while thinking this new option might well suit his intentions. That is, if a bench trial was held before the "right" judge.

"Perhaps this is for the best," he replied.

Abbas repeated the question asked of Jon Wolf earlier, but this time directed to the Silvers. "Did Abbie or Jon have any enemies that might wish either of them harm?"

In the course of their professional duties, Abbas and Silver understood all too well that everyone has enemies, some more desperate than others in seeking revenge for wrongs committed, actual or perceived. Even murders have occurred under seemingly petty circumstances and without much provocation.

Marney appeared puzzled, "I don't know about Jon, but everyone just loved my Abbie!"

Malak Abbas then asked Marney if anyone else had been in the room beside herself within the past 15 minutes or so. She told the officer about a seemingly rude doctor. Abbas asked her to describe him and Marney could not. The investigator thought better about pushing this possibly minor detail.

Abbas decided to reveal the punctured brake hose finding to observe Jim's reaction. There was none. It was as if she said nothing. Yet, he must have known this information could influence a judge or jury away from a simple conviction. Something was not adding up.

Earlier in the day, Abbas had assigned a subordinate to interview Wolf's neighbors, as well as several of the other attendees at the party. The information gained did not substantiate that Jon had a history of hostile behavior. Wolf's worst trait appeared to be his Type "A," obsessive personality. Yet, perhaps this one time, he could have crossed the line with tragic results for reasons still unknown?

Chapter 17

Silver excused himself so he could privately speak with McNamara. He hoped the latter could speed the legal process along before Jon might reconsider.

"Mr. McNamara," Silver stated with restrained excitement. "I think we have been handed a bit of good luck. My idiot son-in-law wants to waive his rights to trial by jury. Is there a judge we can count on to see things our way? I don't want him near any of us ever again."

"Did you get him to sign all the requisite papers?" Bob asked.

"Everything is proceeding as hoped for," Silver responded. "Wolf is so consumed with guilt he won't give anyone any problems. And I convinced him not to request to attend Sandra's funeral tomorrow."

Bob continued, "We make a good team, like in the old days when we had to bend the law, just a tad, to get the bad guys off the streets. Who says the ends don't justify the means. Is there anything else I need to know?"

Silver mentioned the police investigator's comment regarding Abbie's vehicle and its punctured brake-line. McNamara replied, "I am glad you brought that up. I saw a copy of the shop workup report and noticed that as well. Yet, only 24 hours later, the part in question went missing. Imagine that! Every other part of the car was present."

Silver snickered and then added. "I'll see you tomorrow. Do you know how to get to the cemetery?"

Jim then gave his friend directions and at the same time requested he not ask others to attend. After the services, he and Marney wanted to head back to the hospital to be with Abbie.

Abbas was on her way to check on her own daughter's welfare. Eryn was 12 and deeply troubled since her parent's divorce. Although never taking a side, she was very much aware of her mother's hurt because of her father's insensitivity, as well as his unreliability. Yet, like so many other young, naive girls, Eryn hoped her parents would eventually reconcile. However, this was not to be the case. Malak had been awarded full custody, with only strictly supervised visits allowed with Ekron, her father. Yet, it had been months since his last visit, at which time the smell of alcohol was so apparent Eryn went to her room, locked the door behind her, and cried herself to sleep.

School let out early today to accommodate a teacher institute program and Abbas wanted to make sure Eryn made it home safely. There was a 30-minute gap when she would be alone before the baby sitter arrived. Abbas hoped to make it home during that time. Yet, today the Wolf case proved too demanding.

Fortunately, she was able to reach Eryn on her cell phone. Her child had made it home and the sitter was already there. Mom and daughter then discussed her dinner options, with peanut butter and jelly being on the short list.

That finished, Abbas placed her next call, inquiring, "Is Dr. Monika available?"

"Yes, but she is with patients. Would you like to speak with her assistant Mary?"

"O.K., but I am still on duty. Can I be put through or will I have to wait?"

The office was well aware of the time constraints on their favorite police-lady, patient.

"This is Mary," there was a moment of hesitation. "Malak, I have the results of your C.T. scan. Everything is status quo. However, Dr. Monika would like you to see an oncologist and begin Retuxin treatments. Remember, early intervention might keep it from progressing."

"Thanks Mary, I'll think about it and get back to you." Abbas was all too familiar with cancer therapy. Her mother had it years earlier and the effects of the drugs used appeared more debilitating than helpful. They decreased the quality of her remaining years, before she finally succumbed. Abbas had mentioned this to Dr. Monika, who repeatedly informed her of the significant advancements in cancer drug therapy over the past ten years. Yet, this had not convinced her to go forward with the recommended treatment.

The mental picture of her mother's hair loss combined with her gradual physical weakening frightened Abbas. She was alone and had to be there for Eryn. It was clear Ekron could not be counted upon. However, there was one other person she might be able to look to for help, as a last resort: her father, G.P. Mehmet.

Since retiring from the F.B.I., he chose to live alone in Oregon, preferring fishing to family. The only connection he maintained with his estranged daughter was reading police mystery novels and seeing who could solve the "who-done-it" first and before the end of the book.

What he looked forward to the most was his weekly telephone calls to Eryn. He was the only man in her life she could count on and she loved him.

Although Abbas was outwardly hostile to her father since the death of her mother, practicality of current circumstances made her consider reconnecting with him, for Eryn's sake. "Who knows, he might even be of some use in the Wolf case?" Malak thought as she took the phone and began dialing his number, secretly hoping he would not answer and all she would have to do is leave a message for him to ponder. That was not to be the case.

"Dad, how the hell are you?"

"Baby Girl, you caught me as I was just about to leave." He always said that, never wanting his daughter to think he was just sitting alone in his cabin and doing nothing. In reality, Mehmet had been doing virtually nothing for almost six months.

"Anything interesting happening at work?" he eagerly inquired.

Even though she could not see him, she felt his voice strengthen with this question. Without hesitation, she began relaying all of the details concerning the Wolf case known to that point in time. The one-way discourse stretched almost 10 minutes before her father finally intervened. "Baby Girl, go over the part concerning the doctor sending an electronic message in the midst of all that sensitive medical equipment." She repeated what she knew.

"Would you mind if I called a former contact who works with the National Security Agency?" This was not the only aspect of the case that intrigued him. Mehmet asked if Abbie was Jewish and followed up with another seemingly out of left field question. "Did she have any involvement with Israeli politics?"

"Dad, I am telling you now and I don't want to repeat myself, don't make a big deal about it. Don't break any privacy laws. I don't want this case to be jeopardized by a due process compromise, or a potential civil rights issue. Clear?"

He laughed and said he would be getting back to her.

Chapter 18

Knowing that Eryn was safe and that Malak had an unusually calm conversation with her father pleased her. She decided to avoid the height of rush hour traffic by waiting a half hour before heading home. She turned back from the elevator as she observed Jim Silver enter Wolf's room. Abbas casually looked through the door's observation window and saw Wolf squirming in discomfort and waving to get her attention.

Sensing his predicament, Malak asked, "Wolf, did you inform the guard of you urgency?"

So as not to embarrass myself, I answered in a low tone, "The officer told me to just crap in my pants."

Abbas shrugged her head in disgust, immediately took the handcuff key from the guard, and released me, while asking, "Can you make it to the bathroom by yourself? If not, I am sure Officer Bill will gladly escort you. Correct Officer Bill?"

I ran to the toilet.

Abbas noted Silver didn't even acknowledge his son-in-law's predicament. He was too busy looking out the window, seemingly disinterested. She asked if it was convenient to record Wolf's formal statement. Silver nodded his approval.

I came out of the bathroom and made my way to a chair near the bed, where I saw the recorder being set up.

Abbas asked Silver about Sandra's funeral arrangements. He told her the narrowed scope of the services would minimize or even eliminate the presence of reporters. She understood that, but took the opportunity to ask if Wolf would be attending his daughter's internment.

Jim replied, "Jon thought it best not to attend and neither of us wish to discuss the matter further."

Abbas then turned to me, expressing an unsolicited comment that I might be better served by a trial of my peers. To this, I unequivocally responded that I wanted to declare my guilt before a judge, as quickly as possible. That said she recorded my admissions statement without any objection from my father-in-law. Naively, I asked if the case could be heard, as early as tomorrow. Abbas informed me it usually takes weeks at best for the busy court system to assign an available judge to an available courtroom. She turned to Jim for agreement and observed a smirk upon his face.

Silver then followed up with, "Because of what my client and family have endured, I am working on a way to accelerate the process and will advise you as soon as we know the date, time and room where Jon's case will be heard."

Playing back the recorded statement, and with all sides satisfied, Abbas packed up her recorder after placing the tape in a sturdy envelope at the nursing station. While there, a licensed hospital administrator notarized the seal.

Before leaving the hospital, Abbas returned to Wolf's room, and requested the guard to permanently remove the cuffs and leave them off, unless the officer had to leave him totally unsupervised. She signed the required form and finally headed home.

While stuck in traffic Abbas decided to take the opportunity to clarify a concern and she telephoned Abbie's neurologist, Doctor Shah. When told he would not answer specific patient medical issue questions without a formal release from her appointed guardian, Abbas cleverly changed direction, "If another doctor evaluated Abbie, would this doc be obliged to note down his findings and sign off on her chart?"

Shah replied that is customary, but inquired as to the reason for the question. Abbas simply thanked him and indicated she would be speaking with him again.

Meanwhile, Silver had reinforced the necessity that I avoid Abbie and Marney, at least for the immediate future and most importantly, not to request to attend tomorrow's funeral, since confessing my guilt. He explained it would cause unnecessary distress to Marney who was hanging on by a thread herself.

I asked where my daughter's body was. He informed me that a Jewish funeral home had picked her up, and she is being prepared for burial, as we speak. The thought of this proved overwhelming, and I was unable to discuss the matter further. I decided to follow my father-in-law's requests. The only thing I won't do is to stay away from my wife.

Chapter 19

Bob McNamara placed his last call to Jim for the evening.

"I have news. Just listen and don't comment. I have arranged with the clerk of the court to have the case heard in two days. This will give you a chance to go to Sandra's funeral and then to prepare for Wolf's bench trial. The presiding judge is none other than Ben Forman. He has consistently demonstrated zero tolerance for alcohol related accidents, having overcome the booze problem himself. He has handed down the stiffest D.U.I. sentences in the county, which, barring the unforeseen, should keep your son-in-law occupied for many years to come. Who knows? It could also prove unfortunate if something were to happen to him, while he was incarcerated. The Hearing is set for 10:00 a.m. in Room 240. Listen Jim, I think it best that I not attend tomorrow's service. I'll speak with you tomorrow."

Silver understood his friend's logic. Before leaving the hospital for home, Jim and Marney telephoned Rabbi Ford to firm up the plans for Sandra's funeral. That done and with both of them exhausted they returned to Abbie's room where each kissed their daughter good night. Marney said she would pray for her, while Jim whispered in her ear, "The man who was responsible would never be able to harm anyone else again." For a brief moment, Abbie grimaced, but no one noticed.

Before going off duty, the hospital chaplain, Rabbi Cohen dropped in to check on me, at the request of my doctor. Having just learned of my family's tragedy, he appeared visibly upset. Cohen surmised this to have been an unfortunate accident and he thought my emotional and physical pain to be sufficient punishment. Yet, he also knew the legal system had to run its course. Unexpectedly, he asked if I wanted to see my wife. I thought this an answer to my prayers and eagerly took his hand as we both stood up.

"Are you strong enough to walk or do you need a wheelchair?"

I chose the latter. As the rabbi was opening the door to my room, Officer Flanagan demanded, "Where the hell do you think you are going with my prisoner?" The officer then saw the chaplain's insignia and apologized. Rabbi Cohen asked if he would accompany us so I could see my comatose wife for the first and possibly last time.

"You know that I could get into trouble Father, but I suppose it would be okay, if I wrote in my report that we were taking him to the hospital chapel and on the way we happened to stop by her room for a moment." Rabbi Cohen was pleased and signed off as the officer requested. We made our way to the nurses' station where Flanagan casually inquired as to Mrs. Wolf's floor and room number.

No one spoke, until we arrived at Abbie's door. The police officer looked on as Cohen wheeled me next to my wife's bedside and then the rabbi took a chair at the far end of the room.

I took Abbie's hand into both of mine and slowly stood up. I gently placed my lips upon hers. I ran my fingers through her soft curly hair and my tears began to fall upon her wedding band as I pressed it against my cheek. There was nothing left to say. If I had any qualms about my father-in-law's advice, they quickly vanished. Now more than ever, I needed to pay for the losses I caused. I repeatedly said, "Honey, I am so sorry." Then, I sat quietly by and just looked at her. I had enough medical knowledge to know her situation was grave. This was confirmed by her medical chart, which was clearly initialed by the statement "...advise against extraordinary efforts to resuscitate."

Although Rabbi Cohen was there with my wife and me, nevertheless I felt very much alone. I asked to go back to my room. Cohen opened the door and I took one last look at Abbie. Her coloring, even from afar, reflected a healthy pink glow. Yet, all the tubes connected to her and the machine that was assisting her breathing overshadowed any innocuous appearance. She had so much promise, so much to give that the world would never know what it lost. It was at that moment I vowed never to love another.

As the three of us made our way to the elevator, Flanagan pointed out the chapel around the bend. I asked not to go, but the police officer said, "Listen, you are not going to make a liar out of me. I wrote on my report you were going to the chapel and by heaven you will." He took the wheelchair from Cohen and changed its direction.

Making our way through the hallway, the rabbi received an urgent page and had to leave. It was time for me to make my peace with my Lord, alone.

The chapel was a strange experience for me, with electric candles glowing in the darkness. On a tall bookcase were copies of the Old and New Testaments and a tiny almost imperceptible Star of David, Magen David just above. I lowered my head and began to speak with God.

"Dear Lord, I am not like Abbie who prayed daily and thanked you for all of your many blessings. At my bar mitzvah, I received a prayer book inscribed with thoughts of how to pray, instructing that if it were from the heart, it would be heard. Nothing can be more from my heart than my request to help my wife recover and to take the soul of our little girl Sandra and allow her another chance at life. Perhaps, if you will, then permit me the opportunity to see her one time before I pass from this world. Lastly, please give me the strength to face the prison time due me and when I am able, please allow me to serve our people in the manner Abbie had intended to do, herself."

"Wrap it up!" I heard the police officer bellow, as he poked his head in.

"Okay," I replied. Having decided to accept my fate, I sensed a calming aura surround me. I would put my trust in God.

Flanagan effortlessly lifted me onto my bed. We made some small talk, until I started to fall asleep.

Before Flanagan left, I thought I heard him comment, "What kind of schmuck lawyer does this man have, who advises his client to waive his right to a bail hearing and to not attend his daughter's burial?"

Chapter 20

Mehmet apologized for the late hour telephone call, but felt what he had to say could not wait. Fearful of his blood pressure, Abbas cautioned her father to settle down.

"Okay Baby Girl, whatever you say,"

She smiled upon hearing him call her "Baby Girl." It brought back one of the few good memories she experienced as a child.

"I just spoke with Atour, my N.S.A. contact. He actually was aware of your prisoner's wife. She may have had more interests than simply being a wife, mother, and teacher. In fact, she is suspected of being an unregistered foreign agent, for starters."

"Do you mean a spy?" Malak questioned. "Dad, what's going on? It sounds as if you may have read too many foreign-intrigue novels." Feeling this was an unnecessary cheap shot, she added, "I'm sorry, finish what you have to say."

"My source indicated several State Department operatives and their coordinator, a Mr. Aberdam, had Abbie Wolf's electronic communications with a young Lebanese college student monitored. It seems their discussions had something to do with a well-planned covert operation soon to take place in the Middle East. Incidentally, the kid is currently being detained in a nasty detention facility in Lebanon."

"Does it have to do with Israel and Iran, Dad? Everyone knows of the reported threats. They're in the newspapers practically every day. What's the big deal now?"

"Malak, it is a big deal for any U.S. Agency to deliberately deprive a U.S. citizen of due process. It's against the law. Late in my career, it became part of my job to investigate these types of allegations and, as appropriate, prepare a report for the Justice Department with a copy going to the Congressional Intelligence Oversight Committee."

"Beyond circumstantial evidence of some incidental communications, what actual proof exists that Wolf's wife compromised U.S. security?" Malak questioned.

"Baby Girl, Abbie may have stumbled upon something important without knowing the danger it placed her and her family in. The source put this question on the table. He's not going to do any of the work for us. You know, it's been a while, since we visited. How about I fly in and stay with you and Eryn? It would be good to spend time with my only grandchild."

"Dad, I can see through you. If you are coming in to get involved with the case, don't think about causing me any trouble. Remember, I am Eryn's sole support. I have a pension to think about and we like eating regularly."

"You think I turned foolish since retirement?" he shot back. "Malak, I know how to handle myself."

There had always been a competition between the two of them. They were very much alike in ways that made their relationship uncomfortable, if not confrontational. As a result, Malak was much closer to

102

her mom. While that was perfectly fine, Mehmet sensed that his daughter was deeply ashamed of him. Frequently, she would use her wit to make him feel badly about himself. As a result, the divide between the two of them widened over the years. He knew he should have just backed off, but that was not his style. Although he loved his daughter very much, at some level he knew that he was losing her, and he just didn't know what to do to reverse that sad situation.

When Eryn was born, the bond between the two weakened further. Malak was always trying to prove that she didn't need her father, or for that matter, any man in her life.

In the beginning, Ekron and Malak's marriage was rock solid. Both had much in common with their mutual careers in law enforcement, Palestinian background, as well as life goals. For them Eryn's birth was to be the frosting on the cake. Especially for Malak, who always wanted a baby, as that could prove an opportunity for her to relive her childhood, in a manner she would have liked to be parented.

She was a superb investigator and possessed excellent computer skills. This allowed her to work from home one day per week. She frequently had to take extended leaves to care for Eryn and the department cooperated. They knew they had something terrific in Malak and catered to her. In contrast, Ekron's assignment to the homicide division was stagnant and he resented it. He finally applied for a significant federal law enforcement grant that would have permitted him to attend law school in the evenings. However, this request was denied.

At about the same time, his chief wanted him to consider a covert assignment with the Drug Enforcement Agency. It would involve a year of undercover work that would then make him eligible for a two-year sabbatical, during which time he could attend law school, on a full-time basis with an unrestricted and federally subsidized department stipend.

Ekron saw this as his only opportunity to outshine his wife, even though he would miss a great deal of Eryn's early development. Malak had some reservations, while Mehmet repeatedly and loudly warned him that dealing with low-life drug pushers could adversely affect his personality over time. Malak would tell her father to butt-out of their personal matters and then, out of spite, encourage her husband, even though her better judgment knew her father's warnings might later prove correct.

Initially, Malak would hear from Ekron regularly and occasionally meet for an overnight visit. With the increased demands of his work, Ekron turned hostile and would periodically lash out at his wife. As his assignment intensified, so did his temper. Malak began to fear for her and Eryn's safety. She saw the dark side her father had mentioned.

At the conclusion of his assignment, the department proved unable to keep its word, as the promised stipend funds dried up. Without that source of money, his dream of becoming a prosecutor died. Ekron became increasingly despondent and turned to alcohol for relief. He sought help from the department psychologist, but soon gave up. His and Malak's relationship cooled within the wounds of too many harsh words. Eventually, they separated and his visits with Eryn became fewer and fewer. Malak would become both mother and father to their child after their divorce.

Mehmet had tried several times to intervene, when he felt he could do some good, but his efforts had been angrily rebuffed. Eventually, he stopped trying and moved to Oregon, where he lived alone in his retirement. To fill the male relationship void in Eryn's life, G.P., as he was nicknamed by his only grandchild, would daily check in on her after school, mainly to make sure she'd made it home safely. He was determined to be a better grandfather than he'd been a father to Malak, and the latter reluctantly permitted this bond between grandfather and granddaughter to grow.

Motivated by her health issues and her resultant anxiety over her daughter's future, Malak felt some of the tension diminish with the thought of her father's visit.

"So Dad, when are you coming?"

"Baby Girl, I have some things to wrap up here, and I should be there in a day or so, sooner if I am able. Meanwhile, it might be wise to alert Wolf about the possibility of more in the mix than was apparent initially. Be subtle. After all, even the threat of prison time can maim someone who is not mentally tough, and this guy sounds too sensitive for his own good. I am looking forward to seeing you and what's her name." he joked.

105

"And she you," Malak responded. "Let me know if you dig anything else up. Dad, why would Abbie Wolf, a seemingly ordinary wife, mother and teacher have reason to pose a threat to anyone?"

"That's part of the puzzle we need to delve into. Also Baby Girl, don't be upset with me. I know you don't like to talk about this kind of stuff, but I started a small college savings account for Eryn with an initial $12,000 contribution, and also wrote you in as my Life insurance beneficiary. It's a $250,000 face value term policy that I kept up since leaving my position with the F.B.I. Also, you should know what I have in the bank…"

Malak cut him off, "Dad, you're starting to annoy me. Don't go there. Let's end this conversation pleasantly. Tomorrow, I am going to tell Eryn the news about your visit. Bye." She hung up the phone.

Before preparing for bed, she entered Eryn's room, knelt down, and gently kissed her daughter on the forehead, so as not to awaken her. She looked at her for a while, and then whispered, "No matter what, I will always keep you safe."

Chapter 21

"Jim, its McNamara. It's late and wasn't my intention to bother you. Something has come up. With all that's happening, your daughter and son-in-law's house was ransacked. Apparently, a neighbor saw lights in the house and called the police. When they arrived, they noticed the back door ajar. The officers entered to find the upstairs bedroom drawers pulled out, and the contents emptied on the floor. It was a mess. Someone must have been looking for something more valuable than the jewelry and cash left untouched on the nightstand. Any idea as to why this may have happened? When you're up to it, give me a call."

Almost simultaneously, the department was contacting Abbas.

"Abbas, this is Corporal Johnson. I was instructed to call you. Sorry for the late hour." Out of courtesy he hesitated a moment as she roused herself from a deep sleep.

"Go ahead. I am up now." Her years of on-call duty prepared Abbas for the late evening calls that inevitably woke her. She knew the station would never bother with trivia that could wait, until the morning.

"I have two pieces of information regarding the Wolf D.U.I. case that you are working on. It's scheduled to be heard in court the day after tomorrow. Someone must have powerful connections to move it to the forefront on such short notice. The second piece of news is that Wolf's house was broken into."

Now fully awake, she questioned, "Anything of value taken?"

"No, and that's what's strange. Ferguson, the onsite investigator reported the contents of the drawers and closets appeared tossed about, furniture overturned, and mattresses cut open. It's unclear what they were looking for, or even if they found it. In fact the only apparent actual loss was a smashed computer with its hard drive removed."

"Does the Watch Commander want me to go over there now?" she inquired.

"No. However, with the high priority assigned this case by the State's Attorney, he wanted you made aware of this. The scene is secured and patrol cars will keep an extra eye on the house should the perpetrators return. Good night Abbas." Johnson hung up the phone.

Abbas tried to go back to sleep, but could not. She took her old Walk Man radio with its ear buds and began to listen to talk radio. If that didn't relax her, it most certainly would keep her company until morning.

Chapter 22

I was just beginning to feel the effects of a prescribed low-dose sedative when a man in a white doctor's coat entered my room and began to shake my shoulder. He handed me another pill to take and I complied.

Shortly afterwards, he began to speak in a low tone, "Listen Wolf, our time together has to be brief. Much of what I tell you will only remain a hazy memory and you are not permitted questions."

I felt intimidated. He seemed determined and his physical presence could not be ignored. Therefore, I quietly listened.

"An order had been issued to silence your wife. Although they did not succeed, her injuries may in fact be permanent, and there are highly placed individuals within your government not sorry to hear that. As we cannot directly seek the justice due her, it will fall upon you to ferret out the details, which led to your family's tragedy. Her e-mail exchanges and other correspondences may assist you."

Slowly succumbing to a dream state, I distinctly heard the man say, "Someone in whom you are putting your trust despises you and is arranging to put you away for a long time. In this regard, we have already put into place the means to assist you."

He began to walk away, but paused and said, "We express our condolences on the loss of your child. I am sure she would have been a great asset to our people, much as her mother had been. The pill you swallowed will block visual memory of me, but not what was said."

Chapter 23

Marney drank the orange juice that Jim had freshly squeezed before putting on the black dress she saved for sad occasions. She never imagined wearing it for her grandchild's funeral.

"Jim, put on a warm coat. It's very cold outside and we know how susceptible you are," she cautioned him. "Perhaps you should have made arrangements for Jon to say goodbye to his daughter." She looked at Jim and saw his facial features harden.

"There's no way I would allow that. Jon took both of them away from us and this is the least of the punishment he is going to face." he replied.

"Is that really up to you to say? I'm angry too, but don't you think he is suffering as much as we are?" Marney challenged.

Jim answered, "Look, he voluntarily signed over his responsibility for Abbie and Sandra. Do you think he would have done that so easily, if he really cared?" Silver knew that was unfair, but wanted to set the tone for what he hoped to accomplish.

Marney nodded her understanding of what was said, and both of them left the house. On the way to the cemetery, there was little discussion. She looked at Jim and saw tears in his eyes. That said it all for the both of them.

Jim had heard the voice mail from McNamara regarding the break-in at his daughter's home. He thought the newspaper account of the accident and its consequences might have allowed for a crime of opportunity, yet he questioned why nothing of obvious value had been taken.

As they approached the cemetery, the workers were setting up the canopy, chairs and the laying of the ground tarp. Now their granddaughter would lay forever next to their son, the uncle whom she loved very much.

Within moments, the hearse pulled up with Sandra's coffin. While they would have preferred an ornate metal casket, they knew, and Rabbi Ford made it understood, a simple varnished wood design was required. The finality was setting in. Marney was assisted to one of the ten empty mourners' chairs, while they waited.

Ford arrived and embraced both of them. "This is such a difficult time for both of you. The best thing I can do is to keep it short and according to Jewish law. Because you did not want publicity, last night I telephoned eight men to be here today in order to assure the necessary Minyan. You may not know these people. They're from another synagogue and perform this final act of kindness the way it's meant to be, anonymously. Therefore, it is not proper to thank them individually. A simple nod in their direction will suffice."

Jim excused himself for a brief moment. Marney knew exactly what he was going to do as he lifted the ground tarp that covered their son's grave. He began to speak in a low tone so as not to upset anyone. Marney, meanwhile, had a flashback of Leonard's burial. It was in sharp contrast to today's service. She recalled a hundred or more people who came to pay their respects. He was a popular, charming man and it was a shame he died at such a young age. Yet, he lived 49 productive years, unlike his niece.

Although brief, Marney knew Sandra's life was filled with warmth and happiness. Everyone who had made her acquaintance admired her. Even other children appreciated her confident and friendly manner. None had ever experienced the death of someone so young and it was reported by the school principal that the kids were devastated.

In accordance to custom, the rabbi began the service by pinning a piece of torn black cloth upon Marney and Jim's coat lapel. He explained this symbolized the break in their life's connection with their now departed granddaughter. "Look at the sky. Many mourners like a rainy, gloomy environment, which gives them some comfort in their sadness. In reality, today's glorious sun and sky are a greater tribute to remind you of the opportunity, short as it was, to get to know and love Sandra." The rabbi always knew what to say, as well as the most effective means to convey it. He truly cared for all of his congregants as individuals, but none more so than Jim and Marney Silver.

The rabbi asked Jim and the other men to put on their gray gloves and place the casket on a solid metal support directly above the open burial site. Ford then brought up many happy memories of Sandra, as he knew her well. This was a comfort to the grieving grandparents.

Led by Ford, Marney and Jim recited the traditional memorial Kaddish prayer and then he embraced the Silvers.

"I must tell you, although your friends respected your wishes not to be here, they are nevertheless preparing for your return home. Do not deny them their participation. Members of our Jewish community are required to comfort you at this time of loss. I will stay with the coffin and see to its proper burial. It's time that you get ready to depart for home."

The men placed their gloves on top of the coffin accompanied by a beautiful bouquet of long stemmed red roses, Sandra's favorite flower. Unbeknownst to her husband, Marney had gone over to Abbie's house and took Sandra's favorite stuffed animal, a small white unicorn, which she had hidden underneath her coat, until this moment. She quickly put it in the grave without fanfare. The rabbi saw this and understood. Each then placed a scoop of soil on the casket, while Ford took out a pouch of dirt from Israel and spread it in the grave to lie with Sandra for eternity.

Jim Silver asked the rabbi what his favorite charity was. He knew Ford would not accept money for performing today's burial service. Remembering Abbie's love of Israel and Sandra's many visits there, Rabbi Ford suggested the planting of a grove of trees that would serve as a lasting tribute to her memory within the holy land and to which their family and friends could contribute and someday perhaps even visit.

Re-entering their car, Marney and Jim hugged with both inquiring as to the welfare of the other. They smiled for the first time since this terrible ordeal had begun.

Chapter 24

"Five A.M. checkup Dr. Wolf, and how are we feeling today?" the floor nurse inquired, as she proceeded with her rounds. No officer guarding your door today? Don't think of escaping," she humorously commented, while checking my vitals. "You appear to be getting stronger and that's good, as you are being discharged tomorrow morning. I understand our hospital psychiatrist is to meet with you today. He's a great guy and maybe he can help you find some peace."

Early on, I discovered it best not to communicate more than absolutely necessary with hospital staff. Each had formed their own opinion of me, but none as harsh as I held of myself.

Since the day of our marriage, I could always count on Abbie to be there for me. Now I sorely missed her and actually grieved her loss, even though she is among the living. All the things I took for granted; the gentle kisses, firm hugs, and playful teasing will unless a miracle occurs, be gone forever.

Yet, I couldn't feel sorry for myself, especially when recalling one of my mother's favorite sayings, "…you make your bed, you lie in it…" Although not comforting, its meaning rang true, as I face the consequences of my negligent actions.

An orderly brought in breakfast. It consisted of orange juice, a small canister of decaffeinated coffee, and two pieces of dry wheat toast with jelly on the side. Appetizing or not, it was what I was given, and where I was headed, I had better enjoy it.

I thought aloud, "What a far cry from what Abbie could so easily put together, even on short notice. She was a great cook. I was a good eater and I looked it. Yet, the excess surrounding my gut would little doubt melt away in the weeks and months to come. However, what did I really care about my weight, as I would not have my wife and daughter to look at me?"

Reviewing my "would a," "should a," "could a" list, my biggest regret was not telling my girls often enough, how much I loved and needed them. Yet, there was always time for the nonsense.

"Maybe it's good for me to speak with a psychiatrist," I thought aloud. It might provide me some coping mechanisms to make it through prison. My life experiences taught me there will be other opportunities to do something of value down the road and before my time on this planet is up.

The door to my room opened and Dr. Martin Lang, the hospital staff psychiatrist entered. "Physically you are doing well Wolf. But, I can't see inside your mind."

He sat at my bedside and we talked at length about the concepts of guilt and punishment. "Dr. Wolf, I don't have a prescription to ease your mind's pain. I lost my own child eight weeks after she was born with what turned out to be a previously undetected heart irregularity. Imagine me a respected M.D., and my little girl taken away from me and me helpless to do anything about it. I went into a deep depression and withdrew from practicing medicine for about a year. Blaming each other, my wife and I eventually parted. We could not come to terms as to whose fault our loss

117

was. In fact, it was no one's fault. One loss became another. In the end, what gave me strength was a support group for grieving parents. Perhaps the justice system might allow you to take advantage of this or something comparable. I will write that in my report for the judge to review. What I say, might prompt some special consideration. Obviously, I cannot guarantee that. The best thing for you now, in my opinion, is to get through tomorrow and move on. When all of this is behind you, come look me up and we will talk again."

I pondered his words, but my still open wounds were too fresh to heal, especially as my little girl was being buried, while we were speaking.

Chapter 25

G.P. Mehmet was waiting at the Portland airport for the flight that would bring him to Chicago. He asked Malak not to pick him up, as he had a special surprise for Eryn and wanted his granddaughter to see it first. Yesterday, he purchased a twelve-week-old buffed colored Cocker Spaniel, and early this morning before the flight had the vet crate it, after administering a mild sedative.

He expected Malak to be furious, but hoped Eryn's wide-eyed happy reaction to this lovable creature would mute any overt hostile reaction from her mother.

Mehmet understood life was tough for his granddaughter. Her father was effectively out of the picture and she spent far too much time in front of the T.V. or with indifferent baby sitters. The puppy might be what Eryn needed, an opportunity to experience unconditional love.

Mehmet was happy to be coming home. His daughter also appeared pleased. Coming together to analyze the various pieces of the Wolf case might have provided an opportunity for the family to reunite, but that was far from the only reason.

Hearing the announcement to board his plane, Mehmet stood up slowly and grimaced, as his knees felt painfully stiff. He mumbled, "Getting old is a pain in the ass!"

As a retired F.B.I. agent, he was allowed and even encouraged to travel with his weapon. It had been a while, since he wore it on his belt holster under his sports jacket and the bulge was apparent to those sitting near him. He would flash his badge and a smile to allay any concerns. In fact, one fellow passenger commented how happy she was to be travelling with an F.B.I. agent, whom she personally regarded an unsung heroes.

In actuality, he had been a hero to many people, but not to his daughter. There was the time he was in a bank, working undercover in Portland, tracking laundered mob money. Unexpectedly, two men entered with guns drawn, announcing a hold up. Mehmet got on the floor with everyone else, as he did not intend to blow his cover. Suddenly one of the robbers smacked down a crying little boy. Mehmet rose to his knees and asked permission to take care of his son, the crying child. Seeing the child was African American and Mehmet white caught the bank robber off-guard and allowed the F.B.I. agent time to rise, embrace the child, and lay him gently down on the floor beside him. This had a calming effect on the other frightened customers, as well. Later, the perpetrators were apprehended without incident. Everything could have turned out much differently, but G.P. Mehmet was cool, in the true sense of the word.

Sitting in his coach seat, the cabin attendant whispered to Mehmet that he had a waiting "priority" radio communication, and could use the cabin phone in the rear of the craft to access the call, as this would allow for greater privacy. Although protocol typically dictated he return unsecured calls on a scrambler line, this was not an option.

Mehmet was surprised to find out that it was Atour from the N.S.A. and was impressed this man could so easily track him down. He listened intently to the information Atour offered, without responding. Yet, the insights came with the caveat that they have no further contact with each other.

Mehmet settled back, closed his eyes and reviewed what he knew, in the context of what he had just been told.

Chapter 26

A young looking man came into my room and introduced himself as the court appointed psychiatrist. He showed his identification and a statement from the hospital administration allowing him to see patients in this facility. The doctor subsequently asked for my written permission to carry on a discussion. Without reservation, I signed the form.

I answered his questions as honestly and directly as I could. He explained that psychiatrists are frequently employed by the court system for unbiased, pre-trial evaluations and he was Judge Forman's first choice for my case.

The doctor took ample notes on my understandings of the chronology of events that had transpired, at least the ones I recalled. He appeared to include observations on my reactions to the questions asked, as well. I sensed he was seasoned and street smart.

Frequently, defendants are directed by their attorneys to respectfully decline answering such questions, or to be purposely vague. However, that was not to be the case with me, as I rattled on and on, even as the doctor frequently reminded me that my responses were being recorded and could be used by the State's Attorney against me. Nonetheless, I kept on my forthright path.

All seemed reasonable, until he asked if I had any other brushes with the law.

I relayed my part in the accidental death of my best friend, and its consequences for my family, which may have included my father's subsequent heart attack and passing, as well as our families near bankruptcy. That said, I also indicated that I never had the opportunity to reconcile my guilt concerning this first tragedy, as I was simply sentenced to community service and a three-year driver's license suspension. Most distressing to me was that I was turned away from Kenny's funeral by his grieving parents.

The community labeled me a troubled kid, which isolated me for the remainder of that high school year. I lost the few friends I had and reluctantly became a loner. Luckily, I never chose to associate with the "Greaser" elements, who bore similar negative labels.

Part of my approved community service involved speaking to area high schools about the effects of alcohol on driving, and the deadly consequences of mixing the two. I served this aspect well.

Family economics dictated that I work part-time to support my personal needs. My father had a small life insurance policy that provided for my mother's welfare. Yet, within the year, the strain of her depression, as well as her physical limitations, allowed for a modest social security disability qualification. This helped us to function at a somewhat more comfortable level and that's how we lived, until I went to college and began a fresh start. The juvenile crime was subsequently sealed.

The doctor felt this session sufficient for his purpose and excused himself.

Throughout the remainder of the morning, I chose to lie in bed and reflect. No court verdict could be harder on me than I already was on myself.

Nurses checked on me periodically throughout the day, but strangely, no guards were seen outside of my door. This would later turn out to be a glitch in the police department's computer scheduling system.

"Big deal!" I loudly proclaimed while adding, "Where could I ever go to run away from myself?"

Later that afternoon, Ira Shefsky, a public defender chosen by my father-in-law to co-represent me, in the capacity of a private attorney at my trial tomorrow, paid me a visit. He opened his briefcase, pulled out a pad of paper, and reviewed the pertinent details of the accident, as well as the judicial format to be followed.

"Wolf, subsequent to the auto accident and after receiving the results of your blood alcohol level, a petition was filed for a preliminary hearing to determine sufficiency to issue an arrest warrant. The State's Attorney was also deciding on the nature of the hearing, involving a judge or going directly to the grand jury to set an arraignment. Then, the police, with approval from the State's Attorney Felony Review, declared the charge of D.U.I., vehicular manslaughter. As your father-in-law told me that you want to plead guilty and seek a bench trial directly, you of course are waiving your right to a trial by your peers. As you also waived bond hearing, I shall ask for a conference with the presiding judge and attempt to reach a fair sentence, while bargaining with the State's Attorney."

Pausing for a moment, Shefsky thought it wise to also remind me of the following: "Wolf, subsequent to your arrest, all records regarding the accident, including but not limited to police reports, medical examiner reports, hospital and medical records, including those of your wife, as well as statements from those in attendance at the party and community character statements, will in all probability, be used by the prosecutor, judge and myself to determine the level of culpability you may bear and your sentencing. In addition, anything you have said, either intentionally or unintentionally, shall also be made available for all involved parties to review and consider.

Lastly, be prepared to answer direct questions from the judge, as well as from the S.A. and myself. You should know that the judge assigned to hear your case has a reputation for being particularly severe in his sentencing of alcohol related convictions. You will need luck. I have other cases currently on my docket and so I will now excuse myself. Unless you have brief pertinent questions, I will see you tomorrow."

"I do have one question."

"Go on," he replied.

"I thought my father-in-law would represent me."

"Look Wolf, your father-in-law is a respected prosecuting attorney whom I opposed many times in court. He is not well since the death of his granddaughter, your daughter, and for all intents and purposes the loss of his only child, his daughter, your wife. He felt I should co-represent you. Do you have a problem with that?"

I shook my head no and turned away, as the public defender left. By that time, I saw a police guard stationed by my door to log individuals coming into and leaving my room. He told me that I had been designated a "minimal-risk prisoner" and therefore was not shackled, nor was a GPS tracking monitor attached to my ankle.

Thinking about my day, I actually appreciated Shefsky and his no-nonsense approach. At the very least, I have an understanding of the legal process and what to expect in court. Now, I have to put my trust in the two men who would represent me, even with the earlier warning left by my white-coated visitor.

Chapter 27

Mehmet's flight arrived at Chicago's O'Hare airport at 2:30 p.m. He headed to the baggage claim area where he quickly located his suitcases and recently acquired four-legged friend. As instructed, and with everything in hand, he phoned Malak. Although he had hoped to arrive by taxi and surprise everyone with the dog, fatigue overcame that plan.

She answered, "Dad I will be there as soon as possible. Just sit tight and get a cup of tea. Remember no caffeinated beverages!"

Whether she meant to be or not, Malak was definitely intimidating to her father who felt her harsh ways towards him were simply a means of getting back at him. G.P. hoped to make amends. He desperately wanted a new chance with his only child. Yet, Malak held the upper hand when it came to dealings with her father.

Anxiously awaiting his ride, he took Buffi out of her crate for a short walk. Unfortunately, the puppy could not wait until they reached the outdoor sidewalk, and instead did her business on the terminal floor, in front of fellow passengers and airport personnel. One of the latter quickly came over and immediately offered to clean the mess up.

"Don't worry sir, this type of problem happens frequently and is easy to get rid of."

Mehmet offered to tip the man, who politely refused. His only request was to pet the adorable cocker spaniel who strongly resembled "Lady" from the animated film, "Lady and the Tramp."

While waiting, G.P., who had courageously faced so many dangerous situations in the past, began to rethink Eryn's gift. He quickly devised a less confrontational story by informing his daughter, Buffi was his dog, and he could not get anyone to watch her, while he was away.

Abbas appreciated many of the benefits of driving a police vehicle. Most impressive was her ability to park in a prime spot with no one to ticket or tow her car, as long as it was left only briefly unattended. She got out of her car, flashed her badge to the airport security officer making his rounds and went to the baggage area to find her father. When she saw him and the puppy, she almost went ballistic, until she looked closely at her father. His aging was apparent and this softened her. She offered a restrained hello, lifted his two heavy bags with ease and ordered him to follow her.

Purposely ignoring the dog, she said, "Dad, this way." He decided not to let her ways interfere with the first meeting they had in a long while.

"Baby Girl, how about letting me hug you?"

"Let's get everything into the car and on our way. You probably forgot how bad traffic is going to get. What's the story with the fur ball?" she questioned, intentionally avoiding eye contact.

Once in the car, G.P answered with the fabrication, and she appeared to buy it. That out of the way, he switched gears, "Let's go over my understanding of the events pertaining to the Wolf case and what I found out about his wife, to date. For starters, the cut appearance in the brake lining was obviously a red flag, as well as the N.S.A. intercept of an electronic text message from the hospital where Abbie Wolf was being treated, which indicated she no longer posed a threat. These aspects alone heightened the suspicion of a targeted action.

The fact she socialized with students at Hebrew University in Jerusalem, who later became Mossad operatives, represents another piece of an increasingly interesting puzzle. Add to that her fluency in Hebrew, Arabic, and Farsi, which allowed her to work as a translator of sorts with the local branch of the Israeli consulate, may have added to her cover. I understand her duties included writing intelligence summaries for consulate personnel to peruse and eventually forward to their superiors in Jerusalem.

Baby Girl, all of this is comparable to what our own Central Intelligence Analyst Agents do. She may very well have been an unregistered foreign agent, whether she realized it or not. Yet, at what level she functioned and what made her so dangerous to others, remains to be seen.

Recently, I found out that Mrs. Wolf had a number of e-mail exchanges with Jabr Mahjub, a Lebanese Christian-Arab student who studies at Hebrew University, where Mrs. Wolf had spent her junior year of college. Incidentally, the boy's father works within the Lebanese Foreign Service and has suspected ties with Hizbullah and several corrupt

Iranian government officials. The N.S.A. had been tracking both the father and son's electronic communications, which interestingly stopped several days before Wolf's accident. Meanwhile, Jabr has disappeared. Malak, do you see any patterns forming?"

Mehmet took a moment to collect his thoughts and then continued. "Baby Girl, that's what I know. It's not enough to affect Wolf's trial, but it does pose some interesting possibilities."

"Dad, can you count on your source?"

"Not as much as I can count on you," he replied. "My source ended by saying he wouldn't be having any further communication with me. Without proof of a condoned hit attempt, I don't have a solid case to go to the Justice Department or to the congressional intelligence oversight committee. That's where Wolf may prove valuable. Why would our government intentionally look the other way or actively participate in an attempt to silence a low level, suspected foreign operative, posing little if any actual risk to our national security? That is, unless she came upon some information we don't know about."

"Dad, Wolf's trial is set for tomorrow morning. Just as a point in passing, either this person has the worst luck in relatives or someone else may be attempting to manipulate him into a long prison sentence, which would effectively neutralize him, as well. Jim Silver, his father-in- law, is also his defense lawyer. He was an effective prosecutor in his time. He certainly knows the system, but doesn't seem too eager to assist his daughter's husband with his rights. To me, he wants him convicted with the least fanfare. One other thing Dad, Wolf's house was also broken into over the weekend and the only thing of value taken was a computer hard drive. Cash and other valuables were overlooked. Weird, isn't it?"

G.P. responded, "It sounds too sloppy for regular federal agents on an assignment. At the very least, the whole computer should have been taken with the other valuables, to cover up the actual intent of the break-in. Who knows? Maybe there was porn on the drive and someone wanted it for blackmail purposes, and the whole situation is just one coincidence after another? Baby Girl, please pull over, I have a distinct feeling the dog can't wait until we get home to do her business. She looks kind of green, probably from your driving."

Less than 15 minutes later, they arrived home. Malak opened the front passenger door and helped her father into the house, while toting his luggage. She gave him a house key, said goodbye and headed back to the police station to attend to paperwork. It would be another three hours before she would finish her shift and return home.

G.P. was early to meet his granddaughter's afternoon bus. He waited on a corner bench and looked about the community. Not much had obviously changed since he retired and left for Oregon years earlier. This old Chicago neighborhood still had a middle class atmosphere with its large brown, single story bungalow houses lining the streets. However, he now saw many unfamiliar faces. In his youth, the block was predominantly a mixed Arab and Irish Catholic working class area where everyone knew everyone else and for the most part tried to help one another.

Upon closer inspection, G.P. saw graffiti on the back alley garages. As people walked by him, they hung their heads low and avoided eye contact with each other, as well as him.

His thoughts turned to Malak growing up. Even as a young schoolchild, she always enjoyed testing the waters with her father, especially following the death of her mother. He chuckled as he recalled one occasion when his daughter glared into his eyes and told him how lucky he was to have her. G.P. thought for a moment before replying in a low tone, "Yes Malak, it's true I am lucky, but so are you." He went on to inform her that he tried to be the best parent he could be under the circumstances. He hoped she might mellow. No such luck, as she walked away in a huff.

"Effective parenting," he mumbled, "never came with a manual of conduct, like the one issued by the F.B.I. academy for new agents."

The school bus stopped, the door opened and Eryn rushed off into his waiting arms. He closed them about her and whispered, "I love you, Te Amo, my young Baby Girl"

She returned a loving smile and a soft kiss upon his cheek.

Eryn was studying Spanish and enjoyed her grandfather's loose attempts to speak in a language other than English. Her mom, on the other hand firmly espoused her belief that in America, everyone should primarily speak English and act as blended Americans, not standing out on a separate cultural basis. Even though they were Arab-American, her family never wore their Middle Eastern heritage on their shirtsleeves.

G.P. told Eryn about the dog. She grabbed his hand and quickly pulled him inside the house to meet Buffi.

Chapter 28

Abbas arrived back at the tree-lined, recently constructed Community Police Department Building, which was located in a well to do area near the lakefront. The watch commander immediately handed her a note. It requested that she report to the chief's private office as soon as possible. It wasn't as if she had not been called-in before. There were occasions when she received commendations for outstanding police work. However, this time it felt different, as there was no advance warning. She knocked and entered.

"Good afternoon chief."

"Have a seat," he replied, as he scanned the Wolf file. "There seems to be a great deal of attention from the powers that be to this case. Any idea as to why this is happening?"

"No sir," she answered.

"Come on Abbas, you didn't get to where you are by being so laid back. Let's cut to the chase, it appears that the S.A. initially wanted to handle the case himself, to improve his low approval ratings, before the election. As we both know, alcohol related manslaughter crimes make great press. Judge Foreman, infamous for his harsh sentencing towards this type of perpetrator, was assigned by the circuit court clerk to oversee the trial. Meanwhile, Wolf's attorney of record is Jim Silver, a former prosecutor and good friend of Bob McNamara, a still influential prior State's Attorney. Bob was the toughest S.A. I ever worked with and was a great friend to cops as well. The Wolf case seemed open and shut. Even the accused admitted his guilt and requested a bench trial where he probably would be sent away for a long time." The chief purposely hesitated, while staring at Abbas.

She patiently waited during the uncomfortable pause and then interjected, "Chief, where is all this leading? Normally, the department's responsibility ends with the arrest, detention and transportation of the defendant to the courthouse."

"Abbas, powerful people appear to be lining up against this man. Do you think this coincidental? Is this more than a routine case?"

She saw the Chief appeared clearly perplexed and answered, "Sir, it's too soon to tell, but I will keep you informed, if I learn anything. My father just got into town. May I have permission to end my shift early?"

Abbas had not been in the car ten minutes, when the chief personally telephoned her indicating that he had just received information that Judge Foreman was excused from the case and replaced. "It just keeps getting stranger and stranger." He abruptly hung up.

Arriving home and quietly entering the house from the garage, Abbas was welcomed by an excited daughter, who quickly pulled her aside to talk about Buffi. Meanwhile, G.P. was busy in the kitchen fixing the only dish he ever perfected in all the years he was married: spaghetti with lumpy hamburger meat sauce. He also put together a "junk-salad" made from left over ingredients he found in Malak's refrigerator served with a freshly compounded ketchup, mayonnaise, and parsley dressing.

It was a comforting scene, G.P. thought, as they sat at the kitchen table and said a prayer before starting dinner. He suggested taking all of them out for ice cream afterwards, but soon remembered Buffi's need for puppy food.

Malak telephoned a neighbor who recently adopted a young dog. She mentioned the food issue and quickly received a gift of enough puppy food to tide Buffi over, until they could get to the grocery store.

Surprisingly, Eryn asked for a rain check on the ice cream, as she wanted to take her dog into her room, while she did her homework. Malak reluctantly agreed, as long as her daughter concentrated on the assignments and "...there was no nonsense going on."

Mehmet was pleased to see how good a mother his own daughter had become. Eryn seemed to want for nothing material, just more time with her mom and perhaps a kind, reliable male influence in her young life.

While G.P. was washing the supper dishes, he inquired. "This guy Wolf, what's he like?"

"Dad, he seems genuinely remorseful for the accident and its consequences. He wants to take whatever the justice system deems appropriate. He's lucky to be alive. As a direct result of the crash, he sustained life threatening internal cranial bleeding, yet miraculously survived brain surgery performed on an emergency room table."

She reviewed her notes. "He worked as an optometrist within an ophthalmologist's practice. He appears to have lost it all: family, job, and friends. I have some concerns about his mental stability, and the doctors at the hospital have kept him as long as they could. He is placing his future in the hands of his father-in-law and God. Dad, he's Jewish."

Mehmet interjected, "I admire the fact their faith, like ours, appears to sustain them, although as a child, my experience with Jews was not the most positive. When they found out I was of Arab descent, they made fun of me. When I wanted to fight them, they simply shrugged me off, as if I were unimportant. As such, I very rarely engaged Jews. Now, with all the historic problems continuing in the Middle East, there is much too much antipathy from all sides to allow rational thought.

I also understand the Holocaust taught them that they needed a homeland of their own, because no one else appeared to give a damn about them; but now someone needs to give a damn about our people. I respect what the Jews have accomplished and it's obvious there is much we can learn from them. I hope they will take the opportunity to learn from us, as well.

Malak, it's amazing that in June of 1967 they took on the surrounding Arab nations, each full of military might, and yet, the Jews defeated them all in six days. Even Christian Arabs felt a biblical prophecy coming true. Now, it appears that the Jews may be losing some of their resolve, preferring to buy-off terrorists with gifts of land. That's a far cry from what they used to do."

Malak abruptly announced, "This discussion is closed. It's time to go to bed." Yet, she still had to review the Wolf case details before the next day's trial. "Dad, I have to tell you that at the last minute I was assigned to be Wolf's transport to the courthouse." G.P. inquired if he could go with and she responded, "Dad you know it's not appropriate to take you with to escort a prisoner. But, should you agree to keep your mouth shut, I might make an exception." He nodded his understanding.

Chapter 29

I woke to find my suit and shirt neatly folded on the table next to my bed. There was a note from the room guard that my father-in-law dropped off the clothes late last evening. I overslept breakfast and found only a cup of cold coffee and a slice of dry toast on the tray next to my bed. Knowing the uncertainty I was about to face and my nervous nature, I concluded that a reasonably empty stomach would be my best option to handle the upcoming day.

As I started to get off the bed to dress, a doctor whom I had not previously met came in and introduced himself.

"Good Morning, I am Dr. Mueller, assigned to pre-discharge. My responsibility is to check your vitals before you are released from the hospital."

He observed my expression change and assumed it was because of his unfamiliar presence. "Sorry sir, but this is a teaching hospital and the docs are frequently rotated." He gave me a cursory evaluation, made some brief notes on the chart, and left.

Shortly afterwards, Officer Abbas came in. I was glad to see her and told her so. In some ways, she reminded me of Abbie. She carried herself with a confident and kind demeanor, someone who could be counted upon to do the right thing.

"I understand you will be escorting me to my trial, is that correct? Were you aware that Silver had transferred some of his litigation responsibilities to his friend, Ira Shefsky?" Not waiting for her response, I lowered my eyes and anxiously said, "Go figure, huh?"

The guard reminded me that I was still a prisoner and motioned me to place my hands in front of me, to secure handcuffs.

"I have everything under control." Abbas told the guard. "Let the man use the bathroom. There's time for the restraints later." He took the hint and left after getting her to sign the transfer of prisoner form.

"Well, this is it Wolf; soon you'll know your fate."

"Please call me Jon?" I asked.

She shrugged and motioned me to get on with my personal tasks, while completing her portion of the hospital release form, which did not take long. Soon I was ready for her to help me on with my winter coat. Sitting myself down in a wheelchair, she secured the handcuffs to my wrists and covered them with a towel so I would be less conspicuous as her prisoner. It seems she went out of her way to avoid embarrassing me. Yet, I started to shiver in anticipation of the unknown.

An orderly wheeled me to a car that was waiting curbside with its engine running and heater on high. Abbas opened the back door and assisted me in. I saw an older man sitting in the front passenger seat and assumed he must be a plain-clothes escort officer. He gave me a quick glance and a nod. Throughout the rest of the trip to the downtown courthouse, all of us were silent. I thought it routine.

From her years of experience, Abbas understood that anything she may say at this point might later be perceived as biased or even provocative. She had seen prisoners change their personalities, attack the wire mesh separating them from the front seat transporting officers and fabricate harassment charges. If that were to happen, she would have a great deal to explain for allowing her father to be in the car with them.

A short ten minutes later their car approached the ramp reserved for police vehicles transporting prisoners into the courthouse. Mehmet stepped out at the curb and entered the building from the street side door, while Abbas parked in an assigned area. Waiting for her was a uniformed sheriff's deputy who assisted Wolf into a previously requested wheel chair.

The elevator they entered was huge, capable of moving 30 or more people at a time. Its sides were padded with a thick green material much like that of moving vans. Within seconds, the doors opened, revealing a private holding area that led to the courtroom where the trial was scheduled to begin. A bailiff then assisted Wolf inside to his seat and took Abbas aside, asking, "Who is this guy? One of the toughest judges in the system was excused and replaced by a softy. The S.A. withdrew as the lead prosecutor and an inexperienced lower level Assistant State's Attorney took over the prosecution. Even the courtroom was changed to this rarely used facility. I haven't seen anything like this in my entire career."

Abbas responded, "I don't know."

From its unusually small size and remote location, this courtroom appeared not meant to house many spectators. Yet, Abbas was amazed there were no waiting reporters, as D.U.I. manslaughter cases are typically fodder for newspaper sales. However, she was

141

at the same time relieved. It was well known that testifying with the press in attendance frequently resulted in misquotes in the articles that followed. Yet, it was indeed strange that not even a single journalist was present.

The bailiff requested all attendees to stand as he announced the presiding judge's entrance. Judge Feinstein was a small man with a pleasant air about him. He took his seat and asked, "Is everyone here that's supposed to be here?"

At that precise moment, Jim Silver and Ira Shefsky rushed in with an apology for being late because of heavy traffic. All parties were now present. They each introduced themselves and the trial commenced.

The judge described the nature of the bench trial, the ten-year prison term the prosecutor was requesting, and then explained to me the legal rights I was giving up by not choosing a jury trial.

I indicated my understanding of the ramifications of my choice. Upon direct questioning from the judge, I plead guilty to the D.U.I and the vehicular manslaughter charges. Shefsky and Silver then explained to the court their co-handling of the case and Jim's relationship to me. Meanwhile, the judge summarized for those present; the contents of the police reports, the court appointed psychiatrist recommendations, and other pertinent medical reports, as well as previously gathered character testimonials.

The prosecutor and my defense team took their turns jockeying back and forth, as the facts of my case were presented. Each side tried hard to impress the judge at the expense of the other. At one point, the young Assistant State's Attorney attempted to introduce my prior sealed offense. He was quickly silenced and Feinstein reminded everyone that information should not be considered. Neither side disputed the non-controversial facts of this case. Yet, each tried to give a spin to favor their case.

Feinstein asked several questions of Abbas and then complemented her on the thoroughness of her documentation. He inquired if there were anything else in the stack of reports either of the trying parties felt to be germane, but not yet brought forward. Both sides appeared content with the facts presented. The A.S.A. summarized the prosecution position as a straightforward driving under the influence case that resulted in the tragic death of my young daughter and unfortunate comatose state of my wife. He stressed the state's desire to make an example of me by having the judge hand down the stiff 10-year prison sentence requested. He believed this would send a clear message to the community at large about the potentially severe consequences associated with mixing drinking and driving.

Feinstein asked me my thoughts.

I responded, "I am solely responsible for this terrible tragedy and deserve the maximum punishment the State's Attorney is seeking." I added, "I seek justice for my wife and daughter who I loved very much and hurt beyond repair."

The fact that I was taking ownership appeared to impress the judge, but he responded with a simple question, "Dr. Wolf, do you understand how damning your words come across?"

I replied, "Yes."

Judge Feinstein then answered with equal passion, while addressing the court. "Dr. Wolf, all present seek a just conclusion. However, 'just' and 'justice,' are not always the same. Let's go over my understandings from this pile of reports. The defendant's blood alcohol level was fractionally over the legal limit of .08 and that is serious. However, other than its presumption, no additional impairment was demonstrated. The party attendees' depositions from the night in question did not report any observable problems including, but not limited, to the defendant manifesting slurred speech or locomotion difficulties."

He continued, "As Wolf and his family left the party, several of the guests reported hearing Mrs. Wolf tell her daughter to make sure her seat belt stayed fastened and under no circumstances to remove it. Sadly, it appeared Sandra did not comply, causing her to be thrown from the vehicle upon impact with the concrete barrier. This resulted in her death. Neighbors' statements clearly attested to her history of intentionally unlocking and removing the restraint mechanism, indicating it was uncomfortable. That said; drivers still bear the ultimate responsibility for maintaining as safe a driving environment for all of their passengers as feasible.

There were no reported prior histories brought forth of Wolf demonstrating alcohol abuses, either with or without driving being cited. This man appears to be an upstanding, contributing member of the community.

Employer and friends respect him. His behavior the night of the party may or may not have been exemplary, but there was no proof of belligerence directed towards his wife or daughter that could possibly later contribute to him losing control of the vehicle."

Feinstein continued, "Speaking of the involved vehicle, the auto pound report, which neither the prosecutor or defense team brought up, describes a cut or punctured brake fluid hose. Its subsequent leaking might have been contributory, yet this was not addressed or investigated by the defense. In fact, the part in question went strangely missing.

Regarding the defense, I believe the level of representation and advice given to the defendant appears questionable at best. While, it may not be grounds for a grievance suit, I believe it to be subpar, especially coming from such an experienced lead prosecutor. It appears almost as if an ulterior motive may have guided your handling of this case, Mr. Silver."

Briefly hesitating, and shaking his head in disbelief he continued, "I was informed you had your client sign over to you general powers of attorney regarding his wife's care, daughter's funeral arrangements, and a 'Quit Claim' Deed. I find that disturbing, considering Wolf's lucid condition. I have the power to reverse the pertinent directives, should you, Dr. Wolf, wish this done. I would be remiss if I did not also comment on what I perceive to be most egregious. Keeping a father away from his own daughter's funeral is beyond the pale. Mr. Silver this man is married to and loved by your only child. He deserved better than what he got from you.

The defense, prosecution and defendant all seem to have forgotten the definition of the word 'accident.' There appeared no premeditation, just a sad chronology of events. Dr. Wolf, I have heard and understood everything you said and requested. Yet, justice demands reason. Your pleas for severity appear excessive and I feel are due to your recent loss and your current state of self-imposed guilt. Your medical reports describe not only your accident-related emergency cranial surgery, but also pleas from a variety of medical professionals who attended to you, requesting supportive mental health follow up. On this, I concur.

Your loved ones were taken away in the blink of an eye. All you can do now is hope that your wife will pull through, and this court expresses that same desire. I think it appropriate for what is left of your immediate family, including your father and mother-in-law, to pull together as a support system for yourself and your wife."

The judge took another moment to collect his thoughts and for a second time looked at Silver with disgust. Then Feinstein spoke. "Before pronouncing my decision, I will ask for any victim impact statements from those directly or even indirectly affected by the events of this case."

He waited and then said, "As there is none scheduled to be heard and as no one here wishes to add to what was brought out, I will now render my decision. Sirs, please have your client stand and face me.

Dr. Wolf, it is the decision of this court that you be sentenced to 11 months' probation with a report turned into me immediately if you are in any way involved with alcohol related issues or any other problems involving breaches of the law. To cushion potential risks involving driving and alcohol consumption, I am suspending your driver's license for 11 months. At any time during this period, I retain the right to render a stiffer sentence. My leniency is predicated on the fact that you seek professional mental health treatments, with bi-monthly reports forwarded to the court. If these reports indicate you are or may be a threat to yourself or to others, I will review my sentence. Dr. Wolf, take this opportunity to do good work in memory of your daughter, whose loss will no doubt be borne by you the rest of your life. Good luck to your comatose wife, Abbie. From what I understand, she is a compassionate woman involved in serious work that benefitted others, particularly special-needs children. Perhaps you could build upon her efforts, as a tribute to her dedication. Reading your medical history and the police reports, your losses and my sentence will serve as sufficient punishment."

The judge looked toward both the prosecutor and defense lawyers, "Sirs, let me remind you that incarceration is reserved for those adjudicated a menace to society for a crime that falls within the accepted legal parameters deserving such measure. In this case, although such punishment may appear superficially justified, I doubt if it were rendered that Dr. Wolf would return a restored human being and an asset to society. This case is now concluded."

Feinstein exited the courtroom to sign the requisite papers in his chambers.

Officer Abbas waited a moment before asking if I required a ride home.

I replied, "Yes, but I need several minutes alone with my father-in-law" She nodded her understanding and sat down behind me. Mehmet joined his daughter and the two patiently waited.

Silver appeared visibly shaken by the judge's remarks. He hoped Feinstein would render harsh justice and I would be sent away for a long time. He could not digest the concept of any mercy shown towards me. His legal objectivity vanished with Sandra's burial and the seemingly permanent impairment of his only daughter. He must have wondered how he would get by without the satisfaction of seeing me punished for his and Marney's losses.

I turned to my father-in-law hoping for some peaceful resolution. Instead, he lashed out at me, "You are a lucky son of a bitch. That said, the papers you signed earlier have been formally registered and it will take some doing for you to reverse them. In the meantime, I have an offer for you. You signed a 'Quit Claim' deed, turning Abbie's house over to us. I will allow you to live there during the term of your sentence, and I will even pay the mortgage. During that time do whatever you have to do to become self-sufficient, but never come to Marney or me. To us you are as dead as Sandra. If you open your mouth and cause us any grief, I will rescind this offer and have you thrown onto the street. I understand you and Abbie accumulated some savings. After your sentence is up, do the right thing and move elsewhere." Silver turned away and hurriedly left the courtroom.

Now I felt truly alone. At that moment, a warm hand touched my hand. It was Malak Abbas, informing me we should leave and that she would take me home.

Mehmet reasoned that would be a good time to fill me in on other aspects of the case not brought up, should I be willing to listen.

Chapter 30

Mehmet stayed with me, while Malak retrieved her car from the garage. This was the first time we had been alone. Neither of us spoke, as we stood curbside waiting for our ride home, while I pondered my next move.

Abbas' horn beeped and we hurriedly entered the car and sat as we had come. The unmarked police vehicle had a drab appearance; yet, it served as sufficient transportation for me, a man who realized his next trip could have been by bus to a state prison cell. With mixed feelings, I began trying to come to terms with the judge's legal decision, as well as my unspoken self-imposed life sentence of loneliness and regret.

After driving for roughly five or so minutes, Abbas inquired if I had been informed of the recent break-in to my home. I shook my head in disbelief and with tears streaming down my cheeks, I questioned, "When is this ordeal going to make sense?"

Mehmet motioned his daughter to pull over so he could join me in the back seat.

I looked at him and quietly said, "Why would anyone stoop so low to do this to a family that suffered so much? Did some ass-hole not have anything better to do?"

Hoping to defuse the tension, Mehmet took the opportunity to mention that his daughter had unofficially sought his opinion on my case, early on. He then asked if I would permit him to delve further into my situation during his stay in Chicago.

I asked, "What's going on? As far as I am aware, I caused an accident that killed my daughter and placed my wife in a coma. I signed over our house to my father-in-law, and may have jeopardized my main means of income, as well. All this sounds like the dumb plots of the soap opera Abbie and Sandra used to watch together."

Mehmet interceded, "May I call you by your first name?

I replied, "Of course."

"Jon, some of what was known, yet not brought out at trial, may cast some suspicion on the actual circumstances of the accident."

Mehmet then referred to the questionable appearance of a leaking brake fluid hose that could have contributed to or even caused the tragedy. Then he brought up the man dressed as a physician and his unrequested and undocumented visit with Abbie that culminated in a suspicious electronic transmission from a clearly labeled prohibited electronic communications zone. Lastly, he mentioned the theft of the computer hard drive taken during the previously mentioned house break-in.

I anxiously questioned, "Is my wife in any danger? With my father-in-law keeping me at bay, I want to make sure she's safe."

Mehmet responded, "I believe she's fine. If someone wanted to harm her, it would have happened by now." Diverting he stated, "It might be a good idea for you to hire an attorney and take the judge up on rescinding the Powers of Attorney papers you signed.

Too much control over Abbie's future has been transferred to Silver. What do you think?"

I acknowledged the obvious. "While my in-laws don't want anything to do with me, nevertheless, they will watch over their daughter's welfare. That much I trust." Still confused, I asked for a clarification about the so-called anonymous doctor episode that Mehmet just referenced. "Did he prescribe anything or do anything beyond examining my wife?"

Abbas responded, "Jon, I ascertained this man wasn't on staff, and how he got direct access to your wife is still in question. However, her subsequent blood tests were unaffected and her brain wave activity, as well as her electrocardiogram print outs, were consistent before and after the visit. A floor nurse saw the man enter and leave within moments, allowing him time only to gaze at the instrumentation and her chart, at best. My suspicion is that he didn't touch her, especially with the Silvers in the room at the time."

I asked Officer Abbas if her father's, off the record, involvement in my case was typical.

"Your situation was and is atypical. It seems to swell with questions as it progresses. I thought my father, a sworn F.B.I. agent with extensive federal jurisdictional experience, might be able to shed some light on multiple areas of concern. Even the nature of your originally scheduled trial seemed to progress extraordinarily fast. Then unexpectedly, the initially appointed trial judge, who more than likely would have put you away for the requested ten-year sentencing, was replaced by a much more sympathetic figure. Subsequently, the S.A. stepped down from trying the case himself and appointed a lesser-experienced underling. Early on, all seemed exquisitely choreographed to effectively get rid of you. Then, as if a guardian angel stepped down from heaven, your rough fate became smooth sailing. Did you have something to do with that?"

I responded, "No," as so many thoughts were now cruising in and out of my mind, I did not know in what order to address them.

Abbas cast an observation, "I can see you may be overwhelmed with everything we've said. Don't try to digest it all at once. Let's proceed slowly and methodically, with each of us exchanging our thoughts. That way, we may arrive at a clearer understanding sooner."

Mehmet again asked to be allowed to help me and, as appropriate, to seek his daughter's input as needed. After all, he was on vacation and, during the day, when Eryn was in school, had nothing but time on his hands. He looked at his daughter and informed her that he had no imperative to return to Oregon any time soon.

Mehmet then addressed me, "Wolf, individually, the pieces of evidence unearthed so far, while questionable, appear inconclusive in and of themselves. Their direction and pattern still needs to be deciphered."

Wolf replied, "It's almost like the jigsaw puzzles that I hated, but Abbie loved to do. The various aspects of my case have yet to be cleverly assembled."

Mehmet continued, "Case in point, the home break-in appeared unusually sloppy, even for a

153

burglary of opportunity. Apparently, whoever gained entry got what they were after and hoped the mess they made covered their true purpose."

The suggestion there may have been a list of other contributory factors as to what put my family in jeopardy was proving to be somewhat overwhelming. However, at the same time my curiosity was beginning to be aroused.

When Mehmet asked me if I experienced anything strange immediately before or after the accident, I reluctantly described the dreamlike encounter with the white-coated man in my hospital room. When asked to describe him, it was virtually impossible for my memory to cooperate. It was as if that aspect was gated off, as were the details of the accident itself.

Malak looked at Mehmet in the rear view mirror and the two of them must have thought "drugs", but neither wanted to trouble me with additional unfounded suspicions.

The usual 45-minute ride to my home was completed in just under a half hour's time. Short as it was, it was still enough for us to set the basis of an agreement we would follow.

Seeing the house without the customary yellow warning tape, Mehmet and Abbas asked if they might accompany me inside. I agreed and the three of us entered through a closed, but unlocked door.

"What the hell is going on?" Malak asked. "Could an additional break-in have transpired?" she wondered. As a precaution, both she and her father cautiously came in the house with their hands on their holstered weapons.

We were all amazed to see the house cleaned up and in perfect order. From the note on the counter, it appeared that Abbie's friends had straightened out the ransacked mess. Unfortunately, it would now be impossible for Mehmet to do his own assessment of the scene due to unintentional tampering by well-meaning neighbors.

In addition to filling my refrigerator with fresh meats and vegetables and cleaning the house, they must have called our home numerous times, as my answering machine was marked full. The callers left condolence messages with the exception of a few hang-ups. Many asked to be kept informed of Abbie's progress.

However, there was one disturbing call from my office administrator, who advised me to take 30 days off with pay before returning to my job. On the surface that appeared reasonable, yet I needed something to occupy my mind to keep me from missing my family so badly. That venue appeared gone.

As there was nothing suspicious heard on the tapes, or seen during their thorough inspection of the house, Mehmet and Malak were ready to leave. He mentioned he would check in tomorrow and that he was going to rent a car for the next several weeks to chauffeur us around. I offered him the use of my car. After all, as part of my sentence, I could not legally drive for the next 11 months. He respectfully declined my offer.

Chapter 31

On their way home a question crossed Mehmet's mind, "Baby Girl, are we in accord that Wolf seems more a victim than a perpetrator? In some ways he appears to be naive, gullible and maybe even a potential danger to his own well-being."

"That remains to be seen. Dad, I purposely waited to tell you about a message from my chief. Since I told him you were in town for a while, he recommended me for a short-term undercover gig. If I take the assignment, and I would like to, I will not be available to assist you in any capacity. Can you watch Eryn for up to two weeks, max?"

"Can you relay any of the specifics of the task or is it on a need to know basis?" G.P. inquired.

"Dad, I am afraid if I tell you, I will have to kill you," she laughingly replied. "I have been waiting a long time to use that corny line. Seriously, I will be involved in a political corruption investigation coordinated by the S.A., the Attorney General's office and the Feds. I am playing the role of a temporary secretary for a few days. There is a very low level of expected danger, unless my cover is compromised."

"Sounds tame, Baby Girl. I am here in any way you need me." Mehmet feigned enthusiasm, even though he was obviously concerned for her safety. He knew all too well that undercover assignments carry the additional risk of no nearby backup should things get out of control. Yet, they are the paths to additional interesting assignments, as well as departmental promotions.

"Thanks Dad." Malak never liked seeking his permission or blessings in order to do what she felt had to be done, but was pleased there was no obvious objection from her father.

"May I offer a brief piece of advice?"

"Is there any way I can stop you, short of a bullet?" Malak said, starting to show she was becoming annoyed.

"Don't talk; just listen as a good secretary should. It's well understood that officers and agents have paid a high price for even a momentary lapse of focus," he cautioned.

"Dad, I don't have time to cook tonight. After I drop you off at the house, I have to go back to the station to be briefed on what this gig specifically involves. I think I may be home late."

"Don't worry Daddy's here. I have not forgotten how to make the specialty that made you the woman you are today."

"I hope that does not include your typical bull-shit with the spaghetti. Seriously Dad, don't forget to pick up Eryn. If anyone I were investigating ever saw me pick up my child that could be used as an advantage against me. I know you understand."

"I know enough to prefer that you decline the assignment. However, I also know that you won't do that. And any lecture is a wasted lecture," he muttered to himself in frustration.

"Dad, are you treating me as an adult? Have you finally come to the conclusion I can make my own decisions and mistakes, if need be?"

Mehmet knew at this stage of his life, he would rather be happy than right.

"One other thing Dad, make sure your dog does not crap up my house. After all, I didn't ask for that responsibility, and don't allow Eryn to become too attached to the fur ball. What's her name anyways?" Abbas asked sarcastically.

"Bye" was Mehmet's reply as he exited the car in front of their home. He needed some rest time before picking up his granddaughter. He saw Buffi standing in her crate wagging her tail. "What's that awful smell?" he shouted and then cringed. The dog not only took a dump, but was happily playing in it, as well.

"There goes my rest time," he said as he opened the cage, lifted her out, held her at arm's length and then threw her into the back yard. G.P. proceeded to disinfect Buffi's crate and then bathe her in the bathtub. "This is too much work for an old fart," he grunted. Nevertheless, he did what had to be done and finished just in time. He saw the clock and dashed through the front door, not even bothering to lock it behind him.

Eryn stepped off the bus smiling. "Grandpa how's my dog?" she asked excitedly.

"Oh fine" he replied, preferring not to give her the details of the recent mess he just cleaned up. G.P. knew whatever he told his only grandchild would soon find its way back to her mother.

"Grandpa, do you know what the Holocaust was? We're studying it and I have to write a report on it. It's due soon. Did you know any Jews who died in it? What did our church do to save children from the ovens?" She excitedly rattled off her questions.

"Let's wait, until we get into the house, wash up and get a snack. That's a powerful subject for such a little girl," he spoke in a quiet tone. G.P. decided not to go into too much detail, but instead to find out what she already understood and then keep his responses brief.

Mehmet thought it best to protect her from the truth as he saw it. His church, as well as the vast majority of other organized Christian churches did nothing, spoke nothing, and did not encourage anyone else to do anything to stop the butchery in Europe at the time. Yet, his personal guilt was not diminished knowing that other religions were equally complicit with their silence. Mehmet rationalized the Jews eventually got a homeland out of it, even if part of it belonged to his people.

Talking about Jews and the Jewish religion was difficult. G.P. had grown up in an era where Jews were thought to be responsible for the death of Christ. This was reinforced at home, when talking with friends and even from the priests at St. George's Academy. The latter made a point of never mentioning the Holocaust; however, it was generally agreed that the Jews got what they deserved.

Attending parochial schools for his elementary and secondary education in the Chicago area, Mehmet found his environment tightly structured, with established group stereotypes rarely challenged. Questions such as Eryn's would not have been tolerated. In fact, she might have been chastised just for asking.

G.P. became part of a group of high school boys, each from different backgrounds, who attended the same school and saw themselves as the local defenders of Christianity. On their way home, they would intentionally seek out apartment buildings where Jews were thought to live and shout out "Kike" or "Dirty Jew" at the top of their lungs.

"We kids were stupid and insensitive," G.P. reflected. He kept in touch with some of his friends who carried their prejudices with them into adulthood and transmitted them to their own children. "It's amazing how contagious hate is under the right circumstances," he would later mention to Eryn.

Mehmet thought the State of Illinois law mandating education on genocide and the Holocaust in particular, had merit. He believed that if his generation had been exposed to such teachings, perhaps they might not have acted as such "intolerant assholes." Yet, even he still held some subtle resentment because Jewish kids were now heir to some of his peoples' heritage in the Middle East.

With this background, Mehmet hoped he and Eryn could quickly gloss over the entire matter.

"Grandpa," Eryn said looking down as she ate her dinner, "Did you..." she hesitated, "do anything to stop what was happening?"

"Eryn, I was born just as World War II ended. There wasn't too much a baby could do, was there?"

Eryn persisted. She asked the same of her great-grandfather, my dad.

160

G.P. knew all too well that his father despised Israel and those who were responsible for its creation, a result of his upbringing and experiences in the Arab Quarter of Jerusalem. It was there he would encourage his family to avoid Jews as much as possible.

"Sweetie, your great grandfather didn't have the opportunities to know too many Jews in a pleasant way. His upbringing in Palestine and the people he hung around with were biased against anything they did not understand. Largely, they feared the Jews, who seemed content to be amongst themselves. Most were financially stronger than his family and he hated that. He and his parents worked very hard clearing the land in order to grow their fig trees, but had little to show for it. He resented the Jews who accomplished so much. He did not appreciate the pain of Jewish history, particularly the Holocaust. Instead, he perceived discrimination against his own people, everywhere he looked. That's why our family came to America. Life was easier here for those of Arab decent, but certainly not easy and some of our historical biases traveled with us."

G.P. continued, "In a culture such as your great grandpa's, they were used to settling disputes with violence. Because of the appearance of primitiveness, Arabs were frequently made the butt of jokes. Here, where I grew up, Jews were taught by their parents to resolve problems with their heads and for the most part not to rely on their fists. That is to say until 1948, when they established their State of Israel and had survived an Arab onslaught from all sides. Then, they were respected for their unexpected strength in battle, while

161

at the same time, resented for what they took away from us. The original plan was that the land was to be divided, but many Arabs would not accept this. Some felt the Jews had no rights to the area allotted to them, and Arabs from many nations lined up to drive them into the sea"

"Grandpa, are you saying your father stood by and did nothing, while innocent Jewish babies were murdered?"

"It's more complicated than that, Eryn. The Holocaust was taking place in Europe and our family lived in Palestine in the Middle East. I think my family really did not understand the extent of what was happening to the Jews. It wasn't a tribal conflict to get even with a group of Jews suspected of wronging a clan of our people. Rather, it was the European governments organized efforts to exterminate every trace of the Jews from the European continent. If it had been successful there, which thank God it was not, I believe it would have carried over to every other corner of the world, with disastrous results."

"Honey, my father, didn't have the luxury to think of anybody other than his own family. He was very involved with keeping them fed and housed. It's difficult to worry about someone else when you are barely making it yourself. Don't judge my father and our people too harshly, as they didn't have the advantages you or I have. Under other circumstances, I would like to believe your great grandfather would have shown empathy in efforts to seek justice for Jews." G.P. hoped this would have been an acceptable end to this distressing conversation, but that wasn't to be the case.

Eryn persisted, "Grandpa, if you were older, during those bad times, what would you have done?" Lucky for me the telephone rang. It was her mom, and Eryn took the phone, happily relaying the events of her day, with just a brief reference about our discussion.

"What would I have done?" I thought aloud. This question would haunt me for some time. Perhaps I would have been my father.

Eryn gave the phone back to me and I received my latest instructions from my daughter. After dinner, I was to clean up, feed the dog, and let her out to do her business in the fenced back yard. Then I was to supervise Eryn's homework, make sure she took her bath and get her ready for bed. Most importantly, I was to supervise her prayers.

I did my job with enthusiasm, but was disappointed when I asked Eryn if I could read her a bedtime story. She declined, informing me that she was too big to be read to. I then asked her if she would consider reading me a bedtime story. She laughed and said, "Someday, Grandpa."

Then it was prayer time. She kneeled by the side of her bed and said her prayers adding, "Dear Lord, please forgive my great grandfather for not saving little Jewish children from their deaths and burnings in the ovens. Give me the courage to one day stand up for what is right."

"That's enough, Eryn. It's time for bed." I tucked her in and kissed her five times on the forehead. She asked me why I did that. I responded, "Honey, I love you five times more today than I did yesterday." She was tired and did not bring up anything else about the Holocaust.

As I closed her door, she shouted out, "Grandpa, I love you!" How lucky I am. Perhaps I may prove to be a better grandfather to Eryn than I was a dad for Malak.

Our discussion, and Eryn's prayer, was repeating itself within my mind as I lay in my bed. What kind of person would I have been, had I been of age during the years leading up to World War II? When I was younger, I pictured myself a hero, the righter of wrongs. This was easy to think then, until one has to face the consequences of their choices, now. Focusing on tomorrow, I planned to telephone Wolf early. Maybe I could give this man some peace.

Chapter 32

I found it impossible to sleep my first night back at home. As early as practical, I eagerly tried to reach my boss Andy, but had to leave a message about me returning to work on his voice mail. Within ten minutes Elissa, the office manager, returned my call. She informed me that Dr. B. was unavailable, but wished to convey both of their sympathies for my losses. She reiterated the necessity of a cooling off period before my return. "Jon, it seems the publicity surrounding the accident with its suspected alcohol involvement is having an adverse impact on the practice. Dr. Andy thinks it best to wait a bit more, before you return. In the meantime, do you need an advance on your salary?" Elissa asked.

"Why didn't Andy return the call himself?"

She simply replied, "It wasn't convenient."

"So much for years of loyalty," I mumbled to myself.

Without my wife and daughter at home and effectively no job, there wasn't much to keep my mind occupied. Although Abbie had many friends, I often felt out of place in their company. Therefore, I avoided them and now I was paying for that poor judgment. At least a few of our neighbors put forth some effort and considered my personal well-being, even if it was only for the short run.

It wouldn't be long, I surmised, before they bore resentment against me for the loss of their friend. This would be especially true during their Wednesday evening Mah Jongg games. I used to tease Abbie and her lady-friends that only death or disability would be an acceptable excuse for one of them missing the game they loved so much. Now that seemed prophetic.

I really missed my wife. All those times I foolishly sat down and watched television, while intentionally tuning out whatever she said will be a loss I can never recoup. When she would talk about her beloved Israel, a subject I had little to no interest in, I would immediately change the topic to something I wanted to discuss. She would patiently listen to my ranting, while her thoughts were shelved. I thought aloud, "What was so damn important about the Middle East that prompted her to continuously churn out those controversial articles?" adding, "What a jerk I was."

All I knew then was that she was a gifted writer who never made much money at that craft, but must have personally affected so many. I remember once being woken up at approximately 1:30 a.m. by a telephone call. We debated about answering. Finally, Abbie picked it up against my better judgment, while reminding me, "You can't hide if someone is trying to find you and I don't plan on running away from what I wrote."

Foolish courage, I thought. With the large number of nuts about, this could put our family at risk. However, there was no dissuading her. I understood all too well that once she took the moral high ground that was it.

The operator identified the call as having originated from Sweden. The caller asked if she was the author of an opinion piece that appeared in a recent

166

international edition of the Jerusalem Post. Abbie responded by first asking if he liked it. Being fast on her feet, she reasoned if he responded negatively, she would simply say, "No, I am not, however give me your telephone number, and my sister will return your call later in the day."

In this particular case, the caller had liked it and they talked for 20 minutes. Usually callers would not identify themselves and some made vague threats against her. It seemed my wife's opinion pieces forced readers to choose a side and not to stand idly by. In fact, as a direct result of one of her articles, demonstrations against the proposed internationalization of Jerusalem were organized within a number of large cities in the United States, Israel and Europe.

She received calls from Israel at all times of the day. Sometimes, I answered and knew right away from the language spoken who the call was for, but never what was said. I referred to my modest Hebrew skills as my 'sign language,' which I had to learn from transliterated scripts and usually convey it back unintentionally with hand gestures, not very practical on the telephone. Sometimes, I was lucky to be able to discern the name of the caller and, if I were even luckier, their telephone number.

Although critical of the controversial nature of her writings, secretly I admired her loyalty to our culture, our people, and the tiny refuge of land biblically ordained to us as Jews.

Early on, my sweet wife unsuccessfully tried to get me involved with her efforts to oppose the Declaration of Peace principles between the Palestinians and the Israeli government. Laughingly, I would say, that the D.O.P. lacked the final letter "E" to make it complete. This would later prove accurate, but at the time not well received within the spectrum of organizational optimistic Jewish thought.

In those days, the Midwest Charitable Organization (M.C.O.) welcomed her services as a successful speaker and fundraiser, but actively frowned on her efforts to call too much attention to the irreverence of the Arab peace partner chosen by Israeli and American foreign policy makers. Indeed, the very people he hated the most had given him legitimacy.

At the time, it was customary for the average Jew to remain quiet and to let their rabbis' and community leaders' act on their behalf. Openly questioning them was unacceptable and potentially dangerous. Not that anyone would come by and slap you around, but rather they would employ social ostracism, an equally effective technique, and thereby send a message to others who might want to deviate from the "acceptable" way of doing things. However, Abbie was the exception. She openly challenged the Israeli government and established religious institutions, with minimal fall out.

Breaking my reverie, the telephone rang. The caller I.D. indicated, Cook County courthouse.

"Dr. Wolf," I answered.

"Wolf, this is Tom Meyers. I am the parole officer assigned to your case. It will be my responsibility to check on you and schedule your mandatory psychiatric evaluations. The first should be within the next week or so and afterwards, your visits may be as often as one or more times per week. I hope you have good medical insurance, because you will bear the costs. I will e-mail you a list of court appointed doctors from which to choose, unless you have a private practitioner you wish to use. I don't see on your sentencing documents that you are required to do community service. Therefore, our conversations will be as frequent as the mental health professional findings dictate. My telephone number and any other necessary information will also be in the email. By the way, who is Pickles?"

I responded, "It referred to her days of dressing up as 'Pickles the clown' to perform at children's parties and now is part of Abbie's e-mail address and I want to continue to use it."

"I don't see a problem. However, for the first several times you e-mail me, just refresh my memory that the message is coming from you and not your wife. Speaking of her, how is she doing?"

I replied, "I'll be checking on her today. Is there anything else? I am getting a signal another call is coming through."

"Two other things to keep in mind," Tom quickly interjected. "Remember, if you are thinking about using alcohol, don't! Any impairment at any time will get you a stiffer sentence and more supervision. Lastly, don't drive. Your license suspension runs concurrently with your probation period. Goodbye and good luck."

Pressing the "flash" button, I heard strange sounds that reminded me of a telephone repairperson testing the line. I also heard what sounded like a faint voice saying, "Done."

Within a minute, the phone rang again. This time I grabbed it and cautiously answered, "Yes?"

"Jon, this is Mehmet. Is this a good time?"

I replied, "Yes, but first I have a question for you. I don't want to sound paranoid, but is it possible my phone is being tapped?" I went on to describe what I just experienced.

Mehmet chose not to address this concern, immediately shifting the direction of the conversation to something more practical. "I hope you don't mind if I start calling you by your first name, especially as we're going to work together and it's going to get stale very soon being too formal. In fact, feel free to call me G.P."

"No problem, G.P. I was hoping to visit my Abbie, sometime today and needed to arrange a ride."

Continuing to ignore Jon's question of a possible wiretap, Mehmet inserted, "This may work out well for both of us. I need to go downtown. Perhaps I can drop you at the hospital, do whatever I have to and then pick you up. Jon, does that sound okay? The only thing, you may have to be somewhat flexible should I run late."

"Sounds like a plan. Did you rent a car yet?"

"Not necessary Jon, as my daughter is on special assignment and she loaned me the unmarked vehicle you previously rode in."

"Hey, how's your dog?" I asked.

G.P. replied, "That reminds me, I have to pick up some food for Buffi and arrange for a neighbor to check on her during the day. I forgot just how much responsibility a dog can be. That said, how about I pick you up around 9:30 a.m.?"

"That sounds great and thanks, but I have to go as the doorbell is ringing. It looks like a delivery truck parked in front of my house. Strange, I wasn't expecting anything. G.P., I'll see you soon"

"Before I let you go, just be careful in general, not that I am saying there is anything to worry about. I'll check later to see if your phone line is actually compromised."

Wolf opened the front door and was surprised that the delivery person identified himself as a volunteer from the hospital morgue. Apparently, there were some personal effects not yet claimed.

My heart began to race as I took the package. I placed it in Sandra's room. It was all too much, too soon to deal with.

I needed to soothe my anxiety with food. Going to the kitchen and opening the refrigerator, I smiled at the large amount of "healthy" food lining the shelves that our neighbors had brought over. Yet, none of Abbie's friends had personally stopped by to talk. Perhaps they felt awkward. I hoped this passed with time.

Cutting up a banana into a bowl of Cheerios, I found myself getting a little nauseous. No matter, I forced myself to eat. After all, the doctors stressed the importance of a healthy diet, as well as not letting myself get agitated. It was made very clear that my recovery, both mentally and physically, would depend upon my choices.

I washed and stacked my dishes. Then I had to find the checkbook, which Abbie probably still had with her. Luckily, she insisted I always carry a blank check, as well as one or two credit cards. As far as cash, Abbie traditionally kept $250 in her dresser underwear drawer. She would always point out to me that was her mad money and I could only touch it in a true emergency, adding in a joking manner that I was her "boy-toy", a kept man, and lest it should ever slip my mind, "what's hers is hers and what's mine was also hers." I heard this so often, I think these words were written somewhere deep within our marriage certificate.

I showered, dressed and anxiously awaited Mehmet, very happy at the prospect of spending time with Abbie.

Chapter 33

On my way over to pick Wolf up, I thought it appropriate to keep a healthy skepticism of my new friend, at least for a little while. Pulling into his driveway, I sensed someone besides Jon was watching me. His earlier comment came to mind. Perhaps, there may be something to his concern. Norm at the Bureau would be in the best position to advise if something out of the ordinary was going on. In any case, I knew better than to bring up a wiretap issue with him, until I was sure one-way or the other. I greeted Jon, while opening the passenger door. He thanked me for the ride and informed me he was not feeling so great today. Jon asked if I would mind if he were on the quiet side.

"Suit yourself," I replied. I knew he was under stress and would open up when he was ready. Just being there for him was a good beginning.

"What's with the sad look?" Wolf inquired.

"Nothing really, I was just thinking about something."

Approaching the hospital entrance and apparently feeling better, Wolf stated, "Do what you have to do and take your time getting it done. Afterwards, let's grab some lunch together, O.K.?"

It took less than ten minutes to get to the Federal Building. Although I could have parked inside at no fee, I chose to pay at the city lot across the street. I entered the building, took out my F.B.I. credentials, clearly labeled "Retired" and the security guard let me pass without going through the metal detector. Poor judgment, I thought. Anyone could have fabricated a look-alike I.D. Since the attack on the Oklahoma Federal building years back, security was supposed to be heightened, but now appeared at least in this specific incident, lacking.

Arriving at the F.B.I. reception area, I again showed my identification to the woman at the front desk and she inquired if I were carrying weapons. I replied "No", as I left my gun at my daughter's home in her locked box.

"I'm here to see Special Agent Ulbrich," I indicated. The receptionist checked the appointment log, which verified my meeting. She stood up and asked me to follow her. I thought this a good move, as the anteroom had a few sketchy characters waiting there. Some reminded me of people I had arrested in the past.

I walked through the floor metal detector and we headed towards a more remote section of the office. We approached his closed door where I was told to sit down and wait.

"I'll let Special Agent Ulbrich know where you are." She then spoke into a lapel microphone that appeared almost invisible. "Sir, it will take a few minutes, as he is finishing up a telephone conversation."

"No problem," I replied and settled myself into a very comfortable chair with a high back. Surrounding me were magazines of almost every description that dealt with law enforcement. Before I got too comfortable, a very young and attractive Asian woman approached me.

"Agent Mehmet, my name is Special Agent Kim. Please follow me."

So many things had changed in the Bureau since my career began. For one, the female agents now appeared younger and prettier. This woman was thin as a rail. Her holstered gun on her hip seemed huge in comparison to her body size. Yet, she projected confidence and authority, definitely a person to be respected.

I was escorted to a private corner office well beyond the numerous agent cubicles we passed. The floor was smoke-free, another welcomed improvement initiated in the not too distant past. We entered and I sat down.

Ulbrich was ending his telephone call when he looked up, recognized me, and flashed his familiar toothy smile. Having finished, he stood up, reached over the desk, and shook my hand with both of his. "G.P., do you want a cup of coffee and a bagel?"

"No thanks. Norm, you look fit and happy," I observed. "Is it okay if we speak alone?" Kim excused herself and I filled him in on everything that transpired from the date of the Wolf accident to the present.

Ulbrich asked, "What can I do to assist you?"

I reviewed the red flags that elevated both Malak's and my suspicions.

He responded, "Unfortunately, my hands are tied without special authorization from my superiors and that's not going to happen now. The Bureau is going through another of its internal audits to assure we are on the same page with Homeland Security.

Outwardly, it's to control expenses, but actually it's to ferret out security breaches."

"Do you think that there are spies within the ranks?" I inquired.

"I don't think foreign spies are what we have to worry about. I do have some reservations about recent leaks and bungled investigations. Look, I don't want to proceed into murky waters, especially as we are on a heightened state of alert. Something big is expected. Just like you cannot tell me what you don't know, neither can I tell you much of what I do know. The only service I am going to allow is for you to use our computer system. I can sign you in with my password; but will limit your access to only one area. What would you like to know?"

"Norm, I would like to get to know this lady, Abbie Wolf. I want to see if she could have posed a danger to our national security and, if so, on what level and who stood to be most compromised."

"I'll have to sign you in on a single half-hour slot so as not to tie up the system and arouse unnecessary suspicion. I suggest starting with her correspondences. That might give you a clue as to where she was going and whose toes she may have stepped on; or it may be an exercise in futility. At least begin to understand her mindset. Remember, the system will automatically shut itself off in 30 minutes and you will not have the ability to print anything. Therefore, if she were a prolific writer, I suggest you skim and not concern yourself too much with the superficial. If you run across something, or if I should hear anything that I can talk about, we'll speak elsewhere at a different time. Follow me. From this point forward, I want you to wear your I.D. around your neck. Here's a cord. Speak to no one and leave the door locked. You should be fine. Come back to my office when you are done. Agent Kim will then escort you out. Remember, monitor your time."

"Thanks, Norm."

Ulbrich added "Once an Agent, always an Agent. There's no divorce from the F.B.I., is there? We're your lifelong family and you are always part of ours." He opened the door to a temperature-controlled room and logged me on to the computer before leaving.

I requested data on Abbie Wolf's background, as well as her published articles. Her biography initially appeared bland. Her younger years, while no doubt impressive to her family and friends, were unremarkable. While studying in Israel during her junior year abroad, there were scattered references to associating with fellow students who later became Mossad or other Israeli intelligence agents. However, there was no definitive activity in that direction from her. Abbie's skills in Middle Eastern languages, including several Arabic dialects, as well as Farsi, were indeed impressive. Her teaching career was exemplary. She stood out as an excellent and popular educator as evidenced by her academic achievement awards. She had only one parking ticket and no citations for speeding. Her political involvement was minimal. She voted in every primary and general election. Abbie appeared to be an all around nice person, good wife, educator and mother who coincidentally possessed special Middle Eastern language skills and wrote frequent opinion pieces.

Her trips to Israel since her marriage to Jon appeared ordinary. She visited the same holy sites on every trip with her family. Yet, she signed in alone at a Knesset government building known to house two separate foreign intelligence agencies. That might serve as a point of interest.

Jon, on the other hand appeared a non-committed individual to anything other than his profession. References to him were only incidental to hers and at best, he was a minor player within her Israeli and Middle Eastern involvement. He had no publications to his name.

Since the 1993 Declaration of Peace proposals, Abbie authored and published 12 controversial op-ed articles. She had a no-nonsense style that tended to guide readers to the same conclusions as hers, without beating them on the head or preaching. She definitely stressed individual Jewish responsibility to ensure Israel's viability. Her mission was geared to impede the transfer or "fragmentation" as she labeled it, of biblical territory for vague promises of peace, especially with a so-called peace partner who was reputed to have shed her people's blood.

She also took local rabbis to task, as well as various well-established Jewish organizations, for what she viewed as their silent compliance in the modern day sell out of the Jew's right to their heritage.

At one time, she requested a case be heard before the *Bet Din*, the Jewish Court System, seeking a religious legal decision on the unprecedented Israeli government proposed "fracturing" of the Jews' biblical heritage, during times of peace. She labeled it as criminal in action, if not intent. She reasoned that all Israeli governments were only temporary overseers with a Shomer, or guardian responsibility, to maintain intact that what was given to her people through the patriarchs Abraham, Isaac, and Jacob, for the benefit of all succeeding Jewish generations.

Nothing resulted from this effort except her being labeled a pest. As I continued to read her publications, it became clear to me that terrorism was gaining a strong foothold within the areas handed over to the Palestine Liberation Organization.

She wrote, "At each opportunity that Jewish leaders moved to oblige their Arab counterparts' demands, more deaths of Israeli civilians soon followed. … Gullible Israelis even secured money and weapons for the Palestinian Authority. Yet, the Palestinian authorities appeared to do little to raise their own people from their poverty. Guns, after all, could not be used as food for the hungry or medicine for the sick…Even the demands for a separate state for the Palestinians appeared to be a ruse, perpetrated by their leaders…who by their very lack of action, appeared to prefer a perpetuation of the hopelessness of the Middle East Arab poor and stateless. This may have been a means to serve Hamas recruiting, as well as the refinement of their most heinous of weapons, the murderous suicide-bomber."

Abbie Wolf also publically took to task empowered leaders of nations who only gave lip service, while cowardly terrorist bomb attacks claimed numerous innocent victims, including those of Muslims, Christian Arabs, as well as Jews. In her view, world opinion was beginning to sway toward the aggressors. Most startling of which, was her assumption that Hamas, Hizbullah, and Fatah firmly believed the Jewish will to fight would soon be exhausted, and the former would eventually inherit the entire Jewish state, should they remain patient and accept the death of their Palestinian children, as the currency necessary to seal the deal.

Other articles contended Jewish leaders were trivializing the deaths of their fellow Jews in the Middle East, by relegating the circumstances of these losses to a "situation," rather than the war of attrition it actually was. She believed, "...Israel was in the beginning grips of a struggle for its very survival."

Although I had been personally somewhat antagonistic to the Jewish occupation of what my family viewed as their land as well, still I was impressed with her reasoning and consideration for the common Palestinian population. Ever cognizant of the threat of potentially offending powerful Muslim and Arab individuals and groups, I viewed her articles as not sufficient to set the stage for her elimination.

A warning light flashed on the computer announcing five minutes remaining. Rather than randomly continuing on, I decided to close down and leave to meet Wolf earlier than expected.

Agent Kim was waiting outside as I opened the door. She asked me to accompany her to a private elevator where she relayed a message from her boss. "Agent Mehmet, I have been instructed to wish you well with your inquiry and apologize for Agent Ulbrich who had to attend to an urgent matter and would not be able to extend his personal goodbye."

I thanked her and left.

Crossing the street, I again experienced the curious feeling I was being observed. Turning around, I found myself within the midst of a large crowd of people walking in different directions. Although years of duty sharpened my instincts, I dismissed this uneasiness. Even so, periodically I would look around.

Chapter 34

Wolf took the stairs up to the I.C.U., but was informed that Abbie had been moved to a private room, on a different floor. Even though her condition had not improved, she was listed as stable and no longer required either the I.C.U. or the Critical Care level of care.

Hospital policy required that I show my I.D. before the floor nurse would release my wife's new room assignment. Under the circumstances, I appreciated the extra security measures.

Before entering her room, I took a quick glance through the door's glass panel and saw Abbie dressed in a pink sleeping gown. Even the numerous monitors, with their leads attached to her head, could not take away from her loveliness. I came in, sat on her bedside, leaned to her ear and whispered, "I have always loved you. For me there will never be anyone else." I then kissed her warm lips and for a second heard what sounded like a sigh.

I looked around for a chair, but could not find one. I sat on her bedside and began to stroke the black curls that gently fell upon her temples and forehead. Again, I leaned and quietly told her, "I didn't intentionally cause the accident that hurt you. If I could only trade places with you..." I hesitated, and just looked at her, preferring not to finish the obvious. Her eyes were not totally closed. Partial irises and pupils were visible. Whether or not she understood my words,

I saw her features soften. "Abbie, are you trying to tell me something?" I held her hand. An unusual calm permeated my being, as if she understood.

Suddenly, the room door opened and immediately swung shut. When I turned, there was no one there. I assumed a nurse came in to check my wife's I.V. or address some other issue and changed her mind.

It didn't matter. Abbie and I were together. The door opened again. This time a nurse returned with the missing chair. She informed me Abbie's parents wanted to see her, but refused to be in the same room with me. Almost immediately, I felt her body tighten.

"I'm her husband. Tell them I'll be out in just a moment."

"Abbie, I am going to check on your medical progress. It's important we let your parents work through their feelings. They have loved you for more years than I have known you and deserve that respect. If I have to come at different times to visit you, that's all right, sweetie." No matter what I said, I felt disgusted with the underhanded legal shenanigans Jim Silver put before me. There will be a day of reckoning for him. I kissed my wife and left the room.

I overheard my father-in-law speaking to a nurse. I approached from behind so I could hear what was said without interrupting. It appeared that Abbie was accepting I.V. nutrition and she was stable. Nevertheless, her brain wave patterns were not normal. The nurse asked if there were any questions. Jim then turned to me and the hate in his eyes was apparent.

He asked the nurse if there were an available room where he and I could speak privately. Sensing animosity, she wisely directed us to an empty waiting area. At the same time, Marney entered Abbie's room without even acknowledging my presence.

As soon as we were alone, Silver lit into me. He blamed me for everything and repeatedly reminded me of the "Quit Claim" deed that transferred ownership of our house to him. The background lighting showed his age and vulnerability. He was not as tough as he thought. That took the edge off the necessity for me to prove anything.

"Jim, we both know what you tried to do. You shouldn't have lied to keep me from Abbie or excluded me from Sandra's funeral. If I chose to do so, I have the authority to keep you away from my wife."

Legally, Silver knew what I said had validity. For the moment, he quieted down, deciding to let time offer a better opportunity to extract the satisfaction, he believed the court system did not supply him.

"I understand you and Marney love Abbie very much and, as her parents, you will watch over her. Nevertheless, I also love her and don't diminish that, or you will be very sorry. We both have new roles to play when it comes to her well-being. Even though you hate me, I hope one day that may change. For now, watch out for your daughter, my wife."

I then hinted that new circumstances surrounding the accident were being investigated and a different conclusion may soon be forthcoming.

Jim cringed. "You almost had me. If you think you can get off for Sandra's death and Abbie's incapacitation that easily, you're sadly mistaken." His facial expression tightened as he went on, "You owe my

184

wife and me for what you have taken away from us. One way or another, I am coming after you. Watch your back," he said stopping short of a defined physical threat. "Remember you have only a few short months to get your act together. Keep in mind we never want you in our lives again. When you run out of money, don't even think of coming to us. Now get the fuck out of my face."

I slowly walked to the elevator, thinking mostly of what Silver had implied. Perhaps, it was simply face-saving bravado. Yet, considering his many years of dealing with hard-core criminals, he could easily arrange my demise, I suspected. Seeing Abbie's nurse, I decided to get my own questions answered.

Although receptive to my inquiries, her responses appeared intentionally vague. It wasn't as if she was trying to hide anything from me, but rather she was sidestepping, as modern medicine was still in the dark about coma. Abbie's brain waves showed dysfunction and her responses to stimuli were inconsistent. I mentioned my wife's body posturing changes, while I was in the room and speaking with her. The nurse listened respectfully, but refused to write any of this down on Abbie's chart. It must have appeared to her to be the wishful thoughts of a loving family member hoping for a miracle, which of course I was. All I could ask of the hospital staff was to provide my wife the best of care and to assure her safety and everyone agreed.

Now I had to sort out the mystery surrounding our tragedy. I wasn't happy, but for the first time, I might be able to gain some understanding of the work my wife valued so much and which may have contributed to our current circumstances.

There was one more piece of unfinished business I needed to complete. I never had my opportunity to say goodbye to my young daughter. Now I felt drawn to her. I missed her so much. I could still feel the warmth of her arms firmly wrapped about my neck and her soft kisses upon my cheeks. Not being able to save my child had broken my spirit, as well as my will to live, until now.

Walking towards the elevator, I looked about and, seeing no one in my vicinity, I gazed at the heavenly sky and said, "Sandra, you'll never be far from me and I hope to be with you, someday. For now, I have to search out the reasons surrounding your death."

Arriving at the main floor reception area, I was surprised to see G.P. sitting in a chair. "I thought I was supposed to call you. How long have you been waiting?" I asked.

He replied that he had arrived ten minutes ago and then took a moment to review what he had learned. "Your wife was a pretty good writer and a critical observer of what she recognized as continuing injustices to your people and your biblical heritage, Israel."

I was embarrassed and somewhat disturbed that a stranger should understand more about my wife's passions than I did. I forced myself to get over that discomfort and filled him in, as to what transpired at the hospital.

After we entered the car and drove away, Mehmet mentioned, "Now that Abbie is stable, we need to find out precisely what danger she posed and to whom she was a threat. I will try to reconnect with my N.S.A. source, even though Atour emphatically instructed me not to contact him again. If I unintentionally exposed this kind man to jeopardy, then we are at a dead end, at least for a while. Where do you want to go to now?" he asked.

It didn't even take a second before I requested to be taken to the cemetery where I could say a proper and overdue goodbye to Sandra, my child.

"Consider it done. Jon I don't quite understand it, but I see a difference in you." Mehmet observed. "You're giving me an impression that you're slowly coming to terms with yourself and your losses. If that's the case, I am truly glad."

Jon replied, "Mehmet, don't think of diminishing my responsibility in this tragedy. Remember there was an illegal level of alcohol in my blood. No one put a gun to my head and forced me to drink as much as I did. For your information, this wasn't the first time I was involved in an alcohol related vehicular death. Let's not give me any credit for anything I don't deserve."

Somewhat agitated, Mehmet said, "Don't go overboard! Let's not forget the suspicious brake line cut. If that were responsible for the brakes going out, your drinking would not have altered the end result, especially if the intention of a perpetrator was to make the scene appear an accident, rather than a deliberate murder attempt."

"What are you talking about?" I demanded.

"Jon at this point in time, I'm uncomfortable giving you more details than you need to know, for your protection, as well as mine." Mehmet responded.

"Look, you brought it up. If you want my assistance, you will have to clue me in as to what you know and where you are going, or let's stop this bullshit. Do you have information that was unknown to the court system? Be honest with me or let me out of the car, right here!"

G.P. started to smile, "Let me understand this, you want me to let you off right here, in the middle of this run down housing project with the highest crime rate in the city. I doubt you would make it to the nearest bus stop with your wallet in your pants. Still want me to let you out?"

Mehmet understood the last thing he needed was a loose cannon with a big mouth who might inadvertently tip off those responsible for the tragic death of Sandra and incapacitation of Abbie. If unknowingly alerted, they might shut their operation down and vanish, until the heat was off, or as a worst-case scenario, they might plot to kill us. The longer they operated openly and did not feel threatened, the better chance of identifying the potential culprits and developing a more prosecutor friendly case. However, Mehmet had to deal with this understandably emotional, yet unpredictable man, now.

Thinking that G.P. knew he was bluffing, Jon suspected he might have over played his hand. Yet, with the exception of a miracle that restored Abbie to the way she was; at a core level, he needed to find those responsible for destroying his family. Having that purpose would be enough to keep him in line. Nevertheless, he required respect from Mehmet whom he respected and needed to work with in order to accomplish his goal.

Continuing to stare each other down, I started to laugh and Mehmet followed suit. He agreed to bring me up to speed on everything, including the information his government source brought to the table, starting with the unidentified doctor, who had evaluated Abbie and scrutinized her chart. He was not on staff and most likely was an operative with medical training. His communication from the restricted hospital area appeared to reveal that Mrs. Wolf be taken off the need to terminate list, at least for the time being.

"Jon, another source indicated the existence of a flagged dossier on your wife. It appeared that her work with the Israeli Consulate, and to a lesser extent; the Midwest Charitable Organization (M.C.O.), may have provided her opportunities to make the acquaintance of high-level State Department policy makers. They may have also led to e-mail exchanges with a young Lebanese student studying at Hebrew University in Jerusalem. His father works with the Lebanese Foreign Service and is thought to have active ties to Hizbullah and their funding sources within Iran. Understand Jon, all this is mere conjecture, until we obtain verifiable corroboration."

Mehmet continued, "Abbie's contact with the Mossad during her college years and briefly afterwards was documented. Some of the Israeli students she

189

befriended went on to become active intelligence officers and possibly foreign clandestine field agents. Although we are on friendly terms with Israel and her leaders, since the Pollard case we are suspicious of any Jewish Americans with possible connections to foreign operatives. Don't kid yourself. We know Israel has undercover agents within the United States, just as we have covert personnel operating within Israel. Are you following my drift, so far?"

"The break-in at your home seemed contrived, as nothing of obvious value appeared to have been taken. Yet, a hard drive was removed from your wife's desktop computer. Police labeled this a random burglary, maybe perpetrated by kids. Or, perhaps the hard drive contained information that needed to be suppressed."

"G.P., let's back-up for a moment," Jon requested with a somewhat perplexed look upon his face." Did you say the hard drive of our desktop computer was taken?"

"Yeah, I did. Why?"

Wolf then asked, "Is the car we are driving in secure?"

"I don't know, I never thought about it. What's up?" G.P. asked.

Realizing he may appear to be sounding a bit paranoid, Jon quickly changed the subject, "How, did you know where the cemetery was, I never told you?"

At that point, Mehmet felt any qualms he may have had about Wolf began to fade. Answering the question, "The Medical Examiner's office requires they be kept informed, as a matter of protocol, regarding the subsequent handling of any deceased that was once in their care. Do you understand? Look Jon, I have a daughter and a granddaughter I worry about every day. I can only imagine your pain and would never minimize it. Let's get to the cemetery to get you some peace."

His understanding of my pain served to gain Mehmet my loyalty, as well as my friendship. The awkward phase of their relationship had ended. Now they could more effectively deal with whatever came their way.

To pass the time during the drive, I asked if Mehmet would turn on the car's radio. Within a minute, the news relayed an all too familiar story of teenagers driving drunk after curfew and their subsequent off-road crash. This time the car hit a telephone pole, injuring the driver and killing two young female passengers, neither of whom was seat-belted.

"Is this too difficult for you to hear?" G.P. inquired.

Even though I brought it up earlier, I thought a moment before responding. "Are you aware of my record as a juvenile?"

At Jon's trial, Mehmet heard the prosecutor unsuccessfully attempt to enter into the record an episode from Jon's youth, which the judge objected to and ruled inadmissible. "Do you want to talk about it?" he asked.

I felt compelled to tell him about my past. I described my adolescent, alcohol related road accident and its deadly consequences, the guilt of which had traveled with me every day of my life, only to be surpassed by my family's recent tragedy.

This was the first time I detailed to anyone my community service obligation that required talks with high school kids about driving under the influence.

"From the youngest to the oldest students, the reactions were very similar. First, there was sadness and then some tears as I described my best friend's appearance in death. Then I told my audience about the unforeseen consequences of my stupid actions, including the loss of many friends and their purposeful isolation of me, during the time in high school that is supposed to be filled with fun. I mentioned that the near depletion of my parents' savings, which was used to defend me in court, may have contributed to the premature death of my father.

I don't know if I reached anyone, but I certainly tried. It's important that kids think before ingesting booze or drugs and have anything to do with a car. Nobody really knows his or her tolerance. It's hard for kids to understand that their reaction time slows and their judgment becomes impaired. It has proven to be an uphill fight to keep young peoples' attention for more than the initial meeting, as alcohol use is perpetually romanticized as a sign of rebellion against society's rules."

After an extended moment of silence G.P. contributed, "It's thought of as a rite of passage with parents frequently overlooking emptied alcohol cabinets; until an accident similar to what we just heard on the radio happens to someone they personally know.

192

Everyone too easily then forgets such tragedies as time goes by and it inevitably repeats itself over and over."

There was nothing left to say on that particular subject as we entered *Shalom* cemetery.

"*Shalom* means peace just as *Salam* does." Mehmet commented.

"You're right." I agreed.

Stopping at the cemetery's main building, G.P. inquired as to where Sandra Wolf's burial site was. He brought back a map with explicit directions and we were on our way, a two-minute journey.

Arriving at the Silver family plot, I asked if I could go to the grave alone.

"Take your time; I'll use this as an opportunity to return a missed call from Malak." G.P. watched as Wolf faced east and began to pray. Then he saw him kneel on the cold, wet ground and cry. It was all too personal for him to intrude upon, and so this hardened, former F.B.I. agent looked away, as he telephoned his own child to make sure that she was safe.

Malak indicated that all was proceeding, as well as could be expected. At least that was what she told her father. As concerned as her father was about her, she wanted to make sure Eryn's needs were being met. She informed her father of the routine she expected for that day and evening. Even though he already understood, he allowed his daughter to continue on, giving her the satisfaction of being heard.

G.P. had been concerned about Malak's health for some time. Nevertheless, she made it a taboo subject. He figured the more she ignored talking about her cancer, the greater the concern. Thinking about the whole issue tied his stomach into knots, having lost his wife to the same dreaded disease, possibly aggravated by her inaction.

Unexpectedly, the warmth of her goodbye offered G.P. some needed peace. He had not heard a tone like that since she was a little girl hugging him before he left for work.

"Please watch over her, Lord," he whispered.

Mehmet failed to notice another call that had come in, while speaking with Malak. It would not have mattered, as he knew how difficult it was to reach his daughter during the day. The caller- I.D. simply indicated "Out of Area" and no message was left. He rationalized, "If it was important, the person would call back."

Jon returned to the car and asked Mehmet to walk with him. He had something on his mind and Mehmet complied.

"Abbie had a laptop computer which I haven't seen for a while. It may be buried somewhere in her closet underneath dirty clothes. She used to write, while waiting out the washing and drying cycles. She enjoyed the privacy as neither our daughter nor I would venture in, fearing we might be put to work."

G.P. replied, "That might be the break we need. Can we get back into the car now? It's cold out here! In the future Jon, just tell me any of your concerns inside a warm car or house."

It was a quiet ride back to my house. I assumed G.P. was thinking about Abbie's laptop, while I pondered happier times in my life.

Mehmet inquired, "Besides the Israeli consulate, what is the other Jewish group Abbie was associated with and what was your understanding of her relationship with them?"

"The M.C.O. is a fund raising group that collects and distributes money to various charitable causes, both locally and abroad. I never cared too much for those who ran it. Yet, it was a fabulous system for creating perpetual charitable funding. Don't misread what I am saying, they also provided great services for individuals and families with special needs and circumstances, both here and in Israel.

Abbie liked the people she got to know there and attended many of their social events, frequently without me and that was just fine."

I observed a bored look come upon Mehmet's face and changed my discourse direction. "G.P., what you may find more useful is the Organization's relationship with the Consulate of Israel. Israeli causes received a respectable portion of the proceeds raised and the Organization's administrators, as well as their biggest contributors were allowed access to Israel's most influential political and military movers and shakers, usually at briefings, parties and fundraisers. It gave the higher-ups a chance to mingle and to learn from those in power."

Mehmet saw some potential in what he just heard, but had a pressing question he was waiting for just the right opportunity to ask. "Jon your wife brought up an interesting thought in a number of her published op-ed pieces. If your own Jewish people truly valued their tiny heritage, their land of Israel, why were they so eager to give it away, especially to those who hate Jews the most?" Pausing to observe my reaction, he then followed up with, "What message do you think that sends to those who are hoping for Israel to be brought down a notch or two?"

I responded, "Even Jews can have stupid leaders, or leaders who make stupid decisions."

For whatever reason, Mehmet's mind shifted to the first time he began to change his stereotypical concept of Jews, which he thought necessary to share. "Jon, while watching a newsreel that was filmed during the creation of the modern State of Israel, I saw former Jewish concentration camp survivors, who did not appear to know the business end of a rifle, use them as clubs against attacking Arab forces. Whether they won or lost the battle appeared not as important to them, as it was a unified action, where Jews put it on the line and fought as Jews for fellow Jews. Seeing that unusual kind of courage struck me at a deep level."

Jon then relayed an experience of his own, growing up Jewish in a predominantly Christian area of the city. "Mehmet, I put up with a lot of crap just for being a Jew and for a long while, I just took it. You see, Jewish moms educated their sons that fighting was beneath them. We were then and I suspect still are being told that we are the thinkers and healers, the raiser of the standards of living of nations, and therefore should not lower ourselves. That said; our fathers secretly hoped we would fight back. But, what you may not know is that it's very difficult to face-off against a tough, determined to protect her child, Jewish mother," Wolf announced with a smile before continuing. "As a result I got regular beatings from the Catholic boys passing through my north side neighborhood on their way home from St. George High School. Then one time I stood my ground and didn't run away. Sure, it hurt as I got pounded, but I decided I would rather bleed than run from a bunch of piss-ants that would likely accomplish nothing of value with their lives!"

Mehmet was stunned by this revelation, but he could not comment out of embarrassment, at least not for now. He asked himself, "Could I have been one of those St. George boys who beat Jon?"

"Let's not talk about Jews and Israel," I said.

"No problem," Mehmet replied.

Chapter 35

While Mehmet was busy overseeing his granddaughter's routine and taking care of the dog, I spent my evening going through boxes searching for my wife's Israel related writings. Going upstairs, I entered our bedroom and picked up a vague smell of Abbie's favorite perfume. Sitting on the floor with my back against our bed, I recalled the way we planned our intimate evenings for shortly after Sandra had fallen asleep.

"I can't think about that now!" I shouted as I felt my body tremble. The thought of Abbie's ways still turned me on. However, this was not the time to create such a frustrating mental scenario.

Continuing with my search, I found Abbie's diary in Sandra's desk. Here was her collection of her most private thoughts, gathered throughout Abbie's adolescent years that she would never let me read. I wondered what Sandra was doing with her mom's diary, and whether she had her permission. Thinking aloud I said, "What does it matter now? Sandra's dead and Abbie is seriously ill. If it gave our daughter a moment of happiness, it was worthwhile."

Opening drawers and boxes in the closet proved unproductive. Reacting to a strange impulse, I got a stepstool and looked behind our daughter's old dollhouse that was gathering dust on the top shelf of her closet. I felt behind it and touched a brief case. Gently pulling it down, I was delighted to discover it held Abbie's small laptop and several disks.

Sitting at the desk, I attempted to boot it up. At last, I had my chance to connect with my wife's thoughts. This could be my most valuable contribution to Mehmet's efforts, as I seek to search out the cause to which Abbie dedicated herself. I fumbled inserting the most recently dated disc. However, nothing recognizable came on the screen. Next, I attempted to open her documents section, hoping that she had saved some insightful information there. Unfortunately, I couldn't gain access, as this required her password. It seems another obstacle blocked my path, so I decided to call Mehmet.

"G.P., I am sorry to bother you, but I found Abbie's laptop and I can't access anything because I don't have her password." Pausing for his reply, I heard a young voice say, "Hi, this is Eryn. Let me get my Grandpa for you."

"Jon?" G.P. questioned. Upon confirming, it was indeed me and having explained the reason for my late evening call, he enthusiastically stated, "Good job! This may prove a big opportunity to gain insights. Listen, take out the batteries, and recharge them if you know how. Then, and this may sound harsh- just leave everything alone! By the way, did you find any hardcopies of her communications?"

I replied, "No, but how can we gain her password when I tried every combination I knew and was unsuccessful?"

"The I.T. branch in the D.C. office has a code breaking computer that field agents can remotely access. Listen Jon, Eryn is asking for my help with her homework before bed, and the dog is barking her head off. I have to go. Goodbye."

I knew how to remove the laptop batteries and where the charger was. However, my desire to be the hero overrode G.P.'s instructions. Repeatedly, I tried to gain access, but could not. Some password choices had too few letters, while two word combinations proved too many. Putting it down, but not away, I decided to check on Abbie.

I dialed the hospital reception number and was informed Beata, the replacement shift nurse, was on her way to my wife's room, and my call would be transferred there when she arrived. I patiently waited, until the call was picked up and then I requested that the telephone be placed next to Abbie's ear. I was elated at the thought of being able to say good night to her. I took the opportunity to tell my wife how much I loved and missed her, but against Mehmet's strict warnings about speaking on an unsecured line, I added a brief synopsis of what I had done that evening.

I told her what we were trying to accomplish. I ended with my frustration at not being able to access her password and added, "I wish you could help."

At that point, Beata interrupted, "Sir, I have to tell you, while you were speaking to your wife, I noted her E.E.G. patterns improve. I will mention that to the doctors, but don't expect too much. Very few onetime observations are repeatable."

Jon replied, "I understand. I have a request. May we do this again, perhaps tomorrow evening?"

She answered, "Yes."

Then I asked for her work schedule for the rest of the week. She gave me the information and we hung up.

Feeling hungry, I went to the refrigerator, pulled out some sliced turkey and made mental notes of what I needed to buy the next day. Being extra cautious, I then put the laptop back where I found it. Afterwards, I decided to lie in Sandra's bed and watch T.V. Starting to drift off to sleep, I remembered about recharging the laptop batteries and quickly did so.

Across town, Eryn was content in her bed reading when Malak telephoned her dad. Hearing Buffi barking, she asked, "Dad, what's the matter? Is everything all right?"

"Everything is fine. The dog is motioning towards the back yard; maybe she has to go out. Would you like to say goodnight to Eryn?" Walking to her room, he peeked in, saw her awake and handed his granddaughter the phone.

She was very happy to speak with her mother and go over her day. Lately, when she told her grandfather what happened in school and he did not respond exactly the way she wished, she would simply say, "Men," in an all too familiar condescending tone.

G.P. overheard her and could not help but smile, as he never understood women, young or old. He knew his only responsibility was to love and protect the two women in his life, no matter the cost.

Approaching the back door, Mehmet had a weird feeling in his gut and made a quick detour to unlock the case that held his weapon. Putting it in his belt and pulling down his sweater so as not to alarm Eryn, he slowly opened the sliding door. Before he could stop Buffi, she ran between his legs and started to stalk a large tree in the fenced back yard.

Mehmet stated in a stern tone, "I am an armed F.B.I. agent, come out slowly from behind the tree with your hands raised so I can see them!"

As the shadow of a man emerged from behind the Weeping Willow, he indicated, "I am also an armed F.B.I. agent."

Recognizing Ulbrich's voice, I asked, "Norm, what the hell are you doing, trying to give an old man a heart attack? You know, we have a front door that most civilized people come to and knock on when they pay us a visit."

"Don't call me by name. There is a problem brewing," Ulbrich warned.

Mehmet immediately picked up Buffi to quiet her.

"Good guard dog you have there. But, she needs about 50 more pounds and 24 more inches of height to be lethal," Ulbrich joked.

"Are you sure you don't want to come in? It's cold out here."

"Listen, you have been outed by an unknown source. After you left, Agent Kim escorted Mr. Lawrence Portnoy, a senior National Security Agent into my office. He demanded to know what we spoke about and when I questioned his authority, he produced a note from my boss requesting my full cooperation. He then chastised me for allowing your

202

computer inquiries, stating they may have compromised an ongoing national security investigation. When I tried to get more information, Portnoy said that he would ask the questions. What could I do, but answer him honestly about your use of the agency computer. He asked for, and I had to supply copies of the pages you read, regarding Mrs. Wolf's activities. Then he inquired about your intentions. Unsure of what he already knew, I had no alternative but to relay what you told me. I am sorry."

Mehmet responded, "You did fine. I would have done the same thing, if I were in your shoes. I hope that your replies will satisfy his boss and your boss, as well. Actually, I am sorry for any grief I may have caused you. Obviously, something big is in the brew."

Ulbrich warned, "If I were you, I would drop your investigation. You're heading on a dangerous path. One thing for certain, your government sources have been alerted. Unless you can make a conclusive case for federal intimidation or for hampering a civilian's due process, stop it now! You have a daughter in law enforcement they know about, from delving into Wolf's background. In fact, both he and you may be under active surveillance as we speak. If Abbie Wolf were an unregistered foreign agent, you could be considered an accomplice, after the fact. Remember all those years you spent building up that comfortable pension; it could easily vanish if you are convicted, as well as your hard earned reputation. After all, who are these people to you? They're not worth the risk. Don't try to be a hero!

Before you go in, I have a couple of more thoughts for you to chew on. After the N.S.A. agent left, I finished my day doing paperwork. Just as I started to pack up, I saw my boss enter his private office. I followed him and closed the door behind us. He didn't even wait for me to speak, before informing me that someone with clout, within the Israeli government had Wolf's case reassigned to a different judge. That's a lot of influence, don't you think?"

Pausing to look around, Ulbrich continued, "It appears that Wolf's wife regularly translated Arab intelligence information for the benefit of the Israeli consulate. As you no doubt are aware, since the Pollard case, American Jews working in this capacity have had their electronic communications routinely monitored. However, it was a covert intelligence gathering sub-agency from within the State Department that ordered the actual oversight. This followed her repeated contacts with a young man, whose father had known terrorist links.

This is serious. You may be in over your head. Understand, G.P. you will have no cover, no friends you can turn to. Every move you make will probably be watched and cataloged."

Norm wished me well as he left.

"I didn't think of the jeopardy I might have put my family in." G.P. pondered aloud, while waiving to Eryn who was watching him intently from her bedroom window.

"Grandpa, is everything alright? Who was that man in the shadows you were talking to?"

"Oh honey that was just a kind neighbor who helped me search out Buffi in the dark."

Fortunately, that satisfied her young mind, yet, I hated the taste of lying.

Getting his granddaughter ready for bed, he knelt with her as she recited her prayers.

"Dear Lord, protect my mommy and grandpa in whatever they do."

I kissed her on the forehead and tucked her in. Now it was time to think what my next move would be.

Chapter 36

My parole officer telephoned early, saying he set me an appointment with a new court appointed psychiatrist in three hours time.

When I complained about the last minute notice, he reminded me that this follow-up was part of my sentence and to shut up, get dressed and get to the doctor's office on time. Fortunately, the "shrink" was seeing patients at his Highland Park location, not that far away.

I wondered if I could hit on Mehmet to chauffeur me around again. In any case, I would have to turn over Abbie's laptop and disks to him, as soon as possible.

I telephoned him and we coordinated our schedules and agreed upon an 11:00 a.m. pick- up time. Being worrisome by nature, I wondered if Mehmet might have been thinking about pulling the plug and walking away from my problems and me. After all, he wasn't being paid and it wasn't his family members who were involved. I questioned myself as to why anybody would want to deal with another person's grief.

As I had some time to kill, I booted up the laptop and closed my eyes, while trying to think of what Abbie might have chosen as her password. I tried family names, as well as her former Israeli school friends with unusual names. In frustration, I even tried optometry flash words, all without success.

I whispered to myself, "Abbie, please help me figure out what you were thinking when you chose this password."

I thought of her best memories, even favorite vacation spots. Suddenly, I had a mental image of her swimming in Nippersink Lake with her wet, black hair dangling in ringlets and her green eyes radiating happiness.

My fingers began typing, "Nippersink."

Bingo! I had hit upon it. I found myself almost too intimidated to read what I worked so hard to attain. After all, if Abbie wanted me to be privy to this information, she would have clued me in long ago.

Perhaps it's best that Mehmet look through these disks first. He could be more objective with what he comes across. Yet, the temptation to be the first to understand the reason why all of us were put in such jeopardy was overwhelming. Luckily the clock dictated the decision to put it away, for now.

While showering and getting dressed, I wondered how the session with a different psychiatrist would go. I made up my mind not to be too open with this stranger, believing it best, as Mehmet often suggested, to weigh my words, rather than volunteer too much information especially early on. Yet, I decided not to lie or be evasive. Perhaps, this doctor might be the one who might help me deal with the aching void in my soul, which was getting worse with time.

Approaching Wolf's house, Mehmet decided to circle the area and look for vehicles that appeared out of place. Suddenly, he saw flashing lights in his rear view mirror and an officer motioning him to pull over. Identifying himself as a retired, but armed F.B.I. agent, he was told to stay in his car as the police officer checked his license and I.D. There must have been a heightened level of security in the neighborhood since the break-in at Wolf's home, and someone called in a suspicious vehicle alert. Approaching Mehmet's car, he noticed the officer's right hand not on the top of his weapon's holster, always a good sign he thought.

The officer asked, "I see you are driving your daughter's auto. I assume you have her permission. May I speak with her?"

"Sorry, officer, she is working unofficially." This was code for an undercover assignment. Respecting that, the police officer inquired, "Why were you circling the area?"

"I wanted to see if there were any obvious security compromises."

"Find any?" the officer asked.

Mehmet responded, "No, but I would appreciate if you kept an extra watch on his house. He has been through a lot."

"It seemed to me that he got off easy with the D.U.I. related charges, his wife's incapacitation and their daughter's death, don't you think so?" questioned the officer.

Rather than argue, Mehmet pointed out there were other extenuating circumstances and no one should rush to judgment.

The police officer seemed okay with that and he motioned Mehmet to go on his way.

I was waiting outside as G.P. drove up. I must have appeared unusually happy.

"What are you so pleasant about this morning?" Mehmet inquired.

"First of all, good morning and thanks again for the taxi service. For an I.T. illiterate, I am very pleased to announce that last evening I solved my wife's password code problem and was able to access her files."

"That's terrific," G.P. explained, "Because my F.B.I. contacts have been frozen."

G.P. went on to tell me all that transpired the prior evening including a request for him to drop the case and distance himself from my problems.

I froze. "Look, I wouldn't blame you if you did quit. It sounds like we may have accidentally tripped a hornet's nest. If you don't want to take me to my appointment, I am sure I can arrange for a taxi."

G.P. considered Wolf sincere and simply replied, "Get in the car and let's go. I don't have anything else on my docket to do. In fact, prior to meeting you and becoming familiar with your case, my retirement was downright boring." He continued on, but in a different vein, "Since you went to the trouble of solving her password, give me some time to read what she wrote and perhaps we might gain an insight about what's going on."

Arriving at the psychiatrist's office, G.P. dropped me at the corner with some sage advice, "Listen to his questions and keep your answers brief. Most importantly, don't reveal any aspect of what we're doing."

I responded, "Thanks for the thoughts. If you come across any questions on Abbie's files, just bookmark those sections and maybe I can shed light on them later. I wrote down the password for you. What say we go to a Chinese restaurant after my session? By the way, where are you going to be?"

"I always like a coffee fix, while reading mystery files and searching for clues," Mehmet responded with a smile.

Jokingly I replied, "When are your buddies in the D.E.A., going to finally acknowledge the addictive qualities of caffeinated beverages and make it a controlled substance?" My attempt at humor was ignored.

Making my way through the building's hallway and to its single elevator, I looked at the adjacent marquee and found Dr. Michelle Tannen's room number. As I pressed the third floor button, anxious thoughts raced through my mind and my stomach began making gurgling sounds. "What if she asks me to re-live the night of the accident and postulate what I could have done to prevent it?" Even something as simple as checking Sandra to make sure her seatbelt was secure might have made the difference. It was this and other thoughts that kept me up nights and put me in a cold sweat now.

I entered an empty office and sank into a couch lacking spring support. Looking about, I spotted a buzzer with a microphone above it with instructions to signal the doctor upon arrival and to wait until called in. I did as requested, picked up a tattered "Modern Medical Studies" magazine and decided to make the best of the situation.

Chapter 37

G.P. drove to a nearby coffee shop and found a table in a secluded section of the store. He ordered a muffin and the large decaffeinated coffee of the day. There was a scarcity of other customers, which would mean fewer people looking over his shoulder. Yet, there was a lineup of cars at the drive up window, which never seemed to diminish. "What a business," Mehmet thought aloud.

He logged in without complication.

"Wolf had done well for a computer illiterate," he thought aloud, as he skimmed the disks; beginning with the one dated a day before the accident and then worked his way backwards.

"It's amazing how uninteresting and routine the entries were. The messages included shopping lists and doctor's appointments, as well as activities to attend to during the upcoming holidays. This was hardly the correspondence of a suspected foreign agent," he whispered.

After 20 minutes of such unproductive effort, he decided to switch tactics and go directly into Abbie's "e-mails sent" section, which might be more revealing.

While many entries appeared inconsequential, nevertheless he gained additional insight into her character.

She appeared a dedicated teacher interested in her students' welfare, as demonstrated by her electronic conversations with their parents, usually requesting their assistance with the educational progress of their children, most specifically homework matters. It seemed a fair number of the parents only spoke Spanish and had limited education.

Israel related entries came much earlier. It appeared that Abbie had just tendered her resignation as an Arabic and Farsi translator with the Israel consulate, citing schedule conflicts and a deepening rift in morale among her fellow staff members.

Before she left, there were a steady stream of translated reports from Al Jazeera and Al Arabiyia, the largest of the Arab language media-broadcasting networks. It appeared her job was to summarize content and estimate the effects of the propaganda espoused. Abbie felt that a significant number of spokespeople were adamant about not making peace with Israel, not even recognizing Israel's right to exist and in that same vein, enticing young Arabs to join in the cause for Israel's ultimate destruction. The names of deceased martyrs like Osama Bin Laden and other terrorists, as well as their organizations including Al Qaeda were frequently referenced.

While all of this was interesting, nothing was new or even mildly incriminating. C.I.A. briefings to the President and the Congressional Intelligence Oversight Committee echoed similar if not more thorough understandings.

I assumed Israel regularly supplied intelligence regarding suspected terror activity to the United States and there was reciprocity. After all, Israel's ultimate welfare was in the best interest of the United States.

Skimming further, this last understanding was starting to show some cracks. At the prior year's Yom

Ha'atzmaut, Israel's Independence Day function, Abbie indicated she spent time conversing with an M.C.O. member who also worked with a pro-Israel lobby. He claimed to have a reliable source that came upon dangerously different views.

My cell phone rang, awakening me from my trance-like involvement with what I was reading. As instructed, Wolf indicated his session was over and that he was waiting in the building foyer. I said I would pick him up in about ten minutes. Making cursory notes on a pad so I knew where I left off, I closed the system, finished my coffee, and asked for a bag to bring home the chocolate chip muffin for Eryn.

As Mehmet's car stopped curbside, Wolf opened the building door and walked towards the car appearing distressed.

"Now what?" Mehmet inquired, a little irritated with Wolf's constantly disturbed demeanor.

"Dr. Tannen asked me to sit in a hard wooden chair located in the center of the room. Meanwhile, she sat behind a full-length old-fashioned mahogany desk. I could barely see her face, let alone the rest of her. For all I know she could have been naked during the interview. She spoke into a microphone system to amplify her voice, as she had been involved in an auto accident that injured her vocal cords and left her with little mobility.

She read from the court transcripts and demanded "yes" or "no" replies as to the accuracy of her understandings. I endured this for about 20 minutes, until she changed the direction of the questioning, and asked if I felt responsible for what took place. When I responded I initially did, she cut me off and proceeded to lecture me on the various stages of grieving."

Mehmet tried to inject a little humor, but without success. "You know, I never met a shrink who didn't need a little therapy, himself. Perhaps, it comes from listening to so much self-serving bull-shit, while trying to make sense of everything within the framework of so-called psychological theory."

Jon responded, "Thank you 'Dr. Freud,' for your invaluable insights. I think I would have made more progress arguing with you than with her. If I remember correctly, there are five stages of loss, which she insisted I learn. They included: disbelief, which she says fades with time; yearning for lost family will probably last four months or so; the anger stage, I forget how long that lasts; and of course depression, which I have to look forward to and apparently is the longest period, at approximately six months or more. All these precede eventual acceptance.

As if the whole session was not depressing enough, she lectured me that both my physical and mental health are in jeopardy for possible alcoholism and suicidal thoughts. When I told her that wasn't going to be the case, she asked me to elaborate."

G.P. gasped, as if he knew where this talkative man was heading.

"I said that I had initially felt the guilt of having caused the accident, but now there are other factors that may have been involved. The 'shrink' then inquired as to what they might be, and I told her what we were doing." Seeing G.P. furrow his brow and hoping to head-off further disapproval, I quickly added, "Understand, there is doctor-patient confidentiality in play and besides, how would she ever know any of the involved parties?"

Mehmet looked at me in disbelief. "How could you have lived so long and be so naive?" He followed up, "Did the doctor take notes or use a recording device during the session?"

I responded, "I don't know. It was all too overwhelming for me to concentrate on external details. I just wanted it to end. She reminded me not to break any of the terms imposed upon me by the court. Finally, Tannen recommended a list of books to read."

Wishing to end this conversation, I asked if Mehmet knew how to get to my favorite Chinese restaurant.

Arriving some 30 minutes later, the self-imposed silence was finally broken when I asked, "What were you able to ascertain from Abbie's notes?"

"Let's go in and order the food first." G.P. suggested. "I had just located an interesting letter in the "e-mail sent" section when you called. Other than that, it was mundane. I have yet to get to the remaining disks."

I asked, "G.P. is it okay with you if I take the laptop home with me tonight?"

"That's fine; you might gain a greater understanding of her thoughts and insights as they relate to Israel, than I. However, do not talk about our business with anyone other than Malak or myself. Jon, do you finally get it? We have to be very cautious.

216

Whoever tried to silence your wife, for whatever she might have known, is no doubt interested in making sure we don't carry on from where she left off."

We then agreed upon a meal without shoptalk.

I picked up the tab as a partial thank-you for all of G.P.'s help. I knew I could never adequately repay this man for the support he had given me.

Dropping me at my home, Mehmet suggested, "Don't stay up all night reading your wife's entries. Get rest and call me in the morning."

As Mehmet drove back to his daughter's home, he spent the time trying to put together what little he knew with what he may have suspected. He felt the perpetrators who arranged Abbie's accident would not hesitate to kill Wolf or himself, if they believed either came upon compromising information.

The thought about the vulnerable position he may have placed his daughter and granddaughter in crossed his mind. Mehmet began to question his involvement in this case. After all, who was this man to him? Various ways to exit his commitment were racing through his mind; yet, all of this was overshadowed by Eryn's question of what he would have done, had he known about the Holocaust, while it was going on. Would he have tried to save innocent Jews, if he could?

Chapter 38

The earlier Chinese meal filled my stomach, and dinner was certainly not at the top of my "to do" list. Yet, it was another of the many realities that I had taken for granted. Abbie spoiled me and always had delicious food ready whenever I arrived home from seeing patients. It was so predictable that I just let whatever cooking skills I developed lapse. Out of frustration with my apparent lack of effort, she would ask in a rhetorical fashion, "Jon, whatever would you do without me?" Without waiting for my reply, she would gleefully insert, "Starve!"

We talked as most couples did, about a future hypothetical should one of us pass before the other. She would say that she would never marry again, while I would try to find someone the next day, as I was so helpless.

Actually, both Abbie and my mother before her did spoil me. They washed my clothes, prepared my meals, and only required me to wash the supper dishes and vacuum the floors. Both women recognized early on that I was a contender for the poster child of male helplessness. In my own defense, they were not so perfect either. Nevertheless, they were strong in the many ways I was weak. Now the women I loved and needed the most were gone, and I'm forced to fend for myself.

The food the neighbors left in the refrigerator was almost gone and my dirty clothes were piled high next to the washer and dryer. Underwear was in particular short supply. I contemplated buying extras, but didn't have access to a car and felt too embarrassed to ask anyone how to run the washer and dryer. It's just a matter of time before these issues would have to be confronted.

Showering before bed, I caught a reflection of myself from the side view in the bathroom mirror and was disappointed. I resembled my father with a pudgy middle. Since the only meal I prepared in the past couple of days consisted of candy bars and ice cream in a big cereal bowl, it was understandable.

I logged back onto Abbie's laptop and prepared myself for an all-nighter, if need be. I began the unfamiliar task of looking for clues as to why anyone would want to harm my wife. The thought of revenge kept me going, yet, I didn't know who to go after. Now I may have the opportunity to find out.

One of her disks revealed multiple pages of correspondence with the Israeli consulate. As I read the material, I began to feel the extent of the danger Abbie suspected. Arab media was filled with vile hatred for Jews, especially those residing in Israel. Nothing, no matter how odious, would interfere with the reclamation of what they viewed to be their lands, including attacks on innocent Jewish children. Arab leaders appeared clever in the repetition of obvious lies. Yet, Abbie became most distressed with Israeli leaders who turned a blind eye, while supplying Palestinian police officers and military militia with weapons that could be used to rain terror on innocent Jews.

Previously, I had read of mistakes Israel made in their dealings with their Arab neighbors. One in particular appeared to bite them in the butt repeatedly. They had relinquished control over the *Temple Mount*, Judaism's holiest site, to the Islamic Waqf following the 1967 reunification of Jerusalem. This was meant to be an act of respect demonstrating Israel's desire to work with Arab nations. Instead, the latter turned it around, implying it was weakness or guilt on the part of the Jews. In fiery rhetoric to embolden their brethren, they repeated the mantra, if the Jews really had license to this holy land, why would they so readily give it up? Palestinian leadership subsequently mocked the Israelis by speaking of peaceful coexistence in English, while stating in Arabic that those who died killing the occupiers would become martyrs, deserving of respect, and monetary compensation would be provided for their surviving families.

Abbie relayed the messages she translated to her contacts at the Chicago Consulate office and later to Embassy staff in New York. Yet, everything appeared to fall upon deaf ears. Neither party appeared to care. Abbie saw the terrorists as only one of the enemies that needed to be confronted.

At a Consulate dinner, she took the opportunity to meet with African-American community leaders from whom she thought the Israeli cause might gain some sympathy, only to find rejection. She tried to remind them that during the dark days of the civil rights movement in the United States, Jews worked overtime, often at their own peril, to change the unfair stereotypes held of African Americans. She hoped this would motivate the African-American community to move towards a more balanced approach in understanding what was actually happening in the Middle East. Unfortunately, some of these former allies seemed to succumb to Arab propaganda.

She helped organize trips to Washington D.C. to educate members of Congress and their staff as to what the Israeli position was, and the need for their continuing support, as ultimately, it was in America's best interest to back Israel. In the earlier trips, it proved an easy task, especially around election time. Yet, recently she found the Arabs had also organized their own lobbying forces, repeating their own self-serving mantras, labeling themselves as the underdog and the Jews as the aggressors. They referenced the deaths of their children resisting Israeli occupation, but never spoke of outright murderous actions aimed at Jewish children.

Reading her entries, I felt bad that I did not appreciate what it took for her to stand up to the organized Jewish community and to face threats of isolation from all sides. I should have been there for her on many levels. Yet, I was no different from so many other Jews who shirked their responsibility to learn the facts and take action.

The disks further revealed that international support was growing for anti-Israel forces. The influence of the "despise Israel" movement was gaining momentum on college and university campuses within western nations. It appeared to legitimatize a more acceptable format for anti-Semitism.

The modern world appeared to be setting itself up for the consensus that it could easily live without Israel. Abbie's translations clearly foretold that western economies could be revived to their earlier greatness, once Israel was out of the picture.

Now I was hooked and wondered how the anti-Israel and anti-Semitic forces could implement such radical thoughts. Looking at the clock, I recognized the hour was late and I needed to reach Beata, before her hospital shift ended. I hoped to repeat the prior evenings experience with my wife, even though it was obviously one-sided.

Dialing the number, I was told Beata was still on her break, but would return in 5 minutes. I felt disturbed, as I needed some connection with my wife, now.

The telephone rang. Happily, it was Beata calling from Abbie's room. She placed the receiver next to my wife's ear. I mentioned having read her writings and my respect for her taking the strong stand for what she believed. Thinking aloud I verbalized my deepest concern, "Abbie, could this be the reason somebody would want to harm our family? Yet, it wasn't as if you uncovered any great secret, was it?"

The nurse interrupted indicating that she only had only a few remaining minutes. I asked if my wife had visitors.

Beata replied, "The chart indicated her parents stopped by during lunchtime, and Abbie had one more visitor around 2:00 p.m., but the name is hard to decipher, it appears foreign."

Rather than upset a kind woman who had gone out of her way, I responded, "Probably, it was one of her old Israeli friends. Anyway, I hope to arrange a ride into town to see her tomorrow. Thanks for all your help."

I began to fret about Abbie's visitor, concerned that he might pose a danger. Fortuitously, G.P. called.

"Just checking in Jon, to see how your evening went?" he asked, while talking in a soft tone so as not to disturb his granddaughter or the dog, who were both sound asleep next to him.

"G.P., I just got done speaking with Abbie's nurse. My wife had a visitor with a foreign sounding name that was not decipherable. Anything to worry about?" I nervously asked.

G.P. responded in a confident tone, "She's in a safe environment and doesn't pose any threat to anyone, so why be worried? Don't stay up too late reviewing the disks. I'll speak with you tomorrow."

Now more than ever, I was motivated to spend all the time necessary to search Abbie's entries for any red flag that might appear. Hours into this work, I decided to take a bathroom break when I heard a noise coming from the back yard. It sounded like someone turning my kitchen doorknob. Instead of calling the police, I took a flashlight in one hand and Sandra's softball bat in the other. As I tiptoed down the stairs, my heart was racing. Thankfully, I saw nothing as I entered the kitchen area. Then proceeding to the foyer I tested the front door lock and found it secure. A quick look at the back yard and I made my way back up the stairs, leaving my makeshift weapon on the first floor landing.

As I sat down to continue where I had left off, I was grabbed from behind. Strong hands covered my mouth and restrained me.

"Wolf," a male voice spoke. "Don't fight me. I am going to blindfold you and tie your wrists. I don't have to hurt you unless you force my hand. If I release my grip, do you agree not to move or speak for at least five seconds? Shake your head if you will cooperate."

I nodded and found the strong grip released. Waiting the required time, I spoke, "Who are you and what do you want from me?"

The stranger replied, "That's unimportant. I know your wife." He continued, "I see you found her laptop. Figure anything out?"

I responded, "Not yet."

The intruder bound my hands behind me, covered my eyes, and threw me on Sandra's bed. He then took my place at the desk. "For you and your friend's safety, I am erasing some memory from this computer. I am emptying the garbage, so to speak. You should know that it's thanks to your Arab friend, you're still alive. Nevertheless, even that won't help you should you continue meddling. If you choose to ignore what I am saying, one or both of you won't see your loved ones again."

I figured if this man wanted to harm me, he could have easily done so by now. In my imagination, I surmised he must have placed a flash drive into the computer, programmed it to search for and delete files of suspected interest. Perhaps, he might be saving selected entries for later viewing. Then I heard him giggle and asked him what's so amusing. The intruder replied. "You are a luckier man than even you know."

Sensing I wasn't going to be made aware of the reason for that comment and wishing to keep the conversation going, I asked his name a second time.

He simply replied, "The less you know, the better chance you have of being left alone. You know your Arab friend is getting instructions to cut you loose."

"Why do you sarcastically refer to Mehmet as my 'Arab' friend? If it weren't for him, I might never have known that I didn't cause the death of my child or the current condition of my wife."

The intruder replied, "All you need to know now, is that both of you are on a collision course that may prove deadly. The people I take my orders from would no more think of crushing the life out of you than stepping on a bug. You will have only this one time opportunity to walk away and live a normal life. If you don't take my advice, even on an assumption that you might come upon something incriminating, an immediate termination order will be issued. Think about that. Can you live that kind of life, looking over your shoulder and not being able to trust anyone? You both are in way over your heads."

I asked what role he played in all of this and if he could have warned Abbie, her life was in danger, the same way he was warning me.

"What makes you think I didn't? It's too bad about your daughter. Had your family taken your car that evening, neither of you would have been involved, as the problem would have eventually passed with your wife."

At that point, I was beginning to lose control, "You took away everything I ever cared about. What makes you think I won't come after you?"

"You're a fool and that makes you dangerous," he replied. "Even with the resources of a former F.B.I. agent, no one in the media or law enforcement would find either of you credible. There is only one resource that might listen and only reluctantly at that. Moreover, you don't stand a chance in hell of getting close to them. Trust me; you will be taken out in a heartbeat and your last one at that. Take the gift you were given earlier of not being sentenced to prison and get on with your life. It seems benevolent forces are giving to you what they couldn't give your wife and daughter, a second chance."

By the sounds of the constant keyboard tapping, he must have continued his work as he spoke.

"The only saving grace for Mehmet and you, and a temporary one at that, is that my assignment is to relieve you of the means of compromising us and now that's done. All that remains on the computer is dribble."

Maybe he's making sense. Perhaps we had gotten into something beyond our abilities. "O.K., let's say we agree not to carry anything forward and let's say no one would believe us, even if we did, I still want to know something about what Abbie had uncovered."

"Listen fool, that's not going to happen and you're trying my patience. Enough already, I said all I

226

am going to say. Now lie down on the bed on your stomach and shut the fuck up. Don't move for 20 minutes. After that, it shouldn't take more than five minutes for you to release yourself. Forget about me, or I won't forget about you, your Arab friend and your lovely wife. Understand?"

I had no clue how he entered or how he left. Nevertheless, he was gone. I immediately tried to free myself. That proved a harder task than I was led to believe. After ten minutes of struggling, all I had accomplished was to force the blindfold from my eyes. Sensing I was alone in the dark, anxiety began to overtake me. Thoughts of this dangerous man gaining such easy access into my home added to the tension. I had to ask myself, what was so important that Abbie put everything on the line? Did the intruder learn anything or simply erase everything of suspected value? Exactly, what had Abbie come upon? I guessed I might never know the answers to these questions.

Attempting to roll over, I misjudged the end of the bed and came crashing down, face first on the floor. Luckily, I hit Sandra's throw rug. My nose was bleeding, but that was the least of my problems. I had to go to the bathroom and had no choice but to relieve myself in my pants. Lying in my own waste was humiliating, but at least I was alive.

Tears, stemming from my helplessness, started streaming down my face. I got angrier with those who were ultimately responsible for Sandra's death and Abbie's incapacitation. It was at this point I vowed revenge, even at the cost of my life. No matter how long it would take, and even if I had to go it alone, I would get even.

Helpless, I closed my eyes and began to think of all that I learned that could shed light on what we are working on. Eventually, Mehmet would check in on me, unless he had already decided to abandon me.

Chapter 39

Having returned from walking Eryn to her bus,
Mehmet was happy to find a message from Malak
indicating her undercover assignment was completed.
She would be home that afternoon, in time to pick Eryn
up and take her to dinner, just the girls alone.

Malak asked, "Dad would you mind fending for
yourself tonight?"

I was thrilled she was safe. Now that her
assignment was over, I could concentrate on my self-
appointed mission. Pouring a cup of hot coffee and
starting some toast, I opened two Jewish newspapers
that I picked up at the local newsstand. This would not
have been possible when I grew up in this
neighborhood. In fact, anything Jewish was restricted
from our home. My father frequently told me and with
the greatest of pleasure, "They don't eat pig, but many
act like them." Mehmet added, "Whatever that meant?"

Perusing the Israeli news, I read several articles
within the first paper, which reported that the president
of Israel was expected to stand trial for alleged criminal
activity, the prime minister was under an ethics
investigation, the finance minister was suspected of
having taken a bribe and the integrity of a candidate for
police commissioner was placed in doubt. Imagine all
this negative news in just one Jewish paper. My father
would have been delighted and not surprised. This
must be quite a day for anti-Jewish forces, I surmised.

If these are indeed the Chosen People, I began to
question the worth of my efforts and the risks that I'm

taking. Then I thought of innocent men, women and children that were and still are being indiscriminately targeted, just for being Jews.

In the second paper, I read that the Iranian President suggested that the extermination of six million European Jews during the Holocaust was a myth. This was reinforced by a Palestinian spokesperson who rejected any connection of the Jewish people to the land of Israel, thereby encouraging Palestinian Arabs to forcefully usurp the land from the Jews.

Still another article proposed that Jews and Israel must be made to appear as illegal occupiers, exaggerators of the Holocaust, and exploiters of conscience money. "...Once this is accomplished, the Jews will lose their moral credibility and be more vulnerable to universal condemnation..," so claimed the story.

A cold shudder shot down my spine. How many U.S. presidents have tried unsuccessfully to bring peace to this region? That said; a growing number of anti-Israel thinkers and their supporters far too easily conceptualize a world without an Israel as a reality that might serve to eliminate all the wrongs we are experiencing. I began to ponder this and other frightening scenarios proposed by the hate mongers.

Could it be remotely possible that the United States might be covertly abetting an as-yet, undetermined hostile action towards Israel, a nation we have openly supported and sworn allegiance to, since its founding? If that were to be the case and I did nothing, I could never look into Eryn's eyes without feeling shame. Perhaps Abbie may have stumbled upon something related to this farfetched thought.

Hoping to run these thoughts and more by Jon, I telephoned him and found the line busy. I then decided to drive over. I began wondering what would happen if it were determined that our interventions in both Iraq and Afghanistan were, in actuality, a necessary predecessor action towards a greater goal in the Middle East? Then these concerns might not be so much of a stretch. After all, Israel is continuously being blamed for our costly involvement in that region and is propagandized as the main obstacle to peace. Perhaps, this might be our ticket out of the no-win, no-end situation. However, if so, how could such a goal be accomplished, without garnering a backlash?

I read somewhere that the father of a prominent kidnapped and murdered Jewish victim was overheard commenting, that a growing "tsunami" of hatred is occurring, while the court of public opinion seeks to relieve the responsibilities of the perpetrators. The scapegoat for all world tragedies, the embodiment of all problems, appears to always be linked to Israel and Jews.

Making it over to Wolf's house in record time and without being stopped by the police, I looked forward to seeing if my intriguing scenarios concurred within Abbie's insights, or if they were nothing more than an overactive imagination.

I rang the doorbell and there was no answer. I saw his car in the garage so I pounded on the door calling Jon's name. I sensed a problem and went to the back of the house. Observing large muddy footprints facing the rear sliding door, I took out my gun and unlocked the safety. Sliding the door open, I cautiously entered and worked my way through the first floor.

As I approached the stairs leading to the second level, I heard weeping. Rushing upstairs, I saw the door to Sandra's room open. Crouching down to make a smaller target, I leapt into the room. Without backup, I knew I could be in trouble, but my intuition demanded immediate and solo action.

Scanning the room for an intruder or intruders and finding no obvious signs, I cautiously approached my friend who appeared tied-up securely. Motioning to Wolf to be silent, I cut the plastic binding from his wrists and feet and then methodically searched the rest of the house. Returning within minutes and inquiring as to what happened, Wolf yelled, "What the fuck took you so long? I have been lying here in my own shit all night, helpless!"

"Good morning to you too, Jon! Glad to see you so well rested and in good spirits. But, you definitely need a bath, my friend," Mehmet joked as he squeezed his nostrils shut.

Gradually, blood circulation returned to Jon's hands and feet. In a moment, he was able to stand without assistance. He then relayed all that transpired, while taking out his frustrations on his only friend.

Jon sarcastically said, "I hope you don't mind, dumb-ass, if I go to the bathroom and shower and change my clothes."

Overlooking the insult, G.P. was happy his friend was not seriously injured and responded, "I suggest you throw out your clothes. For the record, it's

'Agent Dumb-Ass' to you. Hurry up; we obviously have a lot to discuss."

Through the shower door with the steamy water running, I shouted, "I'm guessing the intruder might have been an American intelligence agent, from the command of his English and his ways. He said he deleted the essentials from Abbie's computer and warned both of us to back off. He intimated that our phones were bugged and we're under surveillance. Also, should we carry on with our efforts, there is a potential death sentence awaiting us."

Mehmet logged on and found some of the important information he had read earlier was indeed gone. Other entries appeared fragmented into nonsense. He then took out a memory stick from his pocket and inserted it in the rear-receiving portal. He smiled as the previously erased entries were restored. Yet, his glee was short lived, when he sensed he had made a dreadful error. The virus that destroyed the original pertinent sections could again erase them and this time; infect his "memory stick" as well.

G.P. informed me of his limited victory. Theoretically, we had only a relatively short window of opportunity to see what could be salvaged. Abbie's laptop was a much earlier model that did not allow for rapid conversion between power sources. There was not even a working indicator to let the user know exactly how much time was left on the batteries, before the unit would shut itself down. I knew this was a valid problem, as Abbie had experienced it before. I also knew the batteries, although recharged yesterday had been extensively used by both the intruder and myself.

233

Having done a stint in the F.B.I.'s counter-intelligence unit, G.P. told me he was very familiar with key "target words" or "phrase concepts" to ferret out potentially pertinent information. This skill might serve us well to beat the limitations of the clock. Based on my recollection of Abbie's most recent conversations with consulate personnel, together we decided to program the laptop to look for "spy;" "detonation;" "Holocaust;" "*Jihad*;" "Lebanon;" "*Temple Mount*;" and "nuclear terror."

I remember my wife mentioning having received a telephone call from an Israeli friend. She indicated that a Lebanese Student studying at Hebrew University, with whom Abbie was corresponding, had been arrested. She appeared distraught, but did not pursue this matter at the time.

Later, I asked Abbie if this might pose any danger to her. She then told me that several months earlier a friend working with the State Department was approached by a mutual acquaintance at a Beirut consular social engagement who requested Abbie's e-mail address. It appeared that the son of a high-ranking Lebanese diplomatic official had been following her writings for years and wanted to discuss his thoughts with her.

Mehmet asked the source of the trigger word "*Temple Mount*." I replied, "It was chosen because of Abbie's repeated reference to it in a somewhat prophetic manner. While studying abroad, she had worked on several archeological digs with professors holding expertise in the three major religions: Islam, Christianity, and Judaism. All had come to the same frightening conclusion. The eventual War of the Faiths would have both its beginning and end on the *Temple Mount*."

"From what Abbie also said, it had been foretold that a site, located within the heart of Jerusalem's Old City, would eventually become uninhabitable, as punishment for the Jewish peoples' lack of faith in and unwillingness to defend their Holy gift. It's the one area still hypothesized to house the Ark of the Covenant and its Ten Commandments stone tablets."

G.P. intervened, "You know I am a Christian Arab with family still living in Jerusalem. I knew the Babylonians carried away the majority of the Jews and their treasures, but not the Ark in 586 B.C. Is it possible the Ark of the Covenant may actually be buried within the labyrinths that underlie the huge *Temple Mount*? It was upon this base the second *Temple Mount* structure was built, and expanded upon by King Herod of Judea. If found, this most prized possession could definitively tie Jews to their biblical heritage."

Mehmet programmed the laptop to begin the targeted search. Four results appeared that were multiple pages long. Utilizing a cable hook up, he prepared the printer. Fortunately, Abbie had a reserve supply of paper under the desk.

We agreed to print the earliest dated e-mail first and then work forwards in time. Mehmet hoped he had a handle on the ramifications of the introduced virus; yet, at any moment, he thought the computer might either lose power or self-erase entries, and we would end up with nothing. Suddenly the printer froze.

Suspecting the flash drive by now was corrupted and expecting the laptop to shut down at any moment, G.P. and Jon began to quickly read the e-mails they had previously miniaturized and forced themselves to rely on their joint memory to retain any pertinent facts that they came upon.

The first revealed some limited background on Jabr Mahjub, a Lebanese student. He was a Christian-Arab studying at Hebrew University, much as Abbie had done years earlier. His father's connections assured his son a place at this prestigious university where he chose to study in the school of Foreign Service.

Initially, he relayed hostile feelings toward all Jews. Ironically, he was assigned an Orthodox Jewish roommate whose religious fervor matched his passion for Christianity. Despite their differences, a friendship took root.

Mr. Mahjub had come to appreciate Abbie's numerous articles that were stored in the library reference center. Although he took issue with her strong pro-Israel stances, he nevertheless hoped to correspond with her and introduce his views under the e-mail moniker, "Proud Arab Thinker."

She must have been intrigued, as she followed up with him and addressed each of his concerns in depth. Subsequent questions became less hostile, as both found common ground in their joint desires to ensure the welfare of both of their peoples.

The next communication came several months later and appeared most ominous. There were references to increasing numbers of suicide-bomb detonations, each with escalating deadly consequences,

236

in and around Jerusalem. They occurred subsequent to Israeli retaliatory attacks deep into Lebanon, because of cross border missile launchings and kidnappings. "Proud Arab Thinker" insisted organized resistance to Israel was growing stronger with the eventual intention of testing the will of the Jewish people to fight, perhaps setting the stage for what was to follow.

Mehmet and Wolf were astounded as they read the last and longest correspondence. The student indicated that he had returned to his parent's home the prior Friday evening and found his father hosting a high-ranking Hizbullah political agent, as well as an Iranian diplomatic emissary. Their dinner was uneventful, until his father and the guests adjourned to the library and locked the doors behind them. Jabr became intrigued and went into an adjacent room where he began eavesdropping on the discussion that was taking place.

It seems the guests were trying to convince their host for the necessity of a covert nuclear operation against Israel, years in the planning. "...At first, it was hard to follow what was happening in the room. Yet, within a few moments of listening, it became clear that there was to be a detonation beneath the *Temple Mount*. The Hizbullah representative told my father that he must act quickly to keep me from returning to Hebrew University, indicating that the means for the Mount's destruction would also culminate in a coordinated multi-Arab military ground attack, effectively finishing off the occupier Jewish State, once and for all. Afterwards, there would be an opportunity for its later rebuilding and re-characterization under a Joint Muslim

237

and Arab Authority. A minority of Jews would be permitted to live there, upon swearing allegiance to the new entity. Meanwhile, displaced Arab refuges worldwide would be given incentives to return to their pre-1948 homes, even if doctored property titles were necessary."

The men continued to read aloud Jabr Mahjub's thoughts, "My father was reminded that the Christian-Arab population within Israel had been denied the equal status promised by the Israelis so long ago. When he inquired as to the welfare of the innocent, unsuspecting populations during and after the nuclear detonation, he was told that all Arab brothers and sisters would be called upon to make the ultimate sacrifice in order to regain our Holy Lands. Reacting to the concern they must have observed upon my father's face, the guests unequivocally stated that after the initial shock, Jews would lose passion for fighting; especially after contrived press releases were distributed worldwide, indicating the nuclear destruction was a misstep from Israeli plans. Neutral nations might grimace for the moment, but then they would get on with the business of business. To soothe the situation, oil dollars would be made available by prosperous Arab nations and from others elsewhere, to facilitate the rebuilding and expected population transfers. The world would soon come to the realization for the necessity of appeasement. Lastly, the Iranian representative promised that all current terror activities were being put on hold, in order to accomplish this most important end goal.

Abbie, I stopped listening and decided to e-mail you the above before I could change my mind. Be warned, your weakness lies beneath your most treasured of possessions, the *Temple Mount*. I learned a 500 square meter pit beneath the Mount is being packed with ..." The e-mail abruptly ended and was the last correspondence from this young man.

The men were stunned by what they read. Now they had the probable cause as to why Abbie was targeted. However, who would believe them and even if they did access a sympathetic ear, where would they get corroborating evidence? More importantly, the remaining question as to how the final action would be accomplished had not yet been revealed.

With intelligence resources effectively shut off from G.P. and with warnings of dire consequences should the men persist, there was real danger and no place to turn. Both Mehmet and Wolf were likely compromised and very vulnerable.

Chapter 40

Mehmet shut the laptop down and suggested they immediately leave the house to discuss their next move. Driving in a zigzag manner, he hoped to ferret out any possible "trailing" cars or motorcycles. Then, he abruptly stopped about a mile from my house in a heavily tree lined street and took out a pair of binoculars from the car's glove box. He searched the sky for the helicopter he observed a few minutes earlier. Ominously, it was seen hovering above a nearby tall building. Was it following us or just a mere coincidence?

Merging onto the northbound expressway, Mehmet sped up and then quickly exited at the nearest off-ramp. Pulling into the parking lot of a busy factory, he again scanned the skies and to his dismay saw the same helicopter. Now, he knew they were being followed, and that the agency involved would be trying to access a remote area for our apprehension. While driving, Mehmet explained the repercussions if it were determined we compromised national security, even unintentionally. He went on to tell me what some Federal agencies were capable of, should they wish someone gone and untraceable.

"Rarely, interagency cooperation could be requested to assist with a deemed active national security threat. It was referred to as a 'reciprocal,' and could include assassination. Although understood not to have been utilized by the F.B.I., it was still rumored to be an available option that was always held in reserve. Some within the intelligence community even conjectured such might have been the case in the Kennedy assassination. After all, how could anyone choreograph such a perfect execution to the highest leader in the land, without leaving definitive clues?"

Mehmet began to perspire as our car sped-off, now driving towards the Chicago Loop.

I finally commented, "Enough, you're making me nauseous. What's going on?"

"Jon, I know a restaurant in the downtown area where they serve all kinds of great 'deli' food. It's a bit noisy, but the food is worth it and I want to beat the crowds," is all G.P. would say.

"Whatever, let's get there quickly before I puke," I replied.

G.P. understood Wolf's time as a free man was realistically, limited at best.

Finding a parking spot behind the busy Halsted Street deli, both men quickly exited from the car. They entered the restaurant and joined a long line of patrons at the counter waiting for their turn to order the specialty of the house, corned beef sandwiches and potato pancakes that G.P. said were the best in the city. Waiting for the food, he observed all approaching individuals through the store's front windows.

"All right," I insisted, "What's up? I get the message, we're being followed. But, G.P. is it more than just that?"

Mehmet motioned me to take a table that just opened near the rear exit and against a wall facing the front entrance. Without objection, I followed his instruction and grabbed it before a waiting family could sit there. It was several minutes before he returned with the food. During the wait, my mind conjured up various scenarios. It was unsettling to see Mehmet act in such a concerned manner, as if we were fugitives trying to evade the authorities. He put the tray on the table and sat down.

"Wolf, I think you know we are in deep trouble. We may have come upon the information that cost Sandra her life and debilitated Abbie. I believe your wife was a targeted hit. Sorry to say, you and your daughter were collateral damage. Now you and I are very dangerous to whoever originally felt threatened."

I replied with unusual calmness, "What's our next move?"

"Now we have to assess the safest way to get the information we discovered out, and not get caught in the process."

I responded, "Let me tell you outright, I have nothing left to lose, but you do."

Dismissing what I just said, Mehmet, brandishing a sly smile, informed me, "Whatever is going to happen, I'll be damned if I let it spoil this delicious corned beef sandwich. I paid for it Wolf, and you are going to eat it and enjoy it!" Adding, "When you place your life on the line almost every day, you get used to the fact that one-day you may not be able to eat such a fine meal."

G.P. went on to inform me that the only reasonable resource that might actually assist us was the Israeli Consulate. However, we needed to get an understanding of how the terrorists were going to implement their plan. Knowing that would give us a considerable advantage.

"Jon, for our protection, neither of us can return to our individual homes or for that matter, to the hospital. It's unclear exactly how far whoever is tailing us is directed to go. Keep in mind; if you should put yourself in a position to be abducted, then my family and I are in jeopardy." Mehmet paused for a moment before announcing, "I have a distant cousin, who may be able to get us the answers we're seeking."

Again, I asked, "Is it too late for you to extricate yourself from this mess?"

Now that he was involved with a possible solution, G.P. appeared to mellow as he replied, "The early details of your case smelled of intrigue. An F.B.I. agent actually dreams of such an assignment and rarely gets anything close to it. I don't fear for my life, and I have no concerns at this time for the safety of my family, as long as your location is unknown. They know nothing of how far we have come or what our next move might be. That gives us a temporary window of opportunity."

I took a moment to tell G.P. an idea that just came to me, "For years, Abbie dragged me to boring Israel Consulate Affairs. I am sure I must have passed their security clearances. Perhaps I can get in more easily by myself and convince them of the scope of the danger they are about to face."

Finishing their meal without further conversation, G.P. and Jon got up and left as a swarm of new customers arrived.

As their car entered the lower Wacker Drive tunnels, G.P. stated, "We started this together and will finish it the same way. I don't want to hear any more talk of other alternatives. By the way, maybe I can teach you skills that may come in handy someday, including the best way to lose an aerial tail. However, let's hope a more maneuverable motorcycle has not replaced the helicopter."

As they exited, Mehmet made one final evasive maneuver, swerving the car so fast I was startled.

"What are you trying to do? Kill us with reckless driving, and then you'll have done the work for the very people we are trying to avoid."

Having said that, I put my trust in my friend and just closed my eyes. When the car hit a speed bump, I awoke and looked about. We were proceeding very slowly in an area of the city in which I was unfamiliar. To make it even more confusing, G.P. began driving down back alleyways where I picked up the smell of raw garbage. Finally, he parked in the rear of a strip mall.

"Jon, I know you are not going to like what I am about to say, but where I am going, you can't follow. I need you to lie on the floor in the passenger area and cover yourself with this blanket. You must not be visible for both of our sakes. I hope that I'll be back in 20 minutes or so. Will you cooperate?" Mehmet asked.

"Do I have any choice?" I replied.

Mehmet removed his gun and holster and put them in the glove compartment along with his F.B.I. identification, giving me this final instruction, "Don't touch this weapon, unless absolutely necessary, understand?" He purposely waited for my acknowledgement.

G.P. locked the car door before walking off. I peeked out from under the blanket and saw him ring a buzzer immediately adjacent to a solid metal, grey door. He turned around and catching my eye gave me a stern look to which I immediately pulled the blanket over my head as originally instructed.

Chapter 41

As the heavy door opened, two men forced Mehmet
inside the building and threw him against a brick wall
where they searched for weapons or recording devices.
They removed his wallet, placed a hood over his head
and loosely bound his wrists together.

  I was led down a flight of stairs and told to sit
on a bench. My hood was removed and I found myself
at the opposite end of a long table, in a dimly lit room
facing wall pictures portraying a hooded man holding a
Kalashnikov machine gun. Next to him was a woman
wearing a heavy full-length coat with just enough open
to reveal a bomb strapped to her body. Below was an
inscription in Farsi, which translated, "Eventually, it
will all be ours."
  Within minutes, a bearded man in a long off-
white gown and skullcap entered. He was pulling at his
whiskers, as if pondering his next move. Showing a
trace of a smile, he said, "It's good you called before
coming. Things are tense as we expect a great event to
take place very soon in Palestine. Afterwards, you may
come home with me and my family and we can run
through our grandfathers' vineyards, once again.
"Salam Aleichem, my cousin Mehmet."
  "Aleichem Salam, Ishmael," I replied. Can we
remove the plastic restraints? My wrists are beginning
to hurt."

"You always were such a cry baby," Ishmael said with a grin. It has been too many years since you visited your cousin and a lot, of course, has happened. Even though each of us took a different path, in the end, we are family and I will always extend to you my hospitality and friendship. Come let's cross the street and enjoy Turkish coffee and Baklava and speak of serious matters, just as we did as children, when you visited my parent's home in the Holy Land."

My bindings were cut and the two of us left through the front door of the olive oil shop and walked to a nearby bakery. There we took a rear table.

The other store patrons greeted Ishmael with a look of deference. "Its lucky for you, Mehmet, you haven't lost your good looking Arab features, coming into this neighborhood as you did. As an aside, do you think me so ignorant as not to have noticed the man under the blanket in the back seat of your car? You are indeed comical."

Looking about, I asked my cousin if we could speak safely and confidentially.

"Go on," Ishmael replied.

"Let me tell you what I know, and ask you what I need to find out." I discussed the Abbie Wolf situation and its aftermath, stopping only to taste the flavorful coffee and sweets served. These brought back fond memories of our visits together when, during the hot summers we would stop for refreshment at the various villages we came to, while hiking the Judean Hills. As I finished my story, Ishmael again fingered his beard, but this time with concern.

"Understand what you're asking me to do could easily blow the cover that took seven years to develop. I gave up any chance for a private life to do this for the Bureau and our country. My marriage was sacrificed. Even my handlers have not contacted me in the past three years for fear of exposing me. Is there any other option available?"

"Ishmael, there are no other choices I can think of."

"My cousin, I have to return now. I will contact a Hamas relative in the Gaza to see what she knows. Yes, neither of us would have made it into the Bureau today with suspected terrorist elements climbing out of our family tree. Nevertheless, we did and there are. Do not contact me again. I am giving you the location of a drop box where any information I come upon will be left. Do you remember basic encryption class?"

I nodded, I did.

"Walk out of here speaking only in Arabic or Farsi, arm in arm, and smiling. Remember no eye contact with others, as that could call attention to you."

As we left the bakery, there was a crowd on the corner dancing. "What's that all about?" I asked.

"Let's find out," he replied.

The revelers informed Ishmael there was another rocket attack launched from Gaza. This time it reached Ashkelon, Israel. While no one was hurt, the deep penetration of the thin computer guided rocket caused a near panic throughout the entire city. One man in the crowd began shouting, "The Jews won't be so arrogant now."

Before we could arouse suspicion, Ishmael grabbed me and we began dancing with the crowd chanting God is great, *Allah Akbar*.

Returning through the olive shop's front entrance, Ishmael quickly walked me to the back door, gave me back my wallet, and kissed me goodbye. As our arms and hands were extended in an expression of friendship, a small key was passed to me. I didn't look back as I opened the car door, sat down and turned on the ignition. Pulling away very slowly, I prayed that no ignorance on my part might have put Ishmael in jeopardy.

As the car picked up speed, Jon spoke from under the blanket. "Can I take this rag off?"

"Not yet," Mehmet replied as he drove four blocks before parking on a side street. He then got out of the car and began scanning the sky with his binoculars. Not noticing any air traffic, he climbed back into the car saying, "And now we wait. By the way Jon, do you have cash on you?"

"I have about $50. Why?"

"With my $100 that's enough for several nights at a cheap motel," G.P. thought aloud. "I had better contact Malak. I have a non-traceable calling card that should provide us some cover."

Pulling into a gas station, he telephoned his daughter from one of the few remaining pay phones in the city and left a message on her voice mail, letting her know he was all right and adding, "I am going fishing for a day or so. My cell phone isn't working, but I will contact you soon. Remember I love my ladies."

Returning to the car, Mehmet motioned me to lower my window. "Jon, I have to ask you to break the law. We have to drop off Malak's car at her home, after we get the rental. Understand?"

"Whatever you say," I replied.

Staying within the posted speed limit, they cautiously drove towards the expressway. Going north, Mehmet stated he knew of a small auto rental lot that just opened in Skokie, advertising low rates. "Wolf, we're now on a budget. No more eating out at fancy restaurants or using credit cards that may be tracked."

Twenty minutes after arriving at Allen's Auto Rentals, Mehmet returned and announced, "Surprise, I rented us a black Ford Focus that they are bringing out now. Your driver's license was turned over to the court after the verdict, right?" Seeing me nod, he continued. "Follow me as closely as you can without hitting me. We have to be good little boys and not get caught breaking traffic laws. Jon, you'll pass me by as I park my daughter's car near her driveway. My plan is to quickly enter the house, borrow some cash and leave through the back door. You will drive two blocks east and pull into the Jewel parking lot, where I should meet up with you in 10 to 15 minutes. Stay in the car and try not to be visible."

Without question, I did exactly as G.P. requested. Following too close I could see his look of disapproval in the rear view mirror; I slowed down and put reasonable distance between our cars. As planned, we each drove to his daughter's home and then I passed it. I easily found the Jewel parking lot, and not a minute too soon, as nature had to be obliged. Then I took the opportunity to purchase our dinner, which consisted of bananas, chips, soda, challah bread, and a pound of turkey meat. Leaving the store, I found G.P. in the rear seat holding on to the blanket. I questioned, "Does this mean I get to put a covering on you and disappear for 30 minutes or so?"

He did not respond. Instead, G.P. told me to pull out, go into the neighborhood and stop in front of the house next to the park, which I did. Both of us then left the vehicle and walked along a narrow path surrounded by bare leafless trees. He advised me to, "Take advantage of this fresh air. It may very well be the last you breathe as a free man, at least for a while." I appreciated the sentiment. We got back into the car and we were on our way to locate a cheap motel room on the west side.

G.P. and I drove for about an hour before finding the seediest motel in a slum neighborhood. I asked if he was joking with this choice. He grunted, "No," as he left the car to register. Afterwards, he walked me to our room, made sure the security lock worked and left without any explanation as to where he was headed.

Once in the car and on his way, he telephoned me. At first, I hesitated to pick up the receiver and then finally meekly answered, "Yes?"

"I'm sorry for being short with you, but I am responsible for your safety. Don't leave the room. I purposely chose a motel in the worst and most dangerous part of the city. Cops don't go there without back up. I'll talk to you later. Let the phone ring three times and I'll hang up, and shortly afterwards redial you. At that point, pick it up. Goodbye"

G.P. drove back to Malak's house in time to observe her and Eryn going out, presumably for dinner. Following them for several blocks, he saw her pull over. She turned off the lights, yet neither apparently exited the vehicle. He parked six car spaces behind them and waited. Suddenly, the back door of the Focus was opened and a gun was touching the back of his head.

"Dad, what the hell are you doing? You scared the crap out of me! Besides, you're getting too old for this nonsense and too sloppy, as well. If someone wanted to grease you, you certainly would have made it easy." Waiting a minute to catch her breath, she continued, "I have a message for you that someone dropped off at the police station, while I was out. He didn't even bother going in. Instead, he gave it to a nearby officer eating his lunch outside, simply saying it was for me. What's with the drama and what's with the fishing bullshit, Dad?" Malak asked, as she handed over the envelope.

Ignoring her questions, Mehmet said, "I have to go now, Baby Girl. Kiss Eryn for me. Tell her I'll have an answer to her question very soon." Observing a puzzled look creep on her face, he ended with, "The less you know the better and by the way I will return the money I took from your dresser drawer."

Malak opened the car door, hesitated briefly before leaning over, and then quickly kissed her father. "Dad, don't do anything foolish. Eryn and I need you. Contact me when you can."

Mehmet opened the note that read, "Go to the box tonight."

He began the long drive to a far south side post office whose lobby was open 24 hours. While this allowed easy access to the locked mailboxes, there were no other people in the area at the time and that made him easily visible.

Mehmet parked a distance away, took off his coat and turned it inside out before putting it back on. He then took muddy dirt and rubbed it on his cheeks, forehead, and chin. Pulling down the front rim of his Cubs hat, he bent low and purposely staggered, as he entered the facility. Wearing gloves, he inserted the key and withdrew a letter. He exited the post office walking past the parking lot to the remote area that was not visible to the security cameras and where he had originally left his car.

Looking about and finding no one in the vicinity, he opened his car door and drove away with the lights initially off. He stopped in a heavily industrial area crowded with many other vehicles to read the note.

There were three unencrypted sentences, "Uranium waste originating from the Former Soviet Union and shipped to Iran, where enriched with Plutonium and initiator Polonium before stored within small, solid graphite balls. Sophisticated detonation of British design, to be activated when sufficient nuclear material accumulated inside the chambers beneath the *Temple Mount*. Ensuing explosion expected to render immediate area uninhabitable." The note was unsigned.

At last, Mehmet had the missing piece of the puzzle that no doubt, even the Israelis were unaware of; otherwise, they would have preemptively acted.

The next order of business was to go back to the motel room, get rest and prepare for tomorrow.

Arriving after midnight, Mehmet found Wolf sound asleep on the single bed. He lay on the couch but could not fall asleep, concerned as to why Ishmael had not taken the time to encrypt the message.

Chapter 42

As of 7:30 a.m., Mehmet had not slept. Nevertheless, he was happy to see the sunrise so he and Wolf could get an early start on the day. Opening the curtains, he heard Jon stir and groan.

I opened my eyes and asked, "What did you learn?"

Mehmet gruffly replied. "Let's get down to business." He relayed the events of the prior evening and the contents of the note he picked up. "I hope we're able to reach someone at the Consulate who knows enough to care about this information and the risks it took to get it."

"I can't promise what someone else might do, but I'm grateful to you and your cousin," Wolf commented.

That simple statement pleased Mehmet, who responded, "Let's get some breakfast before we head downtown. You know that's the most important meal of the day."

"O.K. by me, boss. You know I like to eat," Wolf replied.

Mehmet, who was used to telling people what to do appeared mildly annoyed by the "boss" characterization, yet he was the boss and bore the ultimate responsibility for his friend as well as their mission.

After showering, Mehmet and Wolf got into the small rental car and left for a fast food restaurant. The latter sniffed the air and asked, "Is that our clothes I smell or the food we are about to eat?"

"Your senses are picking up one of the many unpleasant aspects of undercover work," Mehmet replied, and added. "If what I am planning goes well, we should get some resolution soon."

Approaching the outskirts of the downtown area, both men noticed the uniqueness of the day's unusual cloud-free, blue sky. Pulling into a parking spot, Mehmet yanked out a single long black strand of hair from his head, licked it and placed it between the front door and back door panels indicating that its continuity would be broken if someone were to try to gain access into their car.

I appreciated Mehmet's bringing me up to speed on evasion techniques. "G.P., you may find this of interest. At one time, I too had a desire to pursue law enforcement as a career. However, the events of my adolescence obviously put an end to that."

Walking to the consulate, Mehmet was aware of a dread-locked African-American woman walking with a much taller Caucasian male. They appeared to be tailing them, frequently darting in and out of view. He thought it useless to employ evasive measures on the sparsely populated streets. Sensing it might not be much longer before being apprehended, Mehmet felt it necessary to take direct and decisive action. "Jon, our approach must have been signaled to those men leaning against the passenger doors of the three vehicles across the street."

Mehmet took his car keys and purposely scratched two expensive unoccupied nearby limousines, setting off high-pitched auto alarms. This caused other suspected agents waiting outside the Israeli Consulate a brief lapse in their concentration. As they focused their attention away from the entrance, Mehmet grabbed Wolf's arm and both rushed into the building. He then flashed credentials to the building security and they went unchallenged through the metal detector and proceeded towards an open elevator door. As it closed, Mehmet gasped a sigh of relief, while I was embarrassingly oblivious to what had just transpired. "Ignorance really is bliss," I heard G.P. mumble.

Now, we were technically on Israeli soil. However, a large female secretary stopped us from proceeding further. Speaking in a thick accent, she instructed us to return in two hours, when her boss might be available. Knowing that to be impossible, I dropped the name of a Mossad agent, that Abbie had known in Israel and who was currently thought to be assigned to the Chicago consulate office. She picked up a phone from underneath her desk and almost immediately two large men quickly came out of an inner office, while a third held the door open, as we were escorted in.

G.P. was placed spread eagled against a wall and frisked. They took his gun from its holster and put it in a self-locking desk drawer. Next, I was patted down. We were told to take a seat. As two of the security detail left, G.P. looked about, and pointed out surveillance cameras and tiny sound recording devices strategically placed within two desk lamps. He motioned for me to remain silent. However, the earlier coffee consumption had kicked in, and I was forced to ask the remaining guard if I could use a bathroom. A door opened and a woman came out. She directed me to an inner office facility, while G.P. patiently waited.

Finishing, I was taken to a different area. There I politely inquired as to where G.P. was. The guard didn't speak; instead he ominously rested his hand on his holstered pistol. The message was clear, so I decided to sit quietly. Moments later, one of the original security team entered with an older individual who took a seat behind a large mahogany desk. Then the guard stood behind me and placed his hand upon my shoulder. I respectfully asked the older man if Special Agent Mehmet would be joining us soon.

"I believe you are referring to former and now retired Special Agent G.P. Mehmet. He's okay. However, I am not so sure of your future. Before we proceed further, how's Abbie doing?"

I responded she was as good as could be expected, considering she was targeted to be killed, but left injured and comatose.

"Wolf, she's a unique woman with feelings for Israel's survival stronger than many of its own citizens." Reading from an open file folder, he inquired, "Now we need to know what you know of her work."

Assuming Mehmet was being questioned separately, I didn't divulge more than general details, as we also needed to know what the Israeli intelligence apparatus was aware of. I held tight to that bargaining chip which I felt might secure our continued safety.

Instead, I diverted mentioning my hope to see my wife later that day.

"We will have to see about that. Tell me what brings you and your friend here?" the old man questioned in perfect English. His gray eyes reflected no emotion at all, as he repeated the question for a second time.

Again I thought it best to answer honestly, if not fully. I relayed most of what was learned from reading the e-mails. Periodically he stopped me and parroted back his understanding of what I had said, inquiring if it was accurate. Being reassured, he then asked me to proceed as if he were certain I knew much more than I had just revealed. I told him what happened most recently in my home at the hands of an unknown intruder who purposely eliminated selected portions from Abbie's' laptop's stored memory. I ended with our suspicion that we were being followed, but did not know why or by whom. This was met with a facial grimace as he softly muttered, "Aberdam."

Glancing at a wall clock, almost an hour had flown by since we had arrived. I then rehashed the tragedy that cost me my family, as well as my father-in-law's betrayal, and stopped with Mehmet's involvement.

The old man spoke into his jacket lapel and coffee and rolls were brought in.

"Wolf, you'll need strength, as we are far from done. Eat something, while I clue you in on the danger you were about to face, and of your wife's importance to us. In fact, the judge reassignment in your D.U.I. case was by no means coincidental. Our resources have been

259

monitoring your situation, almost daily from the time of the tragic auto accident. Everything seemed under control, until the house break-in, the stranger's texting from outside of Abbie's hospital room, and you're accessing her laptop's contents. Then the stakes most definitely were raised. It's truly unfortunate you came across what you did, as it puts all of us in a difficult position. We now have to figure out exactly how dangerous you are thought to be. Once we know that, we will have to discuss what we are going to do with you."

"Well before the shit hits the fan, at least tell me who you are?" I asked.

"Refer to me as 'M', which my American colleagues find easier than my given name Menachim."

I asked, "Are Abbie or Mehmet in danger because of anything I may have said or done?"

Pausing for a moment 'M' replied, "Probably, but less so if you don't surface, as elements within your government would not wish to draw any unnecessary public attention to possible compliance in two accidents. I believe everyone is okay, at least for the present. In addition, it would serve no purpose to harm a retired F.B.I. agent, especially one dependent on a pension who might easily be controlled. Feeling better now?"

"I see your point. That said, I have to know who planned the accident and how close are they to implementing their plan to destroy the *Temple Mount*," Jon inquired.

"Wolf, it appears you do know much more than I had hoped. Are you always that free with such valuable information? You must be in possession of more critical details, I suspect. In order for us to assist, you'll have to be completely open and honest. After all, your life is not the only one in jeopardy. There are thousands more, including my families. Is there something else you want to tell me?" At that moment, the intercom buzzer went off and 'M' excused himself, perhaps to compare my statements with what was said during Mehmet's separate interrogation.

I looked about the room and noticed the doors had no handles or knobs to open them, only a fingerprint recognition device. I felt stuck, but not alarmed. I decided whatever asked, I would offer my fullest cooperation, but only after receiving reasonable assurances of Abbie's future well-being and a credible plan to allow Mehmet to get back to his family and live out his days in peace, far away from my circumstances.

At that moment, a woman entered the room bringing additional coffee, crackers, and jam packets. I must have appeared somewhat out of control to her as she motioned to her gun and informed me in heavily accented English, should I do anything foolish, she was instructed to restrain me by any means necessary. 'M' returned and again sat behind the same desk. He poured freshly brewed coffee and it smelled delicious.

"I informed Mehmet you decided, of your own volition, to remain here and that you wished him to leave. Unfortunately, he's stubborn and won't leave without talking to you first." Menachim added, as he handed me his phone, "If you value Mehmet as a friend, cut him loose, now!"

"Are you all right?" G.P. asked. "They want me to leave now and will take me out by a way they assure is secure. They also told me you'll be okay, but I wouldn't leave without speaking to you first."

"G.P., you've been a friend to me, perhaps my best friend, certainly in a long time. I want to do what's right, but I am not sure what that is. They appear to think I know more than I do. Should I tell them the information we came upon or wait?"

Mehmet responded, "I am instructing you to tell them that you do know something critical to Israel's survival and you will reveal it upon safe arrival at their headquarters in Jerusalem. Let them know that the clock is ticking, so they had better act quickly."

I answered, "I think that makes sense. What the heck, they are probably monitoring our conversation anyways."

"I am counting on that," Mehmet responded.

"G.P., I have several requests of you. When you are able, please see Abbie and tell her that I will return to her as soon as I can and in the meantime, let her know she will always be with me, in my heart. Make sure she's safe by getting to know my in-laws, as they are her link to life, until I return. When you think it appropriate to do so, fill my father-in-law in on what actually happened. Maybe my in-laws might be receptive. Whenever you are in the area, please visit Sandra's grave and place a single stone upon it for me."

"Sandra and Abbie were the best of what life offered me. Not by their choosing, they too became casualties of terrorism. Perhaps, in my daughter's memory and for all of Abbie's efforts, I may yet find myself in a position to do some good for my people."

"G.P., they tell me you and your family will be safer with me out of the picture and invisible to those who are after us. That makes sense. Stay close to your daughter and thank her for her involvement on my behalf. Nothing happens by coincidence. It must have been predetermined we met. Incidentally, you brought out the best in me. Lastly, you and your family contributed, at great personal risk to the saving of numerous, innocent Muslim, Arab, Christian, as well as Jewish families from another potential Holocaust. You are a credit to the better nature of humanity and I hope to see you again. Be well my friend." I clicked off the phone before G.P. could respond. That chapter of my life is now closed.

Listening intently, 'M' smiled, "If anything good came from your tragedy, it was clearly your friendship with this man who truly cared about justice and about you. Now, it's time for you to tell me what you came upon. I give you my word the information you pass on to me will not change our responsibility to get you safely to Israel, but rather it may buy us the time to best handle what we still have to face."

I understood I had no choice but to trust Menachim as delaying the revelation of what I knew could hamper a timely neutralization of the imminent threat. "First, I want you to know it was a Muslim-Arab who risked his life to get us the missing link, as to precisely where and how the nuclear threat to Jerusalem would be implemented."

'M' leaned forward in his chair as I described the transportation of the nuclear waste material, "Initially it was shipped from the former Soviet Union, through Iran where it was enriched to weapons grade quality and encased within small graphite balls. These were then transported by truck, in small quantities and over time, by Palestinian security personnel who turned the finished product over to the *Temple Mount* overseers for placement deep within recently excavated tunnels beneath the Dome of the Rock. All of this was proceeding undetected, with the aim being to build to critical mass and at a later more opportune moment, detonate. This is my full understanding of the events as G.P. described them."

Menachim interjected, "Those clever bastards. By bringing it in as they did, the graphite shields overcame our satellite radiation detection early warning system. Their plan would make any explosion, while potentially less extensive, still deadly enough to render the immediate surrounding areas uninhabitable for years. During that time, Israel would be labeled the cause of the tragedy and Jews conceivably forced from their biblical homeland. Meanwhile, the Arab population would simply wait it out, with monetary subsidy flowing in from many if not all Arab nations, until such time they would be ready to take everything over."

Recognizing the gravity of the impending situation Menachim stood up, saying, "I must forward what you told me to my superiors in Jerusalem. We owe you, Abbie, and Mehmet a debt. The next order of business will be for my security forces to get Mehmet safely out of here and on his way. However, I want to personally thank him before he leaves."

'M' was torn between his promise to Wolf and the necessity to hold Mehmet, until the neutralization of the threat was carried out. If he were captured, G.P. could be manipulated with threats against his family. Menachim rationalized his detainment would be for his own safety, as well as his daughter and grandchild's ultimate welfare. He would be made as comfortable as possible in a safe house under 24-hour guard for as long as necessary.

Unwilling to risk a monitored telephone conversation, 'M' had the consulate computer generate an encrypted letter describing Wolf's revelations. It was then placed in the day's diplomatic pouch and rushed to O'Hare airport for placement on an *El-Al* flight that was being held, pending its arrival.

'M's orders to the consulate guards were understood; Mehmet was to be treated with kindness and respect, while being confined.

Upon being informed of his situation, G.P.'s foremost objection was not being able to contact Malak to prevent her from worrying. He explained her medical situation and Menachim promised he would arrange to get word to her.

"I understand the purpose of what you're doing," Mehmet said. "I don't resent it, but at least tell me how long it will be before I am released?"

'M' evaded the question, as he did not know and preferred not to lie to this man. "I appreciate the risk you took to get this information to us, but with both you and Wolf unreachable, this further assures safety for Abbie, Malak and Eryn, as well as reducing risk to our operation. Moreover, as necessary, I'll see to it you never have to worry about money after this is over."

"Money never was or is any motivation for me," responded Mehmet. "We may be on opposite sides for some of our visions of a separate Palestinian nation, but, we still share the same desires to protect our extended, as well as immediate families. Also, don't ever underestimate the extent of what Mrs. Wolf uncovered for Israel. Your people would have been caught off guard, and probably blamed for any detonation and the resulting death and destruction. From where the charge was to be set, there would also be little doubt that all the Arab and Muslim nations- Shiite and Sunnis would unite to drive your people into the sea."

'M' placed Mehmet in the hands of two of his most trusted Mossad Agents before returning to Wolf.

Chapter 43

"Menachim, will your family remain in Jerusalem during this security threat?" I inquired.

He didn't respond, but I saw the answer in the anguish upon his face. A moment later he said, "What we have to do now is get you out of the U.S. and into Israel, as quickly and quietly as possible. A passport is obviously useless and if you are recognized on an airplane it would be nothing for our enemies to arrange to destroy the plane as easily as they destroyed your family."

I asked, "Who was responsible for Abbie and Sandra?"

Pondering his answer, 'M' felt the inquiry justified, "It appears a rogue element within your State Department may be involved, but without the knowledge or consent of the Executive branch. The former has been researching for years various scenarios for achieving a stable regional peace with Israel out of the picture. Then Abbie stumbled upon their most recent game plan."

'M' continued, "Iran has always been our biggest threat with the deepest pockets. It has been training and arming terrorists on every possible front, with the goal of weakening Israeli and American resolve. This proved inefficient, until their nuclear option came into being"

Astonished, I commented, "I thought Arab Iran was a long way off from having the nuclear capability to deliver a knockout punch to Israel."

"Wolf, Iran is a powerful Muslim, not Arab nation. Muslim and Arab are not synonymous. The language spoken is Farsi and not Arabic. The majority of Americans don't appear to care enough to understand their soon to be, most dangerous enemy. In basic terms, Muslims approach 1/5th of the world population and growing at an alarming rate. What you might find more interesting is that a Fatwa or legal opinion was pronounced stating they could co-exist with others, except Israeli Jews. When the latter were expulsed, then and only then would Muslims be able to carry forth their definition of peace with other nations, encouraging the five practices: Declaring their faith, Fasting, Charity, Pilgrimage to Mecca and Prayer. On the surface, these seem harmless, yet, in reality they are a death pronouncement for Israel.

It's important for America to get a grasp on reality by understanding Iran. For too long, the United States has dismissed the actual threat from this now fundamentalist culture, preferring to see everything in complex shades of gray, whereas in reality it is exquisitely simple. You are either with them or against them, and the latter is simply not tolerated. Yet, a 1300-year historic separation between Sunnis and Shiites is viewed as surmountable if an Iranian plan for a second and final Holocaust action against us, is implemented. Frightening, isn't it?"

'M' paused to take a drink of coffee before continuing, "As far as when Iran will have nuclear capability? In actuality, they already have it! It wasn't that difficult to acquire since the breakup of the former Soviet Union. This allowed unlimited access to technology and technicians who were and are always available for the right price."

I asked, "If you knew so much, why didn't you publicly declare it and put a stop to this threat before it took the life of my daughter and destroyed my wife's future?"

Understanding Wolf's pain, 'M' respectfully informed him, "The real world is not a John Wayne stage where you run in guns blazing and openly save the fair lady from the villain. It's not that simple. In this case, we just found out what's in the works thanks to your detective efforts.

Now we may have to undertake a direct military style assault. If the area is detonated before it is secured, our purely defensive action will be deemed provocative and Israel will likely be labeled as solely responsible for destroying sites holy to Christians, Jews and Arabs. These include the Dome of the Rock, Al-Aksa Mosque, The Church of the Holy Sepulchre, as well as the entire *Temple Mount*. This would definitely inflame and unite all Muslim nations against us, to strike in such a manner as to render our nuclear deterrence effectively worthless."

'M' continued, "It's for that reason I suspect rogue elements from within the State Department, including Aberdam, ordered trusted security personnel to take out Abbie, as soon as they discovered her breach of their plan. I would also bet they ordered the initial bungled burglary attempt to access Abbie's desktop computer, while overlooking her laptop.

Wolf, most high level U.S. and other western government leaders and lawmakers are unaware that their State Department officials and their equivalents elsewhere possess a great deal of latitude and can negotiate actions in the name of the countries they represent without their leaders fully knowledgeable of what's going on. Governments, particularly in the West, are so complex, even their intelligence agencies cannot effectively keep track of what's occurring on a timely basis, let alone why it's happening. Utilizing powerful super-computers, little doubt helps, but with so much data accessible, everything is still relatively uncoordinated. In reality, intelligence gathering and analysis, is more an art than a science."

I asked, "So what are we going to do now?"

"For the present, we have to get you out of sight. That way we can keep your State Department guessing. They are not 100% certain where you and Mehmet are. However, we are hopeful none of this will force premature action from either side. Wolf, since you hung out with an F.B.I. agent for so long, maybe you have a suggestion on smuggling you into Israel?" Menachim asked half-heartedly while smiling.

Wolf's face suddenly radiated with inspiration. "As a matter of fact, I may. Even in disguise, I am vulnerable, correct. However, if my body could be drug-regulated to control my breathing and heart rate, and my vitals remotely monitored and supplied with adequate levels of oxygen and cooled air, how about transporting me to Israel in a coffin. What do you think?"

'M' looked intently into my eyes. "You're almost as clever as the Mossad team that came up with the same idea." He added, "Whatever we decide to do, we have to do it quickly!" Menachim suggested that I rest in a detention cell, explaining that should we have uninvited guests, this area of the office was difficult to detect and access. I was in no position to argue. He got up to leave and told me to sit tight as he firmed up the transport plans with his superiors in Jerusalem.

Chapter 44

Mehmet was blindfolded prior to being escorted out of the consulate by way of a hidden underground passage. Two guards secured his arms as he was carefully led to a passageway of steep stairs. Finishing the climb, the men made their way to a door, which sounded as if it resisted opening.

My eye covering was removed, and with a strong push, we were met with overwhelming brightness. It proved too startling for my already dark-adapted vision. It took a moment to get my bearings. Amazingly, I found myself across the street from the entrance Jon and I originally used to enter the Consulate. Without warning, I was shoved face down into the back seat of a waiting car between two men who introduced themselves as my initial security detail. Mossad agents, I suspected.

The vehicle quickly blended into the downtown traffic. Several minutes into the ride, I was permitted to sit upright, but told to remain quiet. The vehicle drove past the Federal Building and then entered onto the northbound freeway. Not long afterwards, it exited, but this time we were headed southbound on Sheridan Road. We made our way along narrow streets and then back alleyways to a rundown tenement project. The car was parked and we waited for darkness.

The most uncomfortable part of the journey was the total lack of communication. I began to think it likely they might kill me and dispose of my body in such a manner, as I would be untraceable. After all, I was carrying half the burden of the knowledge that put all of us in jeopardy in the first place. Which was worse I imagined, being assassinated by my own country's agents or those from Israel. In the end, I was only another Arab to the latter.

At sunset, we got out of our vehicle and walked though a building passageway before climbing several flights of stairs. We entered the rear of an apartment where I was told to make myself comfortable. At last, a glimmer of hope I might survive, but I couldn't be sure, at least not yet.

Surprisingly, one of my captors let his guard down and turned his back to me. This posed an opportunity, so I quickly took the advantage. I lunged at him, forcing his suit jacket over his head, which exposed his gun, holstered in the small of his back. I pushed him down, grabbed his weapon and flicked off the safety. In this embarrassing situation, he had little choice but to comply with my request to call his partner into the room. It was an obnoxious, but necessary move to demand the truth regarding my fate.

Avi Margolis came into the living room with a chicken leg in his mouth. This poor man looked so foolish and vulnerable I had to laugh. Both of these agents were so young, it would be a darn shame for them to pay the ultimate price for poor judgment. However, self-preservation was and is the first order of business.

"Gentlemen, get down on the ground with your face kissing the floor," I ordered. "Don't do anything

273

stupid. You would be leaving a sad message for your parents, ending your lives in such a manner."

I saw large plastic adjustable ties on the nearby nightstand, and quickly took several to bind their wrists. Each man was assisted into a more comfortable resting position with his back supported by the couch. Opening the wallet of the first guard I over powered, I found Benny Lipshitz's picture I.D. "Benny and Avi, be two good Jewish boys and follow my instructions carefully. First, tell me the code to telephone 'M' without going through the consulate switchboard." Avi reluctantly released the number and I dialed. Within seconds, 'M' answered and started ranting something in Hebrew.

"This is G.P. Mehmet. Now don't be angry with the boys. They are still young and now more experienced. They're okay for the moment. However, their future depends on your answers to my questions and of course, whether I believe them. First of all, what's to happen with me?"

Menachim responded, "Mehmet, rest assured, you were never in serious jeopardy. If we wanted you killed, that could have been arranged at any time, from your arrival to your departure and anywhere along the ride. Both you and Wolf are weak links as long as you are accessible. Therefore, even though my country is grateful for your efforts, you have to remain on ice for about a week or so. My superiors and I firmly believe should Aberdam's operatives detain you; threats against your family would force you to give up everything you knew and still result in all of your deaths. You saw firsthand the damage he inflicted upon the Wolfs. Do you think he would not do the same to your family? Be patient, let my men go and stay put. There is no reason this has to get ugly."

"Good answer," I quipped. "I made a promise to Jon and he is depending on me to carry it out. I need your help in this and one other regard before I can settle down and remain a compliant guest. Will you help me?"

"Are you sure you don't have some stubborn Jewish blood flowing through your veins? Maybe, it would have been easier on all of us if you left with Wolf. Since that wasn't in the approved plan, what do you need done?" Menachim inquired.

"Jon requested that I see Abbie one final time, to let her know the reason for the accident and that her husband is okay. In addition, I need to get word to my daughter letting her know I'm okay, as well. Most importantly, she must not look for me. Do you have any ideas?"

"M" answered, "As far as the first, I can arrange for a physician on staff at the hospital to play a tape recorded message from Wolf directly to his wife. Your situation will require a more thoughtful approach. Is there any pet name your daughter referred to you as, that only she and you would recognize?"

"Well in the past, she occasionally, and under her breath referred to me as 'Donkey Brain.' Does that help?" Mehmet jokingly replied. He then paused a moment before revealing his pet name for her, 'Baby Girl.' Continuing on, "What say you put something in tomorrow's edition of the Chicago Times reading 'Baby

Girl,' gone fishing. I will get back to you when I land the big one. Be patient, Love, the former Donkey Brain."

"I can arrange to have Malak read the personals," 'M' indicated. "That's the best I can offer. Does that work for you, or would you prefer to deal with the reinforcement agents now stationed outside both doors?"

I looked through the peephole of the front door and the side of the curtains covering the rear door's glass panel and saw Menachim to be a man of his word. I picked up the phone and said, "Looks like you're still in charge. Keep your word and I won't hassle the boys. Remember to reach out to Abbie and tell her Jon is carrying on where she left off. Sound strange coming from an Arab?"

'M' responded, "Should you choose to come out of retirement, consider working with us."

Chapter 45

Menachim found Jon soundly sleeping on the cell cot. He had such a peaceful expression upon his face that it was indeed a shame to wake him. That said, 'M' had no choice. Wolf awoke with a startle and shouted, "What?"

"Jon, we have instructions from Jerusalem to prepare you for departure on the next *El-Al* flight scheduled to leave tonight at 11:45 p.m."

"How are you going to get me out of the consulate? It wouldn't be as easy as you described Mehmet's exit, especially at such a late hour when the streets are sparsely populated."

Menachim responded, "First things first, the idea of getting you aboard the airplane in a coffin was accepted. However, getting you out of the consulate and to the funeral home will be a bit more challenging. Already, suspected hostile operatives are stationed at both the front and rear entrances of our building. Unless we create a believable diversion, I am afraid we're in a pickle and a kosher one at that!"

Continuing on, "Jon, here is the consensus thought. We already have someone about your build and height on the payroll. If we dress him in your clothes, add a heavy overcoat and provide him with a wide- brimmed hat, we may just pull this part of the mission off, especially as two of our 'known' security men will escort him from the premises. All we have to do is bait the interest of those we are attempting to mislead.

In addition, we arranged for a garbage truck to come simultaneously with an empty canister, and then to exchange it mechanically for the one you'll be in. Then at a prearranged drop site, we will have other security people waiting to transport you to our funeral home contact. Finally, we'll get you on board the plane in a manner that shouldn't arouse suspicion. Before I forget, we have a linen shroud for you. After all, you have to play the part of a dead man."

"I have a few questions." Jon inserted.

"Go on."

"How are you going to arrange for me to breathe in the coffin? And for that matter, I should warn you, I'm somewhat claustrophobic."

"Wolf, you'll have more than enough fresh air. Thanks to your C.I.A., the technology for 'cool' transport is now a routine process. In fact, you'll be traveling with more leg room than the typical coach passenger," Menachim joked.

"Just to make sure everything goes smoothly, I have received permission to accompany you on your journey home.

Jon, to ease your mind, there will be a physician available to provide the chemical cocktail that will slow your breathing, effectively placing you in a deep trance-like sleep. There will be a different doctor on board the plane to revive you. Your vitals will be continuously monitored and I'll be alerted should there be any systemic distress. Once sufficiently over the Atlantic, I'll go below to the pressurized baggage area, open your coffin's head compartment and assist the doctor in reviving you. From there, you will be escorted up to the main cabin where you will sit next to me. If you can hold it down, a small meal will also be available for you. Finally, an *El-Al* pilot's uniform in your size will be waiting."

'M' warned, "Jon, eating anything now is contraindicated. We do not want your digestive system working overtime, while the narcotic is being introduced. You could potentially vomit and aspirate food into your lungs. I know you must be frightened, but there is no other way we can assure your safety. Remember, as long as you are unaccounted for, we believe your wife and F.B.I. friend and his family are much safer."

Menachim proceeded to open a security door with his thumbprint and we headed towards his private bathroom where I put on the linen shroud. He then introduced me my look-alike, Achim, a Druze Arab, who bore only a minimal facial resemblance to me, but was of my portly build. In disguise, he looked like a blend of an ultra- orthodox man and a cartoon spy character. Yet, in poor lighting and some luck, we agreed the charade might stand a chance.

As Achim was escorted out of one consulate door, my handlers and I left through another. I heard Achim say, "May you return home blessed with peace, Baruch Hashem." I had heard this phrase before and understood it to mean with the Good Lord's Blessings. My new life seemed just about ready to begin.

Menachim's assistant explained that I will be wearing several layers of loosely sealed, heavy duty and pre-punctured for adequate breathing, garbage bags. Once secured in the trash bin and on my way, I can cut through them with a penknife and work my way out. Next to me in a separate bag will be a warm fleece jacket and hat, as well as a red-bulbed flashlight that should give me adequate vision in the dark environment. If I experience motion sickness, a precautionary supply of vomit bags will be within my reach. Lastly, no bags of actual refuse would be dumped upon my head, and the canister will be rat-free, as well.

Another assistant helped me into the oversized bags. Before they were loosely tied, 'M' stated, "Always remember, you didn't get this far and go through so much to not reach your destination safely. Next time we see each other, you'll be that much closer to Eretz Yisrael, the land of Israel."

I was taken to the staging area where I was gently lowered into a large covered trash bin, with only a mild thump. The timing appeared flawless; as I soon heard the sound of a garbage truck come and replace the canister I was in with an empty one. I felt a chain-link lift my temporary home above the ground and secure it to the truck before we drove away. I bounced with every bump or pothole the truck went over, and swayed with each turn it made. Suddenly, the ride became smooth, as we must have entered onto the highway system. At this point, I worked my way out of the bags and into the warm outer clothing provided. In less than an hour, the truck stopped.

Someone climbed on the canister and motioned me to turn off the red-bulbed flashlight. I was instructed to remain very quiet, while I was assisted out. At that moment, I heard a car approach and was quickly transferred to the rear passenger seat of what appeared to be a large, older model station wagon. Two women sat on either side of me and, using hand signals, instructed me to kneel in the foot rest area next to the rear of the driver's seat and to remain quiet.

Twenty minutes or so into the ride, the auto pulled into a garage and stopped. As the overhead door shut, a ceiling light came on. At this point, an Orthodox Jew, apparent by his garb, opened the car door and welcomed me to his funeral home. After a short walk down a narrow corridor, a second man introduced himself as Baruch, the medical doctor. He explained what was to be done and how long it would take the chemicals to work.

Everything was happening so quickly and precisely, I hardly had time to think. I was placed into a plain, wooden casket wearing only the white linen shroud. Next, it was explained that my face would be painted with a wax-like substance, should a curious customs-agent decide to open the coffin.

"Sir, this may sound strange but, in some ways, I wish I could change places with you," the physician quietly told me. "You are about to experience a great adventure, a chance to start over in life with no baggage and hopefully few regrets." He inserted a needle into the vein of my left hand and started the I.V. that contained the chemical cocktail. I was told to count backwards from 100. My last recollection was the number 97.

I would later learn that after being transported to the airport, my coffin was mechanically boarded onto a conveyor belt that traversed to the baggage inspection area where U.S. Customs briefly screened for explosives and drugs, neither of which required the casket to be physically opened. All the while, Menachim carefully monitored my vitals on his modified e-Tablet, which was programmed to receive wireless transmissions of my heart and breathing rates. Although significantly slowed, both were more than adequate for minimal-life support. The surrounding air was thermostatically controlled and continuously exchanged, proving adequate oxygen availability.

The plane took off at 11:45 p.m., after Menachim boarded. He had been assigned a seat in the rear of the aircraft customarily reserved for onboard flight security.

The only unplanned event occurred when the flight approached New York City and was instructed to make an unscheduled landing at J.F.K. International airport in order to pick up an Israeli Embassy diplomatic pouch. Traditionally, these communications do not go through customs, thereby not significantly delaying the subsequent take off. A benefit for the passengers was the opportunity to view the Empire State building and Statue of Liberty against a moonlit backdrop.

Regaining height and speed, the plane's pilot announced to the passengers that they would experience a tail wind and should arrive at the Tel Aviv airport close to schedule. This included a planned refueling stop in Amsterdam. After the announcement, most of the passengers turned off their overhead lights, closed the sliding window covers and tried to get a good night's sleep. All went without a hitch.

An hour later, the aircraft was well within international waters. Menachim thought this an opportune time to revive Jon. Although previously told that a Mossad physician was to be on board to direct the revitalization process, this had to be modified at the last minute. Instead, an Israeli Air force flight paramedic was substituted. He would be radio briefed on the specific steps to bring Jon out of his deep slumber. 'M' was not particularly caught off-guard by this last minute change, as there might not have been a security-cleared anesthesiologist available on such short notice. Luckily, it proved to be an unimportant point.

As Menachim observed, Jon's vitals slowly returned to normal. Warm compresses were placed upon his forehead and after several firm taps to his shoulder, he regained consciousness. Unexpectedly, he shouted Abbie's name. 'M' thought it just a bad dream, possibly recalling the tragedy that befell his family less than four weeks earlier.

'M' carefully helped me out from the coffin. I began to shiver uncontrollably as the cold from within the baggage department was beginning to get to me. I was escorted to a nearby elevator and as the doors opened, I welcomed the gust of warm air that struck me in the face. Reaching the flight deck, I saw a small gangway that led to the cockpit where the pilots were busy flying and conversing in Hebrew. In the opposite direction was their private lavatory where, with assistance, I put on the uniform that was waiting for me. The paramedic assisted me out and we followed 'M' to our assigned seats, where I immediately fell asleep.

How strange, Menachim thought to himself, a man in a chemically induced state of sleep for hours would wake and still be consumed by fatigue. Several hours later, 'M' was requested to go to the flight communications center, adjacent to the pilot's rest area. Before leaving, he asked the paramedic to stay with me, until he returned.

There was a telephone call from the Chicago Consulate Director. Unfortunately, there was an attack at the apartment where consulate security had been holding Mehmet. Two guards were killed and G.P. was missing.

Menachim asked the Director to arrange for extra security in and about Abbie's hospital room, as a precaution. He was then informed that the operation to neutralize the threat to Jerusalem, labeled "Escaping the Abyss" had been assigned the highest security priority. No current information regarding Abbie's status was available.

As the large jet approached the Amsterdam airport, its shift in direction caused me to stir. I saw observant Jews getting ready to put Tefillin on and recite Shacharit, morning prayers.

After a smooth landing, the other passengers, eager to stretch their legs, stood in the aisles, while awaiting the aircraft doors to open. As I began to rise from my seat, 'M' approached with a distressed expression upon his face. He asked that I remain as he had something important to go over with me.

"It's about my wife, isn't it? While asleep, I had a strange vision. Abbie seemed to float away from me. I couldn't hold on to her and no matter where I looked or how loudly I called, I couldn't find her. Then I caught a brief glimpse of Mehmet and noted his gray complexion. He quickly faded away. I was alone."

'M' took a hold of my shoulder, "Wolf, pull yourself together. While in flight, I was called to the communications center and told by the radio officer that a message had been received from the Chicago Consulate. Unfortunately, Mehmet went missing."

He waited for my response. I became quiet, lifted the window shade, and just looked upon the bright lights of the Amsterdam airport. My eyes watered as I thought of the risks my friend took for me, as well as for all Jews. I uttered a silent prayer for his safety.

I thought of Abbie and G.P., two unlikely partners set upon the same course of action: justice and mercy for helpless victims of powerful forces they could not control. Sadly, these two might never get the opportunity to meet in better times.

Menachim told me that when the time was right, he would see to it that Abbie and G.P.'s services for Israel were respectfully acknowledged. I then requested to be involved in the operation to neutralize the threat, in any capacity I could serve. At that moment, I began to hear the other passengers re-board and joke about having seen Amsterdam from the window of the airport

285

for only 30 minutes. It was hard for me to see so many happy faces, while I was hurting so badly inside. Entire families were on their way to establish roots in Israel and had no idea of what they would soon be facing. The children, although appearing exhausted, were excitedly preparing to see their tiny biblical heritage for the first and possibly their last time. This made me more determined than ever to stop the problem that awaited them.

Menachim tried unsuccessfully to engage me in serious conversation, while breakfast was being served. During the remaining flight time to Tel Aviv, he also became quiet. This whole ordeal had taken a toll on him, as well. His family lived in Jerusalem, yet, he could not move them away from the danger zone. He mulled over his options, just as everyone within the involved intelligence community was doing.

As the plane began its final descent, an excitement began surging within me and the other passengers, as we began singing, *Hatikva*, The Hope, Israel's anthem.

After safely taxing to the arrival area, there was an orderly departure from the aircraft to the tarmac. Menachim and I were met by military personnel and escorted to a side door and avoided customs. I laughed to myself, as I didn't have a suitcase or anything to declare. All I possessed was the *El-Al* uniform on my back.

Menachim must have read my mind as he mentioned, "Don't worry I'll supply you with all you'll need. Be prepared, it might only be baggy army fatigues." Unexpectedly, he gave me a hug. "Now you and I will be like shadows to each other. We will eat and sleep in the same area. In fact, you are to be my family's honored guest. However, first we have to attend a briefing in Jerusalem and later one in Arad."

An entourage of various military and security people welcomed us with a table laden with fruit, cheese, and smoked fish. The coffee was the strong Turkish blend I remembered from my family's last trip here. As everyone participated in the food and each began speaking to the other in Hebrew, I felt very much alone.

Most of the Hebrew overheard was a mystery to me. Then I got a flashback of Abbie and her Israeli friends chattering in fluent Hebrew, while I was unintentionally excluded. Abbie would see this, lean over and gently kiss my cheek and whisper, "It's really not that difficult, if you are willing to try." At best, my knowledge of this strange language was rudimentary, primarily limited to religious services on Friday nights and occasionally on the Sabbath day. Although I would try to keep up, like many American Jews, I just turned pages to look for the English passages and the end of the services. Here, once again I found myself in a foreign environment where the others were speaking unintelligible words and my wife not there to translate.

Sensing my predicament 'M' informed me, "You'll have to learn some basic Hebrew. Perhaps my youngest daughter will assist you, while you stay with us. Until then, I'll tell you what's going on. It seems we made the right decision to get you out. You're a targeted man. In fact, the U.S. State Department has involved other federal agencies, as well as an underground network of confidential informants to be on the lookout for you."

Menachim continued, "For now, it might be best if you say the least possible and just listen, I will translate the salient aspects of the conversations you're hearing. Meanwhile, let's get comfortable in the Humvees and enjoy the scenery. After our meetings, you'll receive a warm welcome from my wife Kala, our daughters and even the cat."

The ride was pleasant. I turned and saw portions of the Mediterranean coast come into view, as we got higher into the Judean hills. I sensed the faint aroma of orange blossoms, which quickly faded. Suddenly, we found ourselves in a traffic jam. Even with our military status, we had to wait it out. I felt vulnerable to a terrorist attack. When I verbalized this concern, everyone within the huge vehicle began laughing. Apparently, they had me at a disadvantage, as they understood my English. I joined in with the laughter as I thought about the foolishness of what I had just said. After all, we're not on patrol in Afghanistan, but rather on the main highway from Tel Aviv to Jerusalem, a reasonably secure area. The others immediately warmed up to me and 'M' whispered, "Well done!"

At that point, my fellow passengers began conversing in English for the remainder of our ride to government buildings located near the Knesset. We drove into an underground garage and then escorted to a large boardroom. At a single round table were several faces I thought looked familiar, including a cabinet minister Abbie had introduced me to on a much earlier trip. All were in a heated discussion regarding the deadly offensive being planned against Israel. As a courtesy, I was provided with headphones that translated the Hebrew spoken into almost simultaneous English.

The military chaplain opened the meeting with a prayer for heavenly guidance to direct us towards wisdom, safety, and peace. Then he related a brief word of historical incidence taken from the Passover Haggadah, "In every generation, they rise up to destroy us, and the Holy One, Blessed Be He, delivers us from their hands. We Jews have learned not to rely on anyone but God and ourselves. Even within our own homeland, many of our Arab brethren question the Holocaust, as if it did not happen and voice their concern that we fabricated it in order to take the Land of Israel for our people. We share our educational goals with their children, provide the best of our health care and opportunities for a better life for their families, yet they dislike and distrust us."

He continued, "Iran subsidizes Hamas to our south and Hizbullah to our north; both conceived in a dedicated mission to our absolute destruction. Iran receives billions in trade revenues that underwrites their hate. Now they have nuclear capability and a plausible, sinister plan to level Jerusalem. How long will it be before Egypt, Saudi Arabia and Syria have the same capabilities? The noose is being tightened about our neck and we are expected to exercise restraint, while Hamas rockets rein upon our cities and Hizbullah rearms with ever more sophisticated armaments. Hostile border nations are building their military preparedness at a pace not seen since just before the Six-

Day and the *Yom Kippur* Wars. Their leaders call for Jihad inspired continuous resistance, while demanding the right of return for all Palestinian refugees from every corner of the world, even those born abroad long after 1948. They plot and plot again our destruction. If they can't destroy us from within, they marginalize us with untruths internationally."

"Now, thanks to 'Devine Providence', we discover beneath the "Old City" of Jerusalem, a booby-trapped explosive circle of numerous, enriched nuclear weapons encased within fragile graphite balls. And if the news could not get worse, we are also informed that rogue elements, from within the U.S. State Department, may have conspired to coordinate our destruction with our enemies."

The chaplain ended with, "We seek divine guidance to assure future generations of Jews a life in our land, our tiny heritage. Please Lord; inspire us to face and to overcome that which we cannot escape."

All present responded "Amen." Then the business of brainstorming began. One group of attendees advocated for immediate worldwide publicity in the hope that it might stop the planned action. That was shelved, as Arab leaders could easily say a Jewish conspiracy planted the devices to destroy the *Temple Mount* and *Al Aksa* mosque, and were caught.

Next, a Golani Brigade General sitting to my left commented, "If we move to secure the tunnels, we have to assume they have the capability of remote detonation. Even if a nuclear reaction did not occur, the damage and immediate loss of life could prove devastating." Another attendee agreed and added, "The Arabs always keep the *Temple Mount* area purposely populated with their children. Even in self-defense, we Jews have the obligation to minimize loss of innocent life wherever we are forced to engage our adversaries."

An intelligence officer brought up, "Depending upon the winds, radioactive dust could prove to be a long-term health hazard for the entire Jerusalem area, if not Israel and Jordan proper." He added, "That said, we are mandated to neutralize this threat to our very existence, by any means necessary."

For the next 20 minutes or so, mostly implausible ideas were bandied back and forth going nowhere, until a petite, dark haired woman not in uniform stood up. "When my husband and I visited Israel before our Aliyah, we swam in the Dead Sea. The water was so heavily salinated; it destroyed the electronics of our expensive watches. Would it not have the same effect on electrical wires, eliminating their ability to conduct a detonation signal?"

'M' seemed startled by the simplicity of this insight.

Additional thoughts were also brought up, including a consideration for pumping inert gas into the tunnels beneath the *Temple Mount*, which might suppress the detonators from exploding. A senior military advisor added, "This in combination with the salinated water from the Dead Sea might provide a good but not guaranteed chance the threat would be neutralized. Yet, understanding there was always the unforeseen."

291

She added, "If successful, we could then contact various news services and demonstrate the seriousness of the situation we faced. Should the Palestinian leaders revert to form and say we orchestrated all of this; at least this nuclear option might not be tried again."

A public safety expert reinforced an earlier concern, "A consummated nuclear action could serve as a precursor to a joint military operation from our bordering neighbors, as well as a signal to our Arab population from within, to rise up against us."

The group fell silent. The thought of such a possibility was overwhelming and maybe indefensible. In the hypothetical, every militarily trained Israeli citizen above age 18 could be pressed into service. They would have immediate access to weapons, but the following question was put forth. "Would they have the will to fight for the very survival of their families and homeland?" The consensus was a resounding, "Yes!"

With this to chew on, the group boarded bomb-proofed buses that would transport us to a remote, security-cleared location near Arad. There we would finalize the means to be employed.

Chapter 46

We arrived at the outskirts of what was simply referred to as "The Site," which was rumored to be one of several locations housing Israel's strategic nuclear reserve. It was decided that we take a small detour first to an overlook of the Dead Sea and its surrounding areas.

Easily visible were the borders of Jordan, Lebanon and the Golan Heights, proximate to Syria, as well as the Mediterranean Sea. This sent a chilling realization as to how vulnerable this tiny Jewish refuge really was.

Viewing the limited road accesses to and from the Dead Sea brought into question the feasibility of transporting heavy salinated water utilizing a convoy of trucks. The noise, even with muffled diesel engines, could certainly call unwanted attention to our task. One of our party then suggested assigning specially equipped military aircraft or helicopters that could siphon up the liquid cargo and bring it to an airfield. There it could be transferred onto waiting trucks for the relatively short run to the Old City. Again, noise could be an issue.

'M' suggested they run the operation during the day, as the operational noise would be at least partially concealed by the normal hubbub of traffic congestion. I then inquired if they possessed enough electric vehicles, which are reasonably silent. Being told this was not currently practical, I decided to remain quiet and just listen.

Re-boarding our vehicles, we made our way past a security checkpoint. There escort jeeps joined us. They took us to what appeared to be a camouflaged mountain entrance, which I was told led to an underground stronghold. Amazingly, this entrance could have been so easily overlooked. Gates opened and our buses disappeared inside. A military doctor was waiting for me and performed a cursory exam that confirmed I was fighting off an early infection and was given fast acting antibiotic pills.

I rejoined the others in a huge subterranean logistics room with extensive digital maps of routes to and from the Dead Sea, as well as the Jerusalem street system, all projected on wall screens. The roads immediately adjacent to the *Temple Mount* were highlighted. Also impressive were the imaging studies taken from overhead flights noting the gross extent of recently dug excavations beneath the Mount.

As we took our seats, a blindfolded man referred to as Mr. *Aleph*, dressed in military fatigues was brought in. It was explained he was the senior Arab engineer of the crew who originally planned the *Temple Mount* excavations for its ultimate nefarious purpose. He and his family were now the guests of the Israeli government.

The man proceeded to describe the location and dimensions of the various chambers. His testimony was then compared to the data gathered from flight reconnaissance studies. Demonstrating consistency of results, it was decided that he be allowed to remove his blindfold, but was instructed not to face the audience. This extra security measure was necessary to protect the identities of the various Israeli intelligence officers present. Some were actively involved in clandestine operations within Iran.

In response to direct questioning, he revealed anticipated numbers of military personnel thought to be stationed within the caverns. He also mentioned comments from his superiors indicating that if any compromise to their security were discovered, they would implement counter-hostile operations immediately. This would include detonation of ordinance. Subsequently, he was escorted out and we were ready to proceed. This man's cooperation proved invaluable.

Our discussion initially geared itself toward our enemy's suspected time line. The urgency to determine the most efficient manner to transport the heavy salinated water was made a priority. Another equally important task involved the best method to target specific areas that required flooding.

Exhausting hours of discussion followed before the decisions were finally summarized by an aide to the ranking General, "It is our agreed upon decision to utilize garbage trucks as a front, each lined with molded plastic water tanks. The hauling into the city would begin early on Monday morning, just as the noise of congested traffic began. Street crews would block off specific access routes and road repair maintenance was an excuse to jackhammer streets, offsetting noises stemming from the underground aspects of the "Escaping the Abyss" operation.

Drilling through a known thinner layer of subterranean rock that separated the Kotel, Western

Wall from the *Temple Mount* catacombs would be accomplished utilizing a recently developed high-powered laser system. Fortunately, the optimal point of entry was discovered years earlier by a group of university archeologists conducting excavations, shortly after the Old City area of Jerusalem was recaptured in 1967. Nevertheless, there exists a statistical risk that any crack in these thousands of year old stone structures might weaken the ancient weight bearing supports and result in a cave in.

The means of flooding the chambers would employ flexible tubing of various diameters that could easily interconnect to any desired length. This technology has been in use for many years by Moshav farmers for irrigation of vast crop areas. In fact, their water trucks, if necessary, could also be commandeered at the last possible moment, to gather additional salinated water reserves from the Dead Sea, as soon as the Sabbath was over.

Finally, the Air Force prepared several medium sized, construction helicopters for low altitude forays over the Dead Sea where they would siphon the liquid, utilizing rapid vacuum technologies and deliver it to a military base on the outskirts of Jerusalem. Once there the cargo would be pumped into garbage truck storage bins for transport to the Old City." He ended with, "Any questions?"

None were forthcoming.

I took 'M' aside and quietly asked, "If this Arab man was so important, won't it look strange that he and his family suddenly disappeared from their home in Jordan?"

Menachim walked over to the Mossad liaison and relayed my question. They conferred for several minutes. 'M' returned, retook his seat next to me and whispered, "The Arab engineer had initiated a request that he and his family be allowed to visit relatives in Canada several weeks ago. He informed his superiors he could save a great deal of money flying *El-Al* rather than taking the 'Air Jordan' flight originating from Amman. His leave was subsequently approved, and that's his cover. Funny, the world considers Jews the only ones thought to be frugal."

Everything was beginning to fall into place as the meeting ended. We walked to the buses and I again overheard several of the military officers beseeching God's help for our success, *Baruch Hashem*.

While the others boarded the buses, I was told to report to the physician who checked me earlier, presumably to drop off a post-antibiotic urine sample. While waiting in the reception area, I was surprised to see the Arab engineer who had testified earlier being escorted in. His guard was asked to briefly step outside. Before leaving, he turned to the man, said something in Arabic and then turned to me and in an equally harsh manner said something in Hebrew, which I obviously did not understand.

I took the opportunity to thank him for his efforts on Israel's behalf and, at the same time, told him of my personal loss. At first, he just stared. After an uncomfortable pause, he approached me, leaned towards my ear and proceeded to warn me; "Beware, one of the men who questioned me had a voice I had heard before. Even though my back was to the audience, I knew that voice. It was from an Israeli who assisted in determining the best location for the tunnels and the most effective sites to place the graphite balls for maximum destructive results."

He quickly moved back to his original seat and ignored me, until being called in for his medical evaluation. For just a brief moment, he stopped and simply nodded in my direction, little doubt to acknowledge the seriousness of what he just said. I never saw him or the man who originally accompanied him again. I was in shock and was uncertain what to do next.

Then it was my turn to be seen by the site doctor. I easily complied with his request for a urine sample. He took my body temperature, which read 99.6, and listened to my breathing, which fortunately appeared uncongested. A repeat scoping of my ears and throat were relatively clear. Apparently, I was making some progress in fighting my infection. The necessity of continuing the antibiotic was again stressed and I was excused to rejoin my group.

We boarded the buses and I sat next to Menachim. Before I had the opportunity to relay what the engineer told me, he informed me we would be making an unscheduled stop in the Negev desert just outside of Be'er Sheva, at a forest named La Hav. He then got up to confer with an intelligence officer and stayed with her, until we arrived. Everyone exited the buses and a Jewish National Fund site overseer took us to a stone-wall that supported a tablet showing many engraved names.

I read the last inscription, stating a grove of 1000 trees had been planted anonymously in Sandra Wolf's memory. 'M' translated the accompanying Hebrew text, "As long as Israel endures, so shall Sandra's spirit find peace in the Land of her heritage, forever." I broke down. Tears uncontrollably flowed and I was given several minutes to regain my composure.

Our group was then directed to a bare spot where a kneeling pad, digging tools and a small, tree were laid out. I was asked to dig a hole and plant the baby pine sapling. Everyone took his or her turn lightly watering the plant. The chaplain offered a prayer that it take root and thrive throughout the ages and led the Kaddish memorial prayer for Sandra.

With only one hour remaining until sunset, we rushed back to the buses so everyone would arrive at their homes before the Sabbath. During this time, I told Menachim of the disturbing conversation I had at the doctors' office. He simply said he would look into it.

Arriving in Jerusalem, 'M' invited me to his nephew's wedding on Sunday. I accepted even though I had been given the option to privately mourn Sandra for the balance of the thirty-day traditional period.

Chapter 47

I was not raised in an observant Jewish home, yet always felt a strong connection to my Judaism, perhaps because I was so often reminded of it, every time I was called a "dirty Jew" or "kike."

My mom enjoyed the Jewish holidays and my father encouraged my religious studies, even though both were more secular in practice. It was not until I married Abbie that the Sabbath seriously challenged my lifestyle. Even though I always had to work seeing patients on Saturday, I rationalized it by thinking I was serving the health and welfare of my community and therefore allowed some kind of dispensation. Yet, I yearned for any opportunity to share this day, away from work, with my wife and daughter.

Now, because of dire circumstances, none of my choosing, I was in Israel with people who believed as strongly as Abbie did, in a land where Jews were given biblical authority to reside. However, it's also a place where we found our fundamental right to live peacefully, continuously challenged. My wife loved observing the Sabbath, but nowhere more so than in Israel. She always took the opportunity to remind me of a famous quote that I was told was ascribed to Ahad Ha'am, "More than Jews kept the Sabbath, the Sabbath kept the Jews." It was her gentle reminder to me that we did not just stumble upon our life as Jews with daily obligations.

Arriving at Menachim's apartment, his wife and daughters welcomed us. The smell of freshly baked challah and the Sabbath preparations were inspiring. As I had no clean clothes to call my own, I was supplied garments from a neighbor who lost her husband, as a battle casualty during the Lebanon conflict, years earlier. Fortunately, his clothes fit me well and by my wearing them, she informed me that I honored his memory.

I was given a *Kippa*, head covering, with a clip to secure it to my thinning hair. The family gathered in the dining area where the Sabbath candles were about to be lit. As Menachim took his place, the women spoke the solemn prayer welcoming the Sabbath evening. Menachim blessed the wine and then bid me to wash my hands, before allowing me to cut, lightly salt and bless the now uncovered twin twisted challah loaves. Fortunately, this was something Abbie had trained me to do.

Lifting the ornate cutting board and with just a little assistance from 'M', I spoke the appropriate prayer. The family again welcomed me.

In deference to me, the girls spoke in English of their school experiences, and politely answered my many questions. Yet, I observed an unusually quiet, humble manner about them. They laughed and giggled as children do, but seemed very reserved; as if they understood, the threats daily about them could change their lives in an instant.

Dinner completed, the dishes were left in the sink, and 'M' and I left for services at the neighborhood Shul, which was within easy walking distance. I again found myself warmly received. When I appeared lost within the Hebrew text, my seat neighbors pleasantly guided me through the liturgy. The only thing I felt uncomfortable with was the obvious separation of the sexes. It appeared to concern me and not concern them, so I kept this to myself.

The Friday night service was nearing completion when I was motioned to stand. The rabbi recited Kaddish for those whose family members were recently lost to death. The community offered a special prayer of comfort to me and another man, whose wife and young children were murdered, as they commuted from Hebron to their home in Jerusalem. I could no longer feel so sorry for myself.

On the way back to his apartment, 'M' reminded me that my knowledge of the nuclear plot makes my very presence, a continuous threat to the sinister forces, until their objective was either carried out or stopped. For this reason, I had to be invisible, even within this observant community. Although I felt relatively safe here, I would later learn that a bounty had been placed upon my head and I was targeted for assassination.

Arriving, we found Menachim's home crowded with neighbors who brought sweets to welcome this special day. Again, I was invited to join the group, but after a few minutes, I chose to excuse myself and go to my room. It had been an overwhelming day and I needed time to be by myself. Lying in my bed, I couldn't get out of my mind what the Arab engineer told me. Was it possible, someone within the Israeli government was a collaborator? Finally, I succumbed to sleep.

I awoke refreshed and eager for the day to commence. We ate a breakfast consisting of fruit, fish, and strong coffee. Dressed in freshly donated clothing and shoes, I walked down the three flights of stairs and left for the local congregation we had attended the evening before. I was amazed at the number of people present. There was hardly an available seat. We were beckoned by 'M's friends to sit in a section near the front, facing the pulpit. Today was to be a bar mitzvah observance.

At the appropriate time, the 13-year-old boy was called to read from the Torah, his *Parsha*, or portion for the week. Menachim and his friends were given an *Aliyah* or honor, just before each of the sections were read. I was not called upon, and wasn't disappointed, due to my lack of confidence in my Hebrew reading skills. The boy, now recognized a man, proudly undertook his responsibility. Just before he finished, I was motioned to go to the bima where the rabbi and other honorees were standing. With Menachim at my side, he instructed me to lift the Torah scroll, with each hand holding a side. It was heavier than I thought it would be. Pivoting the Torah and using all of my strength, I was barely able to lift it. He whispered in my ear, "Wolf, if you drop it, the whole congregation must fast for 40 days." At first, I forgot to rotate it so that its letters were visible to the various sections of the congregation, but that error was soon rectified.

As we left the Shul, a friend of the family introduced himself to me, wished each of us, "Good Shabbos" and invited all over to his house for Sabbath lunch. The invitation was accepted. After consuming the bountiful spread, the men adjourned for their traditional afternoon discussion, today held in English for my benefit.

The discussion centered on what was learned from previous military incursions, specifically within Lebanon, Israel's northern border neighbor. I was amazed by the participants' candor. After many penetrating questions were openly discussed, this group of combat veterans concluded that the Israeli military, as well as the government should have reacted faster and more efficiently to the missile strikes and hostile border crossings. Command objectives might have been achieved with less loss of life if more experienced leadership were made available, and the reservists should have been provided greater access to necessary equipment.

The homeland command appeared to have failed miserably with their responsibility, in that Hizbullah was able to listen in on intercepted radio dispatched directives. This was inexcusable and atypical of the Israeli army that appeared invincible during the Six Day War in 1967, or the army that was able to recover from almost certain defeat and go on to victory in 1973.

Then the subject matter unexpectedly shifted to one man's impression that the Zionist belief that had established and maintained the State of Israel, as well as cemented together the varieties of citizens in the early formative days, had seriously weakened. The stresses of overseeing the territories acquired since the 1967 victory appeared to lessen the will of some Israelis to understand what they were fighting to protect. Another individual, a former ranking officer, expressed a highly controversial view that without clear objectives, the only reasonable option was to reduce the size of Israel.

I chose to sit quietly by and listen.

The discussion lasted late into the afternoon, until the men went to the Shul for Havdalah prayers. I returned to 'M's apartment for quiet time.

Sunday morning, Whiskers, the family cat woke me. It seemed I usurped his bed because of my stay. Until that morning, the girls kept him in their room, where his toys were temporarily stored. I jumped into the shower and shaved my 48-hour stubble. After all, I was to be attending an orthodox wedding. Graciously, more donated clothes were awaiting me, including another pair of polished shoes.

Early in the afternoon, the family, with me in tow, took our place with the rest of the community awaiting the ceremony. The men initially went to a large room where tables were loaded with cakes and different brands of various hard liquors. I tasted a bottle of Scotch that was the smoothest I ever encountered. Just to make sure, I sampled a second. Again, the service would separate the men and boys from the women and girls, with the only exception being mothers with their infant sons.

We prayed in fellowship, even though I was lost the majority of the time. What I lacked in competence I more than made up with in enthusiasm. Prayers completed, and the wedding Ketuba read, signed and witnessed; next came the custom of the breaking of the plates, something that appeared strange and out of place. Although the crowd surrounding the mothers of the groom and bride effectively blocked my vision, nevertheless I heard the sounds of fragmenting china. This was explained as signifying a commitment from both families from which there was no turning back.

A short time later, the men joined the women in another hall, once again gender separated, by a mehitza wall, for the actual wedding ceremony. The significance of the bride circling the groom seven times was explained as a symbolic reference to the walls of Jericho falling and the subsequent opening of the city to the Jewish army under Joshua's leadership. Currently, it conveys a meaning that any walls previously separating this young couple from each other must now also fall, so they will be able to share an open and honest life as husband and wife.

As the ceremony concluded, I asked 'M' why the groom and bride did not kiss, as is the accepted norm in America. I was enlightened that in this community, modesty discouraged public displays of affection. However, there was sure to be plenty of private affection immediately following the wedding ceremony, as the young couple is expected to have consummated their marriage, prior to being introduced to the community, as husband and wife. That's some pressure, I imagined.

As the dancing began, I saw young men put down their Uzi machine guns and M-16 assault rifles to join in the festivities. For a brief moment these Hesder Yeshiva students were able to set aside their heavy responsibilities and just be young boys, joyfully participating in this holy rite of passage.

Walking to our table, 'M' suddenly grabbed my arm and informed me that we were being summoned away. Our mission now had an unexpected urgency that required our immediate attention. Both of us were handed bags of food quickly prepared by Menachim's wife, who waved goodbye, as we hurriedly left. I saw Menachim return and passionately kiss his wife. I thought of Abbie.

Outside of the Shul, a government limo was waiting with its motor running. In the backseat was one of the key generals present at the Friday meeting. There was no small talk, only the command to enter the car quickly. The man avoided any eye contact with me and instead began speaking to Menachim in an agitated fashion. The two occupied themselves in an intense and often loud discussion.

A short while later, 'M' turned to me and, with tears coming from the corners of his eyes, informed me that the President of Israel was under house arrest. "The information given to you by the Arab engineer at Friday's meeting was taken seriously. There had been some prior questions that one from within our ranks, or someone we had been reporting to, may have been passing information to suspected terrorist agents. We never thought it could reach the level it did. While the President did not deny his involvement, he also didn't admit to it. That said, an intelligence officer present at the Friday meeting was observed conferring privately with our President. At his level, that wasn't protocol and therefore suspect. Late last evening, the officer agreed to make an arrangement with the Justice Department to relay the content of their meeting. What's not so clear, is whether our Prime Minister had any involvement. He and the President are very close allies, personally and politically, and that cast a shadow upon the P.M., as well"

Menachim paused before continuing, "Because we don't know the actual extent of any potential compromises, we have considered altering our time table. The trusted essential players and support personnel are being called to active status, as we speak. In all likelihood, the counter-measures will be implemented sometime on Monday."

I asked what the President or the Prime Minister would gain by sacrificing their country and its citizens.

"Israel has never dealt with this level of a potential betrayal in its history, and everyone is just winging it, making it up as we go along. Meanwhile, we are continuing to assess various potential damage scenarios; including the execution of a premature detonation of the nuclear devices, along with a subsequent joint Arab military response that is anticipated to follow. If attacked on all fronts, we may not be able to count on assistance from any nation, including the United States. Jon, fate picked you a most difficult time to be our guest."

Weighing his words, Menachim continued, "Jews worldwide, as well as Israelis, are more vulnerable now than at any other time in our history. Our enemies possess the technological means and trained personnel to deliver a severe knockout punch. Our tactical research indicates that we may not have the time to recover and regroup from such a strike. What happens next surely rests in "Divine" hands. The remaining few hours may well test our viability."

Chapter 48

After disposing of his guards, Mehmet's captors injected a strong sedative directly into his neck. He was then transported to a destination thought virtually impossible to track down.

To assure control over him after the effects of the drug began to wear off, Mehmet's feet and hands were tightly bound, his mouth gagged, and his eyes blindfolded. The killers knew he was a force to be reckoned with and were not taking any chances. Slowly regaining consciousness, Mehmet was reminded that he was a prisoner and that disobedience would not be tolerated. To bring the point home, the tightly placed duct tape covering his mouth was removed in manner to assure maximum pain and he was brutally and repeatedly slapped across the face.

Recovering his senses and to let them know he was not so easily frightened, Mehmet firmly asked, "What do you intend to do with me?" This question was immediately followed with a calculated demand that his still unknown captors remove the highly restrictive wrist and leg bindings, as well as his blindfold.

The men conferred before addressing his requests.

"Everything depends on you, Agent Mehmet. We know who you are, where you live, and everything about your daughter and grandchild. If you agree not to be difficult, we will consider making you more comfortable. I understand what you are going through must be unsettling, even to a hero-type like yourself. As for the blindfold, it probably won't matter if we take that off."

Hearing that statement sent chills down my spine. I immediately interpreted it as my death sentence. No field operative willingly reveals his identity to those he is interrogating, as this could ultimately compromise his own security. Fearing I had little left to lose and wanting to confuse my captors, I responded, "You know you have nothing to fear from me."

With this assurance, my blindfold was lowered, but immediately, a pungent liquid was forced into my eyes.

"What the hell is this? Are you trying to blind me?"

The lead interrogator spoke as the blindfold was quickly reapplied. "An Atropine compound was put in your eyes. Within minutes, your vision will blur, you will not be able to recall seeing us and your mobility will be limited. Don't even try to get off the couch without assistance. Injuring yourself will only complicate what all of us hope to be a short-term ordeal."

After what seemed like five minutes, the restraints and blindfold were removed. Now, even the dim room light proved too harsh for my vision. "Tell me who you are," I asked.

The response was, "It doesn't matter who we are, who we work for, or where you are right now. What is most important is that you tell us what we need to know. If it's what we suspect, all of this can be over in seventy-two hours or less, and you can return to your family. You control their future as well as your own. Understand?"

The threat to my family was heard loud and clear. Yet, my value to my captors would immediately cease once they got what they came after. I didn't think they had picked up Malak and Eryn, otherwise they would have played that trump card early on.

"What happened to the two Israeli guards?" I inquired.

Again, only the lead captor spoke. "The same things that will happen to you should you play with us."

"Doesn't your friend have a say in all this?" I foolishly asked.

"Billy, show our guest how you speak."

In a fraction of a second, the man pulled out a knife, held it to my throat, and made a painful incision only inches from my jugular vein. I touched the area and felt my warm blood dripping from the fresh wound. Just as quickly, the man who cut me placed a handkerchief layered with a white powder against my neck, and the blood flow abruptly stopped. Cocaine, I suspected.

"If you need a name to call me, just refer to me as Tommy. Don't talk to Billy, as that makes him nervous. Moreover, when he is nervous, he becomes unpredictable and very dangerous. Now, let's take care of business."

For the next several hours, I was repeatedly asked about Jon and Abbie Wolf. Each time, the questions posed varied only slightly from the earlier inquiries. Tommy was a professional. He knew exactly what he was doing and proved it by frequently trying to catch me in a lie. At first, the questions seemed innocuous. "How did you come to know these people? Did Malak get as close to Jon as you, or was it strictly within the course of her police work responsibilities?"

As the questions put to me were getting more complicated, I became somewhat confused. This annoyed Tommy, who tried to control his frustration. When he finally reached his limit, his tone became loud and threatening, and I became fearful.

"What the fuck do you care about those Jews?" he ranted. "They should mean nothing to you, because they are nothing. So many of them are just little more than self-absorbed rats. Your family history should have taught you that much. They took your heritage away from you and are responsible for us being in the never-ending Middle East quagmire."

I foolishly followed up with, "Next you're going to tell me they're responsible for 9/11."

Billy stood up, took two steps towards me, grabbed my throat with one hand, and began to squeeze the life out of me. Just before I was about to lose consciousness, I heard Tommy say, "Now that's enough Billy. Aberdam doesn't want him dead; at least not yet. I'm sure our guest didn't mean to insult us and surely won't do that again."

Tommy was right on that account. Death didn't suit my purposes. Perhaps a more delicate approach would gain me the time I needed to assess my situation and my options.

I caught my breath and in a raspy voice responded, "I have no love for Jews as a group, but this man had a terrible tragedy forced upon him, without any apparent personal involvement." I then purposely hesitated and observed both men assume a more relaxed posture.

"I understand what you're saying. He and his daughter were unanticipated collateral damage. What should have been a simple traffic accident fatality quickly became a complicated mess that needed to be resolved promptly. Frankly, I'm astounded Mrs. Wolf came upon the information she did, and in the manner she did. Some might say, (he paused and snickered) that there was heavenly direction to all of this. Yet, none of this would have been necessary were it not for a loose lipped son of a Lebanese diplomat, who has since been effectively dealt with. Now we have options of eliminating everyone involved or selectively, depending on what you tell us. In other words Agent Mehmet, you control the fate of many people."

Not being able to see the two men caused me to second-guess all of my responses. I didn't want to accidentally let anything of importance slip, but rather to purposely spoon-feed the least information so as not to force their hand.

In a moment of inspiration, I took a chance and burst forth, "Just kill me and be done with it! My family knows nothing. I have no idea where Wolf is and I am too old to put up with this bullshit anymore."

Tommy replied, "I, too, don't suspect your family knows anything of importance, yet that doesn't diminish their value to us. The harm we will inflict upon them is of little consequence to us, but should be of sufficient importance to get you to cooperate. Going

314

under the premise I am correct, tell me exactly what you know about a planned nuclear action against Israel, more specifically Jerusalem. Before you answer, remember, should you lie, you'll regret it on many levels. Remember, G.P., there are worse things than death."

I understood where he was heading. In fact, the way these two handled themselves seemed somewhat familiar. Then it came to me. At an interagency conference on counter-espionage training techniques, a presentation conducted by State Department clandestine and protection agents demonstrated an interrogation scenario similar to what I was experiencing. I also remembered that they were rumored to never leave witnesses. That understood, I had to stall for as long as and in any manner I could, in order to let those damn eye drops wear off and then await an opportunity to overpower them. I told Tommy, "The eye drops are making me queasy. I am going to vomit!"

Billy picked me up and effortlessly carried me to the bathroom where I forced myself to gag. As he turned his back, I knelt down and lifted the toilet seat. Unobserved, I proceeded to take the toilet water and place it into my eyes. Then I put my finger down my throat and regurgitated what was left undigested in my stomach. The smell got to both of us and I quickly flushed the toilet. I was picked up and brought back to the couch where Tommy was sitting and drinking a cup of tea.

"I thought you might need this," he said as he pushed a second cup of freshly brewed hot tea in my direction. When I hesitated to take it, he responded, "Don't think less of me for my methods. We are both professionals and know what's necessary to get the assignment accomplished. We have more in common than you know."

I picked up the cup and carefully drank its steaming contents. Between sips I asked, "What could we possibly have in common?"

He responded, "The pursuit of justice, my friend. In other circumstances, we could have found ourselves to be tight friends. Eventually, I promise you and those like you a different way of thinking. Mehmet, I became Muslim after growing up Catholic. I see from your background report you chose not to pursue your Muslim roots and instead chose Christianity. It's not too late for you to reassess where you will be, when what's in the works finally goes down. Many world leaders are starting to appreciate the benefits of associating with Muslim nations, including influential Jews. We are quietly amassing great wealth, and formidable power. If implemented properly, we will have the ability to make the world a healthier, safer place. Imagine G.P., lands where people don't go hungry, child poverty nonexistent, most disease eradicated and standards of living raised for all. Wouldn't you like to be a part of that great adventure?"

I thought this man to be continuously testing my resolve, in any way he could. I sensed the need to shift the direction of the conversation; otherwise, it could easily turn confrontational. "Tommy, I am not political by virtue of the nature of my profession. While your goals appear worthy on the surface, I find it difficult to

316

see them so easily achievable. With all due respect, what you say sounds almost too good to be true." I held my breath as he contemplated his response.

"It's simply the Jews, Mehmet. They're holding all of us back from the one world order where all of this is possible. The stage is set. It has been a long time in the works. First, the 'Saturday People' are to be dealt with and then the..." Tommy suddenly stopped, fearing he may have crossed a line. Regaining his composure, he continued on, "Mehmet, the end is almost in sight. Remember what American blacks said during their civil rights struggle. 'Keep your eyes on the prize.' Well, our prize is within reach. Now it's time for you to tell me everything you know."

Chapter 49

"Driving to the operational headquarters, I turned and saw a military jeep trying to keep up with us. 'M' told me it was a security vehicle assigned to escort us since there had been terror activity in the vicinity. Reassured, I turned towards the direction to which we were originally headed, and saw threatening skies approaching. That certainly would make enemy observation of our plans more difficult, I surmised. Within moments, hard rain began to pelt our car. Instead of slowing down, our driver sped up. While I felt a strong sense of danger, General Orin and Menachim acted as if all this were routine. However, this time the security vehicle was nowhere to be seen."

"Suddenly, a powerful force altered the direction of our car.'M' pulled me down between the seats and covered me with his body. Then a second stronger jolt flipped our vehicle several times. The last image I recall seeing was a mangled body under the weight of our overturned car. At that point I lost consciousness."

"Doc, why am I rehashing all the same details over and over? Nothing has changed from my original deposition statement. I appreciate you're getting me prepared to testify before the U.N. tribunal, but the details I told you the other two times are not going to change. I don't have intricate facts to keep straight. That's the big plus about the truth. It makes everything easy to remember. Trust me; I am ready to answer any questions asked of me."

Pausing for a brief moment, I opened a British newspaper that arrived early this morning. At the same time, the telephone rang and I picked it up. Menachim informed me the President of Israel fled the country and was seeking asylum in a traditionally hostile neighbor nation. In addition, corroborated intelligence was finally acquired, linking him to the Iranian based and U.S. State Department assisted plot, intent on bringing down Israel and replacing it with a larger entity, overseen by a Joint Muslim-Arab Authority. Jerusalem would serve as its provisional capital. "M" then unexpectedly hung up on me.

I relayed all this to Doc adding, "Who knows, I might not have to testify at all now. On that premise, I am not going through with any recommended cosmetic facial surgery, even if it's for my protection. Now, I can concentrate on getting back to Abbie, as soon as possible. Not being able to speak with her or her caretakers has been my biggest disappointment. Doc, perhaps her health may have improved, while I was away, and soon we can be together and get on with our lives. It's that hope that keeps me going."

Feeling content in the hope the end to my ordeal might be at hand and wishing to celebrate, I made a request of Doc. "Please get me a soda and while you're at it, get one for yourself."

Reflecting on the past two weeks, I had been a virtual prisoner, confined to a tiny room with two shifts of Mossad guards, changing every 12 hours, as my only companions. I had not been allowed any access to the streets of Marseille, or even the option of sticking my nose out the window to smell the fresh French air.

Instead, I'm sharing space with non-stop smokers. If Aberdam does not get to me first, I think the cigarette smoke will surely do me in.

Hearing some commotion in the walkway leading to our apartment and thinking it the guards returning with lunch, I asked Doc if I could let them in, unsure if he had heard me.

Without waiting for his okay, I put my hand on the doorknob and started to release the safety bolt when a cold chill came upon me. For a moment, I hesitated and then just as quickly felt foolish at my hesitation and finished turning the knob. At the same time, Doc re-entered the room, dropped the two sodas and loudly shout "No!" all the while reaching for his holstered pistol.

The door burst open. I heard a muffled pop and blood began spurting from between Doc's eyes, as he fell to the floor. I turned and found myself face to face with Aberdam, the man responsible for my child's death and wife's incapacitation. With a sinister smile he asked, "Wolf, did you think I wouldn't track you down? You were warned and now you will share the same fate I personally delivered to your wife and traitor Arab friend. In the end, all of your efforts will have proven fruitless. You think your stopping us for the moment will bring our plans and actions to a sudden conclusion. We have come too far to give it up so easily. If the surrounding Arab nations cannot have Jerusalem, then no one shall live in it. The nation that you fear the most already possesses nuclear capability, and now has the means to deliver it. The end is inevitable and you and Mehmet will not be here to stop it."

A bright flash of light momentarily blinded me, as a bullet grazed my forehead. Instinctively, I grabbed the barrel of this man's gun and deflected it away as he fired once again. The heat burned my left hand, but I didn't feel pain. Suddenly, an inspiration came upon me. I released my right hand grip of his jacket, clenched my fingers at the middle knuckles and forcibly lunged at his throat. He dropped his gun and grasped his neck with both hands. The color quickly faded from his face. He was finished, I thought to myself.

I hurried to check Doc's pulse when a powerful thud knocked me over. A bullet must have struck my back. Summoning whatever strength remained, I grabbed Doc's gun from his lifeless hand, turned and fired, until I could fire no more.

Aberdam's body trembled as his head wound pulsed blood high into the air. Nothing recognizable was left of his face. I had killed this cruel, inhuman man and felt no regret. Aberdam would not be able to hurt anyone else's family, as he had mine. Yet, I was saddened knowing that the sacrifice of my family and friends had not assured Israel and my fellow Jews at least a brief period of the peace that they had been seeking for so long. I finally understood what my wife had sacrificed her life to accomplish.

I fell to the floor and lay there feeling my life oozing away. Yet, I didn't fear death. My only regret being, that I could not say goodbye to my wife. Staring out the window at the bright blue, cloudless sky, I visualized Abbie laughing, as she happily played with Sandra in the lake behind her parent's summer home. Looking so young and beautiful, she turned towards me and beckoned me forth with her smile, and I rushed to her open, waiting arms and kissed her passionately, while feeling a contentment that had eluded me my entire life.

Made in the USA
Charleston, SC
14 February 2015